THE SHIKARI

SPACE HUNTER CHRONICLES 1

The Shikari

SPACE HUNTER CHRONICLES #1

Unlike her brilliant xeno-zoologist father, Mikaela can't keep an alien creature alive. During her futile attempts, an alien rat bite triggers superhuman mutations, changing her into who knows what, and it might be killing her. Desperate to keep her late father's ship running, she accepts a lucrative contract to tag and bag a dragon-like creature. She teams up with her childhood crush, Kiros, and his merry band of mercenaries.

En route to the faraway Cetus constellation, while fending off attractive Kiros, downright erotic dreams of a yellow-eyed man named Tieren torment her. When Kiros steals her prize and lures her into danger, she must rely on the real and gorgeous Tieren to stop Kiros. The xeno fauna injuring Kiros *and* Tieren forces her to choose who to save, her lying friend or her new flame who's stolen her heart across parsecs.

Also by Sevannah Storm

The Blood of Legends Series

The Huntress

The Healer

The Gifting Series

Soul Forged

Fate Forged

Sun Forged

War Forged

Star Forged

Shadow Forged

Earth Forged

Lust Forged

Standalones

Xiaxan Fox

Ire of Silver

Sol Survivor

Seven Cursed Sisters

The Lady and the Assassin

Plump Playwright Series

Plump Jane
Seducing Amelia
Loving FinleyKeeping Tessa
Kissing Navy
COMING SOON
Inkoded
Fire Forged
The Crucible of the Eternal

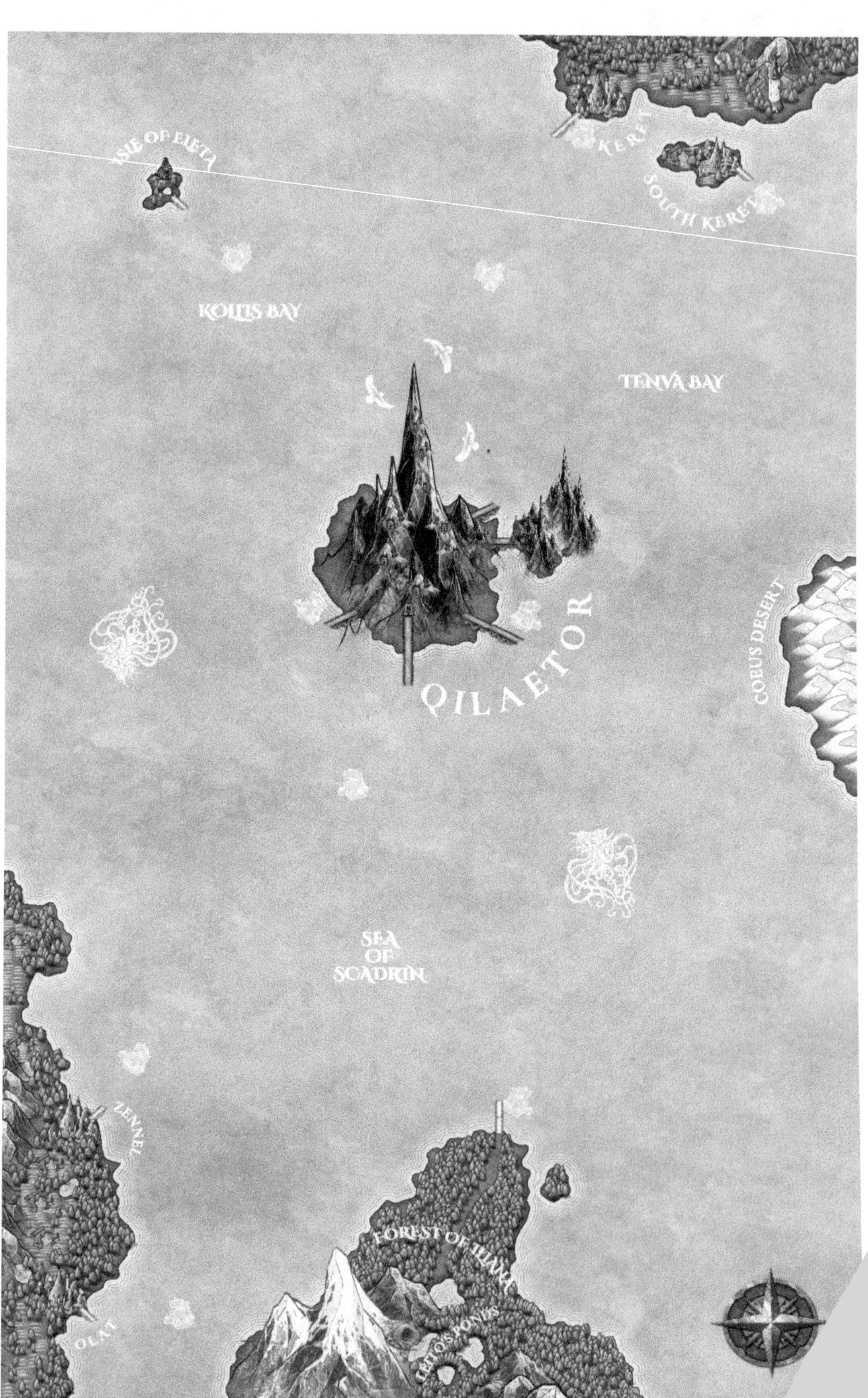

ISLE OF ELETA
KERET
SOUTH KERET
KOLLIS BAY
TENVA BAY
QILAETOR
COEUS DESERT
SEA
OF
SCADRIN
ZENNEL
FOREST OF ILIANA
LETTOS PONDS

GLOSSARY

Characters

Mikaela Danvers – Mick-ay-lah Dann-verse

Thomas Danvers – Tom-ass Dann-verse – Mick's father, xeno-zo-ologist

NOX – Nocks · Nano Omnipresent X-class A.I.

Cason Themis – Cay-sonn Themm-is – hired messenger

Selira Myers – Suh-leera My-hers - Mick's mother

S.o.S. – Soldiers of Solomon – mercenary group.

Solomon Burger – founder of S.o.S. – now retired.

Kiros Caldwell – Keer-ross Cold-well – Current Solomon

Drys Lyons – Dry-s Lions - older man

Wyatt Palmer – Why-it Palm-her - pilot, listens to audio books.

Aidan Woodard – Ay-dinn Wood-hard - Scar left eyebrow.

Lanek Spencer – Lah-neck Spen-surr - Next Solomon – shoulder length blond hair.

Seth Reynolds – Seth Ray-nolds - buzzcut, slashing eyebrows, scar right side of face.

Ru (Ben) Holcomb – Roo-bin Hole-comb - bald, brown eyes, chews on a matchstick.

Elias Morton – Ee-lie-is More-tin - mechanic

Tieren Fanyell – Teer-in Fan-yell

Braon – Bray-on – Tieren's younger brother and future king of Rianus.

Pengfei – Peng-fay

Meilo – May-low – Tieren's valet and friend to the throne.

Assalan – Ass-a-lann – General Assalan, an adviser to the throne.

Sugard – Soo-guard – Ambassador Sugard, an adviser to the throne.

Karlez – Car-lez – Cousin Karlez, an adviser to the throne.

Fresaie – Free-say-eh

Ghilian – Gill-ee-in – Tieren's friend and Meilo's brother.

Petey – Pee-tay – Tieren's grandmother and true ruler of Rianus.

Rassin – Rass-in – Meilo's sister.

Zabbica – Zab-ee-kah – Meilo and Ghilian's mother.

Greeven language

tsiliyo - zill-ee-oh - strangers

teeko – tee-koh - hearts

ateeko – a-tee-koh - my hearts

teek - teak - heart

ateek – a-teak - my heart

bucaah – boo-car - child/squawkling

abucaah – a-boo-car - my child/squawkling

takaag – tah-karg - brother

tui takaag – two-ee tah-karg - little brother

Tsuna – zoo-nah - prince

Tsunar – zoo-narr - princess

atsuna – a-zoo-nah - my prince

atsunar – a-zoo-narr - my princess

Gawen – Garr-win – the Greeven gods

malin – mah-linn - thief

kekaseea – kekk-a-see-ah - mate

Zelet – zeh-lett - shit

benf – ben-f - friend

benfo – ben-foe - friends

abenf – a-ben-f - my friend

Nona – No-nah - grandmother

Moma – Mo-mah - mother

Miscellaneous

Fentus – Fenn-tiss – Science Research Company

Great Siege of the Drusoht – Droo-sott – historical battle between the Drueen and Greeven.

The Auviphis Order – Ow-viff-is - guards chosen from birth to train and protect the heir to the throne.

Sibatu – see-baa-too – jeweled ceremonial blade

Emlo – em-low – glowing rocks mined for their light. When that light dies, the stone is used for tables, chairs, etc.

Trial of Tolend – Tow-lend – a test of survivability all royals must pass in order to be considered worthy rulers of Rianus.

Creatures

Hokou – hoe-koo – albino monkey with three tails, three-fingered hands and feet, and razor-sharp teeth.

Pauszor – pows-zorr - whale-like creature (amphibious) with rhino horn for teeth

Bebbayaya – bebb-a-yah-yah - worm-like creature with sharp spikes and gaping mouths. Yellow acidic venom and massive mandibles.

Battusk – bat-tusk – rock rats that live close to ocean waves.

Skkeens – skee-ins – multi-colored birds.

Iwaki – ee-wuck-ee – fish with their iridescent skins in reds and whites, rose to greet him.

Ferila – fur-rilla – alien rat.

Consumables

Jaketta – Jah-kett-ah – blue fruit

Ersik – err-sick – peach-like pink fruit

Styaha – sty-a-ha – weed used to trigger visions

Places

Tau Ceti – Tow Seh-tee

Cetus – Seh-tuss

Rianus – Ree-ann-us

Greeven – Gree-vin

Drueen – Droo-een – dragonlike shifters in the realm of Levion.

Levion – Leh-vee-on

Qilaetor – Kee-lay-torr

Eleta – Eh-let-ah

Bircier Mountains – Burr-see-err

Contents

Chapter One

MICK SPLAYED HER GLOVED fingers and pinned herself to the glistening stone wall. She slowed her heavy breathing behind the mask. The luminescent pink and yellow flowers hanging like droplets on the orange trees burned spots into her retinae. She squeezed her eyes shut while the drums thumped, reverberating through the soles of her magno-boots. Semi-naked tribesmen chanted and hummed, facing a dais. The chieftain or high priest, with the white plumage and black stripes painted across his torso, danced to the front. When he ululated, she winced, wishing she could cup her ears. Behind him towered a gold-carved deity—a three-man high statue with plump breasts, a hefty belly, and a penis resembling a thick snake.

Beside the chieftain sat her target.

Trusting the exo-suit to camouflage her, she wove through the kneeling humanoids to the altar at the center of the dais.

On the smooth rock squeaked a hokou male—so named for the swirling patterns of stars on their skin. Dad had been creative when

1

he'd named his discoveries. She planned to steal this one since these unclassified humanoids would kill it as a sacrifice to their statue. Flicking a glance at the god's eyes embedded with precious gems, she wrapped her fingers around the hokou's pale elongated torso.

It chirped in panic.

The chanting ceased.

She swallowed a chuckle at the spectacle of a male hokou hovering in mid-air while she, invisible, carried it.

The closest she could compare it to an animal on Prime Earth would be an albino monkey. Except a hokou had three tails, three-fingered hands and feet, and razor-sharp teeth. It scratched her gloves, twisting to do so. Her exo-suit sparked under the abuse, and just like that, she uncloaked amid the worshipping humanoids. Silence reigned until she clutched the hokou to her chest and ran. War cries and bellows trailed her mad dash through the jungle. She retraced her steps to the shuttle at breakneck speed. Ducking as befeathered spears whizzed past her, she scrambled in her haste, sprinting up the ramp. As she dived onto the metallic flooring, she yelled at NOX to get her the hell out of there. At the same time, the hokou sank its teeth into her shoulder.

She screamed. Its teeth sank so deep, the bite numbed her arm. Blood flowed, plastering the suit to her body as she struggled to tear the creature off her. Each yank had more fire burning along her veins and nerves. She sobbed. In desperation, she punched it in the face. It unclenched its jaw for a second. She caught it by a tail and tossed it into a cage before ripping her mask off.

After a stagger and a tumble into the pilot seat, she gripped and released the console, drawing in deep calming breaths. Trembles gripped her, shuddering her limbs. The pain blazed through her, spasming her muscles.

"NOX, I'm wounded." She coughed and blinked at the crimson droplets on the fore vids. The metallic taste of blood registered. "Prep the pod."

"Your pain markers *are* elevated," he hummed.

Elevated? Her eyes stung too hard for an eye roll, but she was tempted.

On auto-pilot, the shuttle breached the atmosphere. She didn't admire the planet's beauty or the dark embrace of a cold expansive universe. Instead, she squeezed her eyes shut and focused on breathing.

When she'd scanned the planet in passing, she hadn't expected to find the hokou's homeworld. Thinking to have a mating pair, she'd observed the capture, chant, and slaughter that formed the humanoids' religious ritual. Not once had the male hokou killed or bitten a local. Not once had she suspected they drugged it.

The shuttle tucked into Dad's research ship, the *Jinsei,* and landed. Time ticked by as she waited for the bay door to close.

"Air pressure restored," NOX said. "Pod powered up and open."

Climbing the ladder to the raised walkway took forever, one hand above the other. Sweat dripped off her chin when she reached the top. There she hesitated, bending over to gasp in ragged breaths. Straightening, she stumbled forward, trailing a hand along the passage wall, needing the cool surface and its stability. She clung to the medbay doorway. Dizziness, dripping sweat, and the lack of sensation in her limbs had her fighting for air. Her chest tightened. Pain followed the crushing weight pressing behind her sternum.

She crawled into the white pod sitting centerstage of the stark-white medbay. Rolling over drained her remaining strength. The transparent lid closed, entombing her, and holographic stats flickered on its surface. Normally, she read the scan results but not today. The colorful lettering had nausea tightening her stomach until tamping down the vomit rising up her throat became a priority.

Drifting in and out of consciousness, she caught a few of NOX's words, a stat here and there before darkness dragged her into its merciful depths. Time slowed. When the lid opened, releasing her, cool air brushed along her skin, raised the hairs on her arms, and drew a shiver.

"Results," she rasped as she pulled herself into a sitting position. She raised her arm, flexing her fingers to test them. The bite had shredded the suit and along the edges of the tears, blood had hardened the soft nano-bio fabric. With a groan, she climbed out of the pod, calculating how much a new exo-suit would cost.

"You are at peak capacity."

She arched a brow at the bulkhead. "But?"

"I am glad you caught that, Mick. I have been working on my human inflection."

"But?" she asked again, striding along the passage to the small loading bay she had used that now housed a pissed-off male hokou.

"The bite has infected your blood." NOX, her Nano Omnipresent X-class A.I, paused for effect; something he was working on too. She hoped he didn't master it.

"Why didn't the pod cleanse it?" While she studied the sleeping creature, she gripped and rolled her shoulder with no hindrance in movement.

"No record of such a conversion exists. The effects occurred before you entered the pod. It could only address the conditions it recognized."

"I'm dying?" She sat, leaning an elbow on the workbench to drop her face into a palm.

"No, quite the opposite. You have never been this healthy."

"What? I was unhealthy before?" She stiffened. The surprises kept coming.

"Space travel affects human bones, muscles, tendons even with artificial gravity. You no longer exhibit that deterioration."

"Huh." Grabbing the handle, she carried the cage to the lower levels where the *Jinsei* housed Dad's menagerie. There were fewer creatures, almost as if they died from grief, sensing he wasn't with them anymore. It was why retrieving a male hokou had been important to her.

On a bench under UV light waited a caged female hokou her father had bought on some backward docking station. Mick slid the male's cage alongside it. "Emma, what do you think?" She waited, but Emma did nothing but blink at her.

Dad could spend hours down here, and they'd interacted with him. She had teased him about being the universe's xeno whisperer, something she was not. Why she thought she could follow in his footsteps, she'd never know.

She had to find something she could do to keep his legacy alive. What did other xeno-zoologists do? Not once had she met another in this field. They couldn't all be lab-bound, right?

She paused, staring at the hokou male. Bagging this one had been easy, well, except for the bite. What if... She grinned. Tagging would be easier. Just sample data to send to scientific research companies might be lucrative enough. She tilted her head and studied the metallic walls of Dad's barely space-worthy bread tin.

"NOX?" She chuckled. "Investigate whether there's a demand for blood and tissue samples from alien creatures. If so, document which companies and who to contact."

"On it, Mick."

Spinning, she leaned over the workbench to note what type of guns and gadgets she might need. Dad had a rifle. She'd start with that, maybe add modified bullets or extractors. After all, killing the creatures wasn't the intention. She tapped her foot, excitement sparking along her nerve endings and thrumming in her ears.

A tick-tick came from the rear of the bay. It grew louder until it engulfed her thoughts.

"NOX, check out that racket, will ya?"

"What noise, Mick?"

She hitched a thumb behind her, expecting him to watch from one of the many hidden cams.

"Oh." He whirred in thought. "Um, Mick, I have prepped the pod again."

She straightened and glared at the ceiling. "Why?"

"It seems you are hearing minute sounds originating from the engines."

She scoffed. "Those are bays behind us, NOX."

"Exactly."

Ice spilled down her spine, raising the hairs on her skin. She exploded into action, bolting along the passage, only to bump into the sides.

"Preternatural speed too." He sighed, grinding bolts to mimic the sound. "Do hurry."

Gripping the railings, she hoisted herself up the ladder and ignored the crumpled metal beneath her hands. With a shuddering breath, she sprinted the final distance and dove into the opened med-pod seconds later. *Unnatural speed and strength? What next?*

While the pod scanned her, she sifted through what a xeno-hunter might need in the field. Red text on the glass caught her attention. Not that she understood the medical jargon. She waited for NOX to elaborate, but he remained silent.

"And?" She huffed.

"Fortified and mutated muscles could explain your speed and strength. But the creation of an abundance of nerves could be why you have sensitive hearing."

"And touch," she muttered. "Will these fade with time?"

"I cannot say."

So, no help at all. She gritted her teeth and ran a hand up and down her arm. The texture of her skin and flesh beneath felt normal. The pod slid open, and she hopped out. Now wasn't the time to deal with this when she couldn't control whatever *this* was. She had a new career to plan, a way to save Dad's legacy, and she was going to grab onto it with both hands, mutations or not.

She headed to the menagerie and carried Emma's cage to the playpen Dad had built. As soon as the tiny door slid open, Emma scampered out and climbed the fake tree. Motion triggered the UV lights set into the bulkheads, bathing the terrarium with warmth.

Mick clipped the male hokou's cage in place and flicked the door. He didn't leave as quickly. She supposed she should name him.

"Hey, Horatio." She grinned at her creativity. *Yup, that will do.*

The food dispenser hummed as it spat rehydrated fruit into a tray. He peeked out of his cage, then crept into the terrarium. Emma dropped from the branch to swipe a piece of fruit. Startled, Horatio leaped aside. In a blink, he lunged at Emma. She squealed, deafening Mick. Instead of cupping her ears, Mick yanked open the access door and shoved Horatio off Emma. He leaped onto her arm. Fire burned along her veins from where he'd sunk his teeth into her forearm, again. She swung her arm, sending him flying to the rear of the terrarium. Pain radiated, pulsed, rose, and fell like a tidal wave while blood dribbled to her elbow. She couldn't focus on this now, fearing a worsening of the mutation.

Glaring at a sprawled Horatio to make sure he didn't attack again, she gently scooped up Emma. Blood matted the fur at her throat. Her limp body said it all. The air in Mick's lungs froze. She couldn't breathe. *No, no, no. Not Emma.* A tear slipped off her chin and faded into Emma's fur.

"NOX, prep the pod." Mick croaked, spun on a heel, and slammed the terrarium door behind her, ignoring her own blood speckling the metallic floor.

"She's dead, Mick. There's no pulse."

"No," she gasped, cradling the little body against her chest. The tears flowed while anger and sorrow engulfed her.

"The male's dying too. His abnormal behavior has to be a side effect of whatever the natives fed him."

"What?" she squeaked. "I...did all this for nothing?" She slid Emma into a biodegradable capsule, taking care with her tiny hands and feet, even tucking her tail in with the gentlest of touches. "How long does Horatio have?"

A whimper from the terrarium snagged her gaze. Slumped in the corner lay the male hokou. Grief weakened her knees. Perhaps Horatio had been dying all along, and her "rescue" had doomed him to an excruciating death. She sniffed and flicked tears aside with her wrist.

"Could the pod—?"

"You can try." NOX sounded doubtful.

When she picked him up, he didn't resist. His sad gaze rested on her, and each breath shuddered his chest.

"Prep the pod." She carried Horatio, speed walking while trying not to jar him.

"Done," NOX said.

She lowered him onto the pod's bed she'd recently vacated. When she stepped back, the capsule sealed. The red writing flickered like birthday lights—sad and hopeless. It didn't bode well. She splayed her fingers on the glass and waited.

"Internal organ failure, too many to heal. As soon as the pod heals one, another collapses. Something in the hokou's blood—"

"That makes no sense. Why would his bite grant *me* healing but not him?"

"A mutation, Mick."

"Perhaps this is my fate too," she muttered. "Because *I* did this. I...couldn't save him...*them*."

With trembling fingers, she ordered the pod to euthanize, sure to grant Horatio a sweet death. Everything within her couldn't let him suffer, not a moment more. In an instant, his labored breathing ceased. A last breath rasped out of him, his lifeless gaze on her.

Opening the glass, she gathered his limp body. "I'm so sorry, little guy." Crying, she carried him to the menagerie. She placed him into the capsule with Emma, clipped it shut, and rolled it into the tube. "Fly past the closest sun, NOX, and launch tube one." Spinning the lock in place was her final task in Dad's empty and deathly still menagerie.

She scanned the cages once filled with exotic and colorful creatures.

"NOX, deactivate all feeding programs. Freeze the power and life support to this area." She slumped and left the room, jogging to her father's quarters. Only when she slapped her palm on the keylock did she notice the dried blood. Unblemished skin remained where Horatio had bitten her. She should have the pod reassess her, but that could wait. If she was dying, finding out tomorrow was good enough.

She staggered inside when the door opened.

On his desk sat a bottle of alcohol. She dared not look anywhere else. Not once had she stepped foot inside his room, not since the funeral. Dad's things were as he left them. She hadn't the heart to move into the captain's cabin nor had she sifted through it. Like a tomb, it would go down with the *Jinsei* as is.

Grabbing the bottle and bolting, she paused in the passage, her breathing ragged. She waited, listening for the door to seal.

Up the ladder to the upper level, which had once been the viewing deck, she slapped the keylock and entered her room. A shuddering sob escaped her. She uncorked the bottle with her teeth and raised it to her lips. The fiery sweetness of port hit her tongue and burned her throat and belly. As she drank, something slithered along the glass bottle to nestle against her cheek. She pulled the bottle away and blinked at the amulet hanging around the neck. Catching it in her palm, she studied the hieroglyphs on its edges and an embossed bird at its center. Her tears dribbled into its grooves. She ran her thumb along its hooked nose, smearing blood across the amulet's white gold. Dad had worn this every day, but the funeral parlor couldn't incinerate it. She vaguely recalled slipping it onto the bottle.

"Dad... I miss you so much," she whispered and crumpled to the cold metal floor. She looped the amulet around her neck and raised the bottle amid the tears streaming down her cheeks. Never had she felt more abandoned than at that moment. And she was isolated, in a metal tin, flying through space with no destination in mind. On this ship, she would live and die...alone.

Chapter Two

THAT'S LIFE

Year: 2364

10 Parsecs (32.6156 light-years) from the Orion Nebula.

GRIT, MADE FROM DISTILLED spinach, hit the back of Mick's throat like a mouthful of sand. She swirled the variegated green sludge before slugging it back, clenching her teeth against the earthy flavor and the sweet burn of alcohol.

Rainbow colors against the velvet of endless space filled the ship's fore vids. The *Jinsei* drifted outside a nebula she had stared at for two Prime Earth days while she awaited her next job.

But flicking through the available contracts made her grimace. Her credits ran thin. Keeping Dad's research ship operational was expensive, but she couldn't bear the thought of replacing it with something sleek, fuel-efficient, and pretty. It would be an act of betrayal, tossing away the last thing she had of him.

A migraine pressed behind her eyes, scorching, blurring, with dark sports vibrating at the edge of her vision. She refilled the glass, wincing at what had become an addiction. Grit kept her senses dulled: no incessant humming of the engines buzzing through her skull, no random drafts of air raising the hairs on her neck, and no burning of her nostrils from the stench of ozone permeating every inch of space. A discovery she'd made the day she'd jettisoned the last of Dad's menagerie into a sun.

Slugging back the green liquid, she prayed it drowned out NOX's tinny singing of another show tune. She slammed the glass onto the console and flipped through the contracts again. Fentus Research needed more guinja from Fornax. Easy credits but barely enough to keep *Jinsei* running for one Prime Earth month.

The religious group Followers was after something ludicrous. Rumors had reached their holier-than-thou ears of a dragon-like species. They offered ten times the Fentus amount for evidence. Mick snorted. An excursion for photographic evidence of their stupidity? Doable, except it was to Cetus—a remote galaxy humans had yet to colonize.

If she accepted the Followers' job, she would receive a third now for expenses.

Should her evidence disprove the rumors, they'd pay her the remainder of the credits.

And if she confirmed their existence and drone-delivered a live specimen, that would mean double the payment.

While palming the amulet, she studied the console screen, weighing the distance, fuel costs, and time spent alone against the payment offered. The *Jinsei* had the equipment to scan the planet. That at least guaranteed some of the credits would reach her pocket.

Tilting her head, she hollered at the metallic bulkhead, "NOX, how's the *Jinsei's* reconnaissance equipment?"

Catching him in the middle of '*a modern major general,*' NOX fake-cleared his non-existent throat to answer, "In working order, but a service wouldn't go amiss." He hummed the opening tune to Oklahoma as he calibrated the *Jinsei's* canons, again. He had 'ears' and 'eyes' everywhere, so she wasn't alone, but he wasn't human and lacked the spontaneity of her species.

With two taps on the console, she accepted both jobs. She would pick up the guinja en route to Cetus and drone-deliver them to Fentus. Refilling her glass, she sipped the grit, finding small samples palatable but less effective. Her mutated system worked through the alcohol faster than she liked.

A ping from the console confirmed the Followers had awarded her the job, along with the credits. An addendum had her groaning, downing the grit to smash the glass against the bulkhead, showering shards onto the metallic flooring.

Another party had shown interest, and even though she had dealt with competition before, she wasn't prepared to deal with the Soldiers of Solomon. She had last seen Kiros Caldwell eleven years ago at Dad's funeral. She'd attended in her father's stupid disguise, a last hurrah as his 'son,' Michael, instead of the Mikaela her mother had named her. A shuttle accident had killed her mother and stranded Mick on Earth. With Mick's various allergies, joining her father's air-controlled world, that of documenting unknown creatures across galaxies, was logical.

If a primitive planet necessitated it, Dad had hired Soldiers of Solomon for protection. Mick had grown up among them. They'd trained her, laughed with her, and shared their stories. Kiros had often tossed Mick over his shoulder or pinned her to the ground during their sparring sessions. He'd been younger then and destined to replace Solomon Kruger when the time came. She'd developed a crush on the charismatic Kiros. Something, he, thankfully, hadn't noticed.

What would he say now if he saw the real Mikaela? He had a slow simmer that would build until he snapped. But he'd never harmed her nor did he bear grudges. Those were good character traits for the leader of a renowned mercenary band, and she hoped they would be her salvation. One thing Kiros couldn't tolerate was dishonesty. As Michael, she had hidden her gender from him for sixteen years.

"NOX, set a course for Fornax." She pushed away from the console to stretch, raising her hands toward the flickering low-UV lighting, ignoring the bot clearing the shards of glass. The grit had left her bloodstream, and sobriety pressed on her senses. She closed her eyes and wondered why she bothered with alcohol. Her bed, a cryo-pen, and blessed darkness would suppress her heightened abilities.

"Incoming call from Kiros of S.o.S." NOX patched him through before Mick could stop him. She lunged for the console and activated her avatar the moment Kiros's face appeared on the fore vids.

"Mick? Is that you?" His baritone stroked her memories, inciting old affection.

She forced a smile, trusting the avatar to display a thirty-something-old man, modeled after her father at that age. The cost of it was a little more than standard, but worth it when it added a layer of believability to her role as xeno-hunter.

"Hey, Kiros, it's been a while."

He looked good; his bright and familiar smile dimpling his dark cheeks against his impossibly sharp jaw.

Her heart leaped and bounced, shuddering her breath. The modulator deepened her voice but wouldn't remove its breathless quality.

"You've made quite a name for yourself traversing the galaxy," she said into the stilted silence. Trailing her gaze over his corn-row braids, she wished she could run her fingers along the tight ropes glimmering like licorice.

"I'd say the same. I'm surprised we haven't stumbled into each other." He chuckled. The sound rumbled toward her across who knew how many light-years.

She *had* seen him on Ganymede, but she strode past him with forced casualness. Not that he would've recognized the woman she had become as Mick-the-boy he sparred with. He had looked good then and now having filled out, taller with broader shoulders and a barrel chest.

She shrugged. "To be fair, we don't hunt the same species."

"True enough." He grunted. "The Followers offer way too much to turn down this job. When I spotted your marker, it made sense to combine our talents like we used to."

Her breath hitched, and she sat, her knees weak at the idea of meeting him after all this time. A glance down had her grimacing. An oil and sweat-stained tank top over low-hanging cargo pants? He'd seen her in worse. Her breasts straining the tank's worn fabric were the issue. He'd never seen those. She cupped the amulet and ran her thumb along the hooked beak of the bird. For some strange reason, holding it brought her comfort.

"I accepted another job en route. I wouldn't dare consider detaining you while I hunt guinja." She rested her gaze on his face, watching for any revelation of what he thought. Just a smile, as usual.

"Mm, what do you think, Drys?" He spoke to someone off-screen, a man she wasn't familiar with.

This Drys mumbled a response, and despite her enhanced hearing, she couldn't catch a word. She kept her smile plastered on, not willing to reveal her desperate hope that Drys would advise against this joint venture.

"Still got the *Jinsei*?"

She twitched at Kiros's question and nodded.

"And the menagerie?"

Pain was swift to strike, seizing her chest. Dad's collection of xeno creatures had died one by one after his death, and each time, she'd relived losing him. She dipped her head to blink away the tears while forcing the constant loneliness to the back of her mind.

"No creatures are on board the *Jinsei* at this time." She forced a smile when she met Kir's onyx gaze. "No vacs required." Not that she carried vaccinations for all known diseases or infections, only the lethal ones.

"You're alone?" He leaned closer until she could count each of his long eyelashes. "Is NOX with you?"

"Yes, and I had him upgraded to give me blowjobs." Mick fought to keep a straight face when Kiros's eyebrow shot upward. "I wish."

He chuckled, but his shoulders stiffened. Though why the idea should bother him, she didn't know. Had Kiros always been anti-A.I.? He'd never mentioned anything in that line.

"We'll rendezvous with you and park the *Sentry* in your cargo hold. What's your points?"

She pressed the pause button and sucked in sharp breaths, fighting for calm. How could she extract herself from this? How could she keep him at bay without pissing off the deadliest merc in the known universe? Nothing came to mind. All she had were blank thoughts blinded by panic.

"What's wrong?" NOX asked.

She squealed and smacked the bulkhead, stinging her palm even as she dented the metal. "Don't scare me like that."

He made a whirring sound, modulated after a snort. "Your heartbeat's elevated, and your core temperature is fluctuating."

"Because you scared me." She stuck her tongue at "him." "Now, be quiet, I'm on a call."

NOX tutted. "I shall scan your vitals in the meantime."

"Do a full diagnostic, the works." She grinned. That would keep him busy long enough. Unpausing the call, she forced another smile. "I'll send you my beacon, Kir. Lock onto it, and we'll meet en route."

"Roger." His focus dipped to his console as if he waited. With a sigh, she activated the signal and sent it. Grinning, he met her gaze. "I can't wait to see you. Is my room untouched?"

"It is, but then again, you're Solomon now. Moving up in the world earns better accommodation." Which meant one of the three officer quarters.

"True. See you soon, my old friend." After he ended the call, the fore vid showed the passing stars.

Two shots of grit later, she gripped the console, straining for a way out of this. She had accepted the job, so her reputation was at stake. There was no backing out. Modifying her beacon meant delaying the rendezvous and not bringing an end to the dilemma. Perhaps she should face him, reveal the truth, and have done with it? Like she said, Kiros wasn't one to carry a grudge. She hoped that hadn't changed.

"I have the results from the full scan you requested," NOX said, intruding on her memories and returning her to the Kiros-dilemma.

"Let's hear it," she said, taking a moment to pinch her brow. She doubted the results had changed since her last deep scan, but it didn't hurt to be thorough.

"The infection has saturated your internal organs. It's healing your liver as you consume alcohol and has removed all traces of your allergies." He released a mechanical chuckle that grated, like scraping stone across metal. "I have run a few calculations and expect your speed, strength, vision, and healing capabilities to be superhuman."

"Everything hits a peak, NOX. I have to start deteriorating at some point." She shook her head, trying to rid her ears of the humming engines. "Perhaps insanity is the way I go."

"Your brain remains untouched, for now."

"Great," she snorted, "possessed by hokou parasites. When I lose my mind, scuttle the ship."

Unable to sleep unless aided, she spent hours working through ancient training vids. What she needed was a sparring partner. Some of the fighting styles required an opponent. Using the stored A.I. shell to house NOX cost too much. He somehow managed to damage it. Last time, he'd wedged himself in an air vent. It had taken her hours to dislodge him, and she'd had to remove his arms to do so.

"I was hot. I went to parties a lot, y'know..." NOX hummed the rest of the tune, not one she recognized, which meant he was trawling the bottom of the show tunes barrel.

She shuddered, imagining him discovering space operas. He would drone on about characters suffering from amnesia, then falling in love with their husband's brother's son by accident.

NOX would make it his life's mission to unravel the inner workings of these characters and drive her insane with questions.

When she stepped into the gym, the overhead lights flickered, bathing her in a sickly blue. Since the hokou-incident, the gym had grown as she needed equipment. For now, she crossed the dense sparring mat to the boxing bag in the corner. A round of kicks, punches, and hammerfists would ease the tension in her shoulders and drown out the engines' hum with her thudding heartbeat.

On normal days when Kiros wasn't intent on disrupting her thoughts, she'd do an hour or so of yoga, searching for that elusive inner peace. Or maybe try a little Jiu-Jitsu—made harder without a partner.

Darts of fire rippled up her legs when she connected with the bag, sending it swinging with each roundhouse kick. As soon as her mind registered it, the pain dissipated. Her mutations healed something as insignificant as muscle strain. She punched harder, pivoting on the ball of her foot to bring her body into motion. A knuckle snapped. She yelped and leaped back to cradle her hand. A sliver of bone protruded. Blood trickled free around it. She spun, planning on heading to the medbay. But a twinge of pain froze her. The bone slid back into her knuckle, and the skin knitted.

"What the frig?" Wiping the blood smears aside on her damp leggings, she blinked at her healed skin. No residual pain lingered. She flexed her fingers, testing the movement. Yanking her tank aside, she stared at the unscarred skin where the hokou had bitten her. She'd thought the pod had done a bang-up job. Now she expected it had had nothing to heal.

"NOX?" She angled her head to the bulkhead. "Did you see that?"

"What?" He sighed. "Hang on. Lemme check." Not a millisecond passed before he whooped. "Well, well, well."

"I'm glad you're pleased."

"What else am I supposed to be? Miserable? A pessimist? This here is grade A entertainment."

She gritted her teeth. Sometimes, she missed the old stick-up-his-ass NOX, polite, considerate. Somehow, he'd gained sass, which had her in two minds, either to pull his plug or laugh. For now, she chose not to respond. Her thoughts settled on the tasks ahead.

Hunting guinja on Fornax meant she needed to prep the shuttle, restock the tranqs, and check the drones. After Cetus, she had to venture to Fentus Research and collect the drones they stored for her. She couldn't afford to keep buying new ones.

With sweat dripping off her chin and her breathing evening out, she skulked to her quarters, practicing walking on silent feet. Not an easy task on the grated flooring.

In her quarters, she peeled off the sweat-drenched top and pants and tossed them in the aerator. What she should do is incinerate them. Hell, she might as well stop off at Sculptor for new clothing. After a quick shower, she grabbed a reusable cryo-pen from the wall-mounted med-box and threw herself wet and naked onto her bed. Sedatives or sedi-pens no longer affected her mutating body. Only cryo-pens offered a good night's rest. She didn't know what she would take to numb her mind when her mutations adjusted to the ice-gel flowing through her veins.

That was a problem for another day. Kiros's impending arrival and his reaction to her were foremost in her thoughts. She expected him to hate her, smashing her girlhood hopes. How silly she had been to dream of him confessing his undying love for her when he had only known her as a boy. Now, she would be lucky if he didn't kill her at first sight.

CHAPTER THREE

KIROS GLARED AT DRYS Lyons across the bridge. The man had saved his life too many times to count, and Kiros should be counting. Such debts he would need to repay.

Now Drys paced with furious energy, his gray hair brushing his shoulders as he rubbed his salt and pepper beard. "Something don't feel right, y'know."

The implication that Mick Danvers deceived him was preposterous, downright laughable. The kid was too sweet and naïve, yet in the last six years had developed a reputation for finding rare alien creatures. True, Kiros hadn't liked talking to an avatar, but it wasn't unheard of to use such means to retain anonymity. Hell, all the soldiers answered to Solomon in public, confusing any would-be assassins. To each his own.

Kiros folded his arms across his chest and watched his confidant pace. "He's a good kid, Drys. I had a hand in raising him."

"Then why use the avatar with an old friend? And his voice? Manipulated. My brittle bones aren't happy. We're walking into a trap."

Kiros wondered the same thing. His welcome disturbed him. Then again, it was eleven years since Thomas Danvers's funeral. Kiros should have reached out to the kid, been there for him. Had he failed Thomas? Kiros rolled his shoulders, hoping to ease the burning tension. He expected the same-old Mick to greet him with a hero-worshipping smile like he used to. But the kid had hesitated in his responses, almost as if seeing Kiros scared him. On that, Drys was right to be suspicious.

They'd received Mick's beacon, and soon enough, Kiros would get to the bottom of this. "Have we set course to intersect his trajectory?"

Wyatt, their ace pilot, waved a hand instead of responding. Somewhere in his mass of dreadlocks were his earbuds playing yet another audiobook; his focus intense as he navigated the *Sentry* toward Fornax.

"Think the kid will split the payment?" Drys trailed Kiros to the mess.

"I don't see why not." He paused, his shoulders brushing the sides of the narrow passage. "Before you say anything more, he won't suspect the ruse. Like I said, naïve and sweet."

Drys grumbled under his breath. "His reputation is the perfect diversion. While he hunts for 'evidence,' we'll snatch a creature. The Followers are more than happy to pay double if the kid grabs a live sample too."

Kiros grinned. "If we find rare minerals, De Beer Mining will compensate us for our data. Overall, it's a lucrative project any way we look at it."

"Using the kid's ship is genius." Drys filled a cup with coffee-flavored sludge and poured in too much sweetener.

"I know, and our history won't raise suspicion either. It would be like old times when Thomas hired S.o.S for hostile excursions." Kiros bit into a protein bar and left the mess.

Drys's overactive instincts unsettled Kiros, and as he strolled to his quarters, he frowned. Something was off with Mick. Had he caught wind of S.o.S's other endeavors? Kiros shook his head. Impossible. The kid didn't run in the same circles. Drys's paranoia was rubbing off on Kiros.

His door slid across, and he slipped through the growing opening, too impatient to wait. As captain's cabins go, this one was bigger than a bunk but not by much. A rectangular prism seven feet by ten meant he could install a larger-than-normal bed to accommodate his height. Grooves in the metal crisscrossed a wall from which he could summon a small galley, a shower, a toilet, or a table with a chair. All slid out of sight at a push. A sterilizing aerated closet held his clothing and linen. This was a luxury he had earned from the sweat of his brow and the blood staining his hands.

Tearing off another bite of the protein bar, he flipped onto his bed and folded an arm behind his head. "Access gallery." The screen in the ceiling flickered on, and a directory appeared, divided into many more. "The year 2348."

A robotic voice—neither feminine nor male—said, "No files for that date."

Was it longer than sixteen years since he last photographed Mick? "Display last images taken before 2348."

"Two images located."

The first image was of the S.o.S band. Solomon Burger laughed while sharing a dram of whisky with Thomas. Mick was in the background and in profile, his cheeks hairless. The kid must have been twelve. His spindly arms had yet to develop muscle.

The second image held the smiling Mick he remembered. Kiros had one arm thrown over the kid's narrow shoulders. The skinny runt looked almost feminine. Dark brown hair cropped short, pale skin, umber-colored eyes; a striking contrast to Kiros's mocha skin and walnut-brown eyes.

"Eli says we need parts." Wyatt's tinny voice cut through the bulkhead.

Glaring at the fine holes where the sound traveled through, Kiros said, "I told Eli to hold off on repairs."

"You said that in Andromeda, Kiros. I checked ahead. Eridanus has what I need." Eli's distinctive drawl meant he cornered Wyatt on the bridge. It must be urgent. He didn't like confrontations unless it was in battle. Eli was a tried and tested mechanic, who lived life to the fullest with gung-ho aggression. The meaner the treatment, the better.

"Fine, we'll burn hot to get there, but that fuel's coming out of your cut." Kiros tossed his biodegradable wrapper on the floor, watching a bot slide out to clean it. He kept his quarters spotless, but he often made a mess to give the poor machine something to do. "You will not repair shit until we dock on the *Jinsei*. Understood?"

"For how long will the *Sentry* be stationary?" Eagerness saturated Eli's voice, spiking it.

"The journey between Fornax and Cetus." Wyatt's bored tone drowned Eli's grumbling whose voice faded as he left the bridge.

Kiros sighed. "Give me two hours, Wyatt, and I'll cover you tonight." The quiet of the bridge, while the crew slept was the only peace he could find onboard the too-small rapier-class ship. Their band had grown too fast, and they hadn't found a larger ship more suitable to their needs and pocket.

"Roger that, Kiros."

Silence settled once more in Kiros's quarters.

Mick's image remained on the ceiling vid. He didn't need any delays. Something urged him to hurry, to meet the boy sooner. Before Fornax was preferable. He closed his eyes, drew in a deep breath, and released it in a slow exhale.

"Kiros, we got company." Wyatt's voice jolted him awake.

Kiros growled, exhaustion adding lead to his limbs and making his movements sluggish. Had he slept for a second?

He rubbed his face. "What is it?"

Wyatt chuckled. "I think we struck it lucky. The manifest has it as a cargo carrier with crates of cabbages. Sec-comms has it flagged as a slave ship with its trajectory Ursa Minor."

"Scan for life forms." Kiros swung his legs off the side of the bed and rose to his full height. He stretched, clicking his back and neck. Relief was instant.

"Clumped together as expected of a slave ship." Wyatt gasped. "Over seventy prisoners."

"What's the bounty?" Kiros jogged along the passage, passing a few of his men en route. They trailed him, eagerness for a fight in their easy smiles.

"Hefty," Wyatt said. "Might be worth veering off course."

"No." Kiros burst into the bridge to lean over Wyatt, analyzing the info on the vids. "We'll board and plant a few men to retake the ship. Deliver it to Kapteyn, and claim the bounty. Either hire a vessel and meet us at Fornax, or await our return."

"That could be weeks." Aidan tossed worried glances while he picked at a scar across his left eyebrow.

"We'll wait a Prime Earth day at Fornax. Any longer is unacceptable." Kiros stared down each man. "Need me to lead?" He hid a grimace. If they said yes, he'd have to travel to Kapteyn. But he had made the offer, half implying they were lost without him.

"I got this." Lanek tugged on his threadbare 'lucky' gloves. "Aidan, Seth, and Ruben, you're with me." He swept up his shoulder-length blond hair into a ponytail.

"Action, at last." Ruben rubbed his palms together, a grin splitting his cheeks. His chewed matchstick clung precariously to his bottom lip.

"We had action last week," Seth said, tapping his blaster to check on its power banks. His buzzcut and slashing eyebrows hinted at dark-brown hair, and a jagged scar rippled down the right side of his face.

"That wasn't fun; they knew we were coming. These guys have no clue what's about to hit them." Their arguing voices faded as Lanek led them to the airlock.

Wyatt banked the *Sentry* alongside the cargo carrier and extended the arm with the men inside. Once it latched onto the carrier's hull, the seal would open, and they could either force their entry or Ruben could work his magic. Kiros didn't know of anyone with his talent—the opening of any locked, sealed, or coded door. The latter was the preferred approach. They would need the ship operational to deliver the prisoners alive.

"This don't feel right," Drys said, shaking his head. "Too coincidental."

"I'm beginning to think you see danger in everything." Kiros chuckled. "It could be an easy takeover, or worse, we kill them and scuttle the ship."

Drys grinned. "True." He flipped a switch on the console. "Status?"

"Ruben's working on the door," Aidan said. "Are they aware of our presence?"

"They haven't changed course, and no heat signals await your entry," Wyatt said, his fingers flying across the console.

"How can they not have picked up on the *Sentry's* approach?" Kiros scowled. "Drys's right. This *is* odd." He pressed the comm button. "Lanek, proceed with caution."

No response followed except for the firing of blasters, thumps of falling bodies, and the heavy tread of hurried boots. "Ambush," Lanek growled. "Moving forward."

Silence followed. Kiros clenched his jaw, wishing he'd led the team. Lanek would replace him when he retired, and the ability to trust him and all Kiros had taught him was harder than anticipated. This *was* a simple takeover, regardless of the complications.

The *Sentry* tilted, a creak and whine pierced the bridge, and the engines strained to maintain their position. Wyatt grabbed the lever, cursing a blue streak. "Quit taking a stroll, Lanek. They're attempting to shake off the *Sentry*."

"Heading to the bridge." Blasters, screams, and cursing filled the *Sentry's* bridge.

"Can you tap into their sec system?" Drys arched a brow, his shoulders tense.

"There isn't one. The life system is struggling and the engines sputtering. The ship shouldn't be operational." Wyatt sucked in a breath. "This is a too-elaborate trap. Who have we pissed off?"

"Recently?" Kiros smothered a laugh, finding it inappropriate for now.

"Die, bitches," an unknown voice yelled.

Blaster shots sounded.

Lanek grunted in pain. Kiros glanced at the team's stats. He released a breath. None had died.

"A flesh wound," Lanek said, his voice strangled. "Bridge cleared. Aidan, scan the ship. Confirm the authenticity of the life forms."

"Two levels below," Aidan said. "The heat signatures are jumpy."

"Shit," Seth grumbled.

"I don't like this either," Lanek said. "Aidan, hold the bridge."

"Acknowledged."

Heavy breathing set the soundtrack for their trip down two levels, along with a few blaster shots.

"Ruben, you're up," Lanek said.

"Friggin hell, I hate this," Kiros said, keeping his voice low.

"Suck it up." Drys smirked. "Solomon went through the same shit with you."

"Doesn't mean I have to like it," Kiros said, but the tension stiffening his back eased a bit. He missed his former boss and mentor. They had dropped him off at Moon Station. And with a wave, he disappeared into the causeway crowds, fading into obscurity. That was the way of things, and Kiros expected to do the same when his time came.

"Oh, frig," Ruben said. "Confirmed sighting of the prisoners."

"Shit," Lanek said. "Seth reassure them. Wyatt, give us ten to check the state of their stores."

"Done," Aiden said. "They're fully stocked. Enough for a few trips to Fornax."

"Excellent. Good work, team." Lanek coughed. "Detach, Wyatt, and we'll rendezvous at Fornax. And Seth, get me some medical aid, would ya?"

Wyatt retracted the arm and tilted the lever to the right.

"Happy now, papa bear?" Drys teased, chuckling as he left the bridge.

"Full burn to Eridanus." Kiros hesitated and dropped his hand on Wyatt's shoulder. "Want me to take over?"

"I got this, boss." Wyatt flipped a switch, and a droning voice recited a novel, filling the bridge.

Kiros returned to his quarters, bed, and blessed sleep.

Chapter Four

FORESHADOWING

The planet Tau Ceti, aka Rianus

TIEREN FELL TO HIS knees with fire cinching his chest. Coughs shredded his lungs and tore up his throat as he expelled the tainted smoke irritating his body. The ritual's purpose was to spark a vision. Each year, he returned to the shaman's tent in the hopes of an epiphany.

This time, he'd received his first one. The gods had finally spoken.

Collapsing onto his back, he stared at the pale-lilac sky, mesmerized by the brown-tinted clouds and relishing the sweet air cooling his singed throat.

The unusual creature in his vision was a female. Her image resurfaced, and her delicate face proclaimed her not of his world. And with her exotic features came this sense of excitement, completion, and dread, all warring with each other to take turns shuddering through his body. He was as hard as the Mountains of Bircier, and his arousal tented the loincloth he wore for the ceremony. He rubbed it in acquiescence and acknowledgment, sighing at the bolt of heated pleasure shooting to both his hearts.

"She is a danger to you more than Rianus." Pengfei released the tent flap and waddled toward Tieren sprawled on the floor. His loincloth fluttered, flashing more of the man than Tieren cared to see. "It is time you had a vision, *Tsuna* Tieren."

He pinched his lips at the formal address. Inside the tent, he was a man seeking answers. Outside, the full weight of his responsibilities bowed his shoulders. "A moment of freedom, Pengfei, that is all I ask for."

Pengfei furrowed his brow. "That is something you can never have unless this female chooses wisely."

Tieren scowled. "She endangers my brother, Braon, and my home, Rianus. I cannot tolerate either."

"But you must, *tsuna*, for she brings you peace if you embrace her strangeness."

Tieren leaped to his feet, not willing to discuss his vision.

Pengfei threw his hand skyward in a wild gesture. "She'll fall from the sky and steal your brother during his Trial of Tolend. This is a serious matter, and one we need to prevent."

Tieren grunted and whipped off his loincloth to tug on his loose breeches they called dowo. "Two lunars need to pass before Braon embarks on his Trial. I will attend to my tasks this day, but visit me within a lunar."

Pengfei's pursed lips implied his impatience.

Tieren ignored him and sauntered down the worn path toward the Pools of Condare where the remainder of his clothing waited. He could fly, but the breeze had reached the rolling purple hills of his realm, whipping his ebony plumage across his back. He raised his face to the sky, enjoying the call to freedom.

He couldn't answer, for a ship awaited him. The distance to the Isles of Eleta was too great for his wings to carry him, and many a Greeven had died in the attempt. A two-day journey by ship but necessary, and with his advisers traveling with him, none of his tasks remained unattended. Soon, he would step aside for Braon to reign.

As the shadow in a sea of white Greevens, he could never rule. Every decision he made was scrutinized. Each move he made was judged or argued over. All because his plumage was a darker hue, harkening to their ancestors and when their home had had two suns.

The female in his vision was a paler brown, that of their oceans and lakes, as if her skin reflected the morning clouds and the rock of Bircier. Her plumage had fallen down her back, swaying with the seductive movement of her hips. Regardless of her mesmerizing brown eyes, she would steal his brother.

Bring him peace? If he killed her, then yes.

"*Atsuna*, was it a successful session? Did the gods speak to you?" Meilo, Tieren's trustworthy servant and friend, hurried along the path toward him, dangling a wineskin over a forearm. His beaded and braided black hair brushed his shoulders.

The poor male asked him every year with Tieren's usual response a scowl. This year, he grunted.

"That good?" Meilo uncorked the wineskin and offered it to him.

"The gods have spoken, but the images are cryptic. Do not ask me to explain." Tieren pinched his lips. What could he say? His mate was a star traveler? No, as distrusted as he was, this would worsen his standing in the kingdom.

Braon wouldn't judge him, though. Sighing, Tieren took a long pull of the chilled wine, grateful as it soothed his smoke-roughened throat. He held out his arms for Meilo to dress him, not saying a word when his servant cinched the belt tight. The robe draped to his toes. He slid on his sandals, then knelt for Meilo to braid his hair.

He had often considered taking his dagger to it and slicing it off. Males wore their hair shoulder length. If he did as well, it would admit defeat, a submission to their traditions and their opinions of him. This he wouldn't do.

"You reek. I will order a bath once we board the ship."

Tieren agreed. The stench of the *styaha* weed clung to his skin, and the fabric of the robe irritated him. He said nothing and strode down the hill toward the ship docked at the wooden pier.

Awaiting him were his advisers. Spies, more like it. General Assalan, Ambassador Sugard, and Cousin Karlez, but no spies were from Braon. All hoped to replace Tieren as a confidant, to manipulate Braon and drain him of his authority.

General Assalan, his white hair peppered with dull silver, was the first to speak. Rare gold beads tipped his braids. "How fare's Pengfei?"

"He is well." Tieren clipped his words, hoping to convey an unwillingness to waste time talking.

As usual, they ignored his stiff posture, Cousin Karlez more so, thinking the small amount of royal blood in his veins granted him an advantage. "What did the gods say, *Tsuna* Tieren?" His warm brown eyes linked him to the Fanyell clan, except, where his plumage was white, Tieren's was midnight.

Using his title as a prince of the kingdom was not the way to butter him for information. His cousin didn't know him well despite sharing ancestry. "The gods reveal as they see fit."

He ducked into his tent, allowing the flap to close on their duplicitous faces. The ship lurched as the two-day journey began. The path was treacherous where only the most skilled navigated. The ship flowed with the current, but to veer off it was to encounter ravenous beasts and choppy waters. The parchments spoke of a powerful magic wielder who'd cast the route into existence. Storms pounded the seas on either side but never within the path itself. It was wide enough to carry several ships, and if he raised his gaze to the beige skies, something pale and iridescent shimmered above him.

The only danger on the return journey to Qilaetor was boredom.

"More wine, *atsuna*?"

Tieren hissed at Meilo, who chuckled, dodging a fist.

"Have done, Tieren, I but jest. I mean to ply you with fine wine to loosen your tongue." Meilo poured a goblet of blue *jaketta* wine, taking a deep drink before refilling it for Tieren. "I have placed guards around your tent. None shall eavesdrop this night."

Tieren sipped the wine, allowing a small smile to tease his lips. "I meant what I said, Meilo. I do not wish to discuss it." What could he say? He had to kill his mate to save his brother. No Greeven dreamed of being in such a situation.

"Mm, perhaps after a bath?" Meilo was like a denga with a bone.

"If I give you one word, will you leave this alone?" Tieren swirled the dark-blue liquid, the fruity fragrance rising to tantalize. Meilo had traveled with him each year, commiserated after every failed spirit walk. As one of the few males to truly stand beside Tieren, it was cruel of him not to share when the gods had, at last, revealed something to him. "Vow it."

"I vow, Tieren."

Tieren laughed at Meilo's eagerness. "*Kekaseea.*"

Meilo froze with his goblet halfway to his lips. His white cheeks darkened, and he turned a slow circle to stare at Tieren. "Your mate?"

Tieren shifted his ass, finding comfort on the cushions strewn across the rug. Meilo opened and closed his mouth, then downed his wine, but Tieren ignored him, choosing instead to revisit the visions the gods had shared.

His hearts skipped beats, then synchronized, confirming the connection he had with this female. Perhaps what he should have done was wait a day, redo the spirit walk, and hope the gods shared more. Yet, they had been silent his entire life. He doubted they would deign to answer his curiosity.

True to his word, Meilo didn't mention the visions again, and for that, Tieren was grateful. He needed time to sift through his emotions and decide the best path to take.

Chapter Five

TEMPTATION

Amid gray smoke or clouds, a face appeared. Mick squeaked and jerked back. The man met her gaze as he emerged to stand naked before her. He was magnificent, and as dreams go, she couldn't have designed a more perfect example of sheer masculinity. A molded chest, broad shoulders, and muscled arms to four-fingered hands whispered of long nights and infinite pleasure. His hawk-like nose saved him from being a pretty boy, and she adored his obsidian skin, glowing like heated volcanic rock.

She wasn't one for fanciful dreams. This, with the cinnamon sky and those penetrating cognac-colored eyes meant she had to be fantasizing. He ran his gaze over her. Only then did she realize she was as naked as him. His open admiration halted the urge to cover herself. In a dream, what did it matter if the world saw her so...exposed?

"Like what you see?" she asked, cupping her hip.

He grinned and stole her breath. No way should a man be this devastating. Man? She frowned, studying his hands *and* feet. Four fingers and toes instead of five? And they didn't look like deformations. Nor did he have nipples or a navel. Well, she'd had weirder dreams than a nipple-less man.

"For a strange female, you are beautiful." He squawked his words in a deep, resonating voice.

She scowled. *What is this?* "I can't understand you. You don't speak English?"

He winced. His gaze darted across her face, then he slumped. "I feared this would be an issue." He reached out a hand, as if to plead with her. "I... You..." He sighed. "I want to know everything about you. Without words, what can I learn?" He splayed his fingers across his chest. "Tieren."

At his expectation, she repeated the last word. "Tier...enn?"

He smiled again and tapped his chest. "Tieren."

"Oh." Her cheeks warmed. That was his name. "Mick." She patted herself just below the collarbone. Mikaela would have been preferable, but under the circumstances, too long.

"Mick," he repeated. His accent thickened the 'ck,' turning it into two syllables. Hell no, she wasn't going to change it. Not when heat exploded in her core at her name on his tongue.

He tucked a curl behind her ear, his touch sparking fire. How could she feel that so vividly in a dream? On impulse, she hugged him. Peace along with his warmth seeped into her, more so when he looped his arms around her. His embrace summoned tears, but she refused to release them. A hug from another person was incredible even if only in a dream. She rubbed her cheek across his pec, relishing the spicy fragrance of his skin.

If he said not a word but held her like this every night, she'd be content.

Gentle tugs on her braid forced her to lean back and meet his cognac-gold gaze. He unraveled the braid and buried his fingers into her hair. "Beautiful, *kekaseea*."

The warmth of admiration in his eyes conveyed what he said. And in his arms, she felt attractive. She ran her fingers along his broad shoulders and bulging biceps. Tiny scars marred his skin, some old, a few new. How had he earned these? She stepped back and snatched his hand to run her fingers over his calloused palm. Manual labor or weapons training? She gripped an imaginary sword and swung it.

He nodded. "I have some skill with a blade."

Now if NOX could penetrate her dreams, she would ask him to upload Tieren's language into her mind via her implant. But thankfully, her dreams were her own.

Tieren caught her hand and fanned out her fingers, tracing each one with a fingertip. "Five?"

She echoed him as best she could, assuming it had to do with their differences. That one word scraped her throat raw.

He tapped her fingernail. "Weak. How do you hunt?"

Frowning, she flipped their hands to stroke his solid-as-rock nail and darker than his obsidian skin. "I bet you can kill with these." She flashed a smile to soften her words, then chuckled. He couldn't be offended when he didn't understand her. "You're sexy as hell," she rasped and watched him closely.

He straightened, as if he'd understood her. "Whatever you said, you sound sensual."

She shivered at his husky tone. "Maybe you do understand me."

His brow furrowed, shadowing the confusion in his eyes.

"Okay, maybe not." She let go of his hand and threw hers in the air. "How can I talk to you? This is insane. Worst dream ever. One star. Wouldn't recommend."

She cupped a hand over her mouth to smother a giggle. "If this is a dream, can't I control it? Make you kiss me? Magic a bed out of the ether?" She traced a finger down his bare chest, stopping where his navel should have been. His cock bounced.

He captured her hand and yanked her against his hard body. She hummed, relishing his warmth. Splaying her fingers across his chest, she unerringly sought his non-existent nipples with her thumbs. Odd that he had none. Boy was her mind messed up.

"...running low on sol." NOX's tinny voice intruded.

She groaned and rested her temple on Tieren's collarbone. He tightened his arms around her but didn't respond, like NOX hadn't spoken.

"Want me to do a flyby?"

"Yes, please," she muttered. When she raised her chin to smile apologetically at Tieren, he shimmered.

With a moan, he squeezed her, but his arms slipped through her body.

"*Kekaseea*," he whispered, his touch fleeting along her jaw before he faded.

"Dammit, NOX. You couldn't wait two minutes?" She spun on a heel to rant at a bulkhead. Only gray shadows and mist remained.

"Mick, come on. We're passing a perfectly decent sun. Should I or should I not do a flyby?"

She slapped herself across her cheek and burst awake, sitting up in bed. "Just friggin do it, NOX."

"Whoa, someone woke in a pissy mood," he hissed.

She grabbed a sneaker balancing on the edge of the bed and lobbed it at the bulkhead. *Can't a girl get some privacy?*

Especially during erotic dreams. Well, not erotic, more...sensual. Promising. "NOX, if I give you a word, can you trawl all known languages and find its meaning or origin?"

"Yes, since I have tons of spare time."

She scowled. "Listen, I don't need your sass before I've had coffee."

"To sass or not to sass? Indeed, that is the question. Listen, toots, besides flying this monstrosity and dealing with your shenanigans, a software update just came through. And by just, I mean it took several hours to roll out." He scoffed, sounding like a blown gasket. "I am, after all, a mean machine."

Mean machine?

Shaking her head, she hurried to say, "*Kekaseea.*"

"That's the word?"

"Yup." She pinched her brow. "What's the time?"

"Does it matter?" He huffed. Another shoe hit the bulkhead. It fell to the floor, landing far from the other. "Fine. Prime Earth time is ten-ish, and good morning, by the way."

She ignored him, faced the mirror, and unraveled her frazzled braid. With a quick brush, rebraid, face wash, and her mouth cleaned, she yanked on stained cargo pants that clung to her ass a little too lovingly. Her brown tank top was worse. Scrimping to fuel the *Jinsei* meant she couldn't buy the necessities.

"What's the finances looking like? Any chance we can spare a few credits for—" She grimaced. "I have to, NOX. I've outgrown everything but my boots."

"It's all that grit you consume. Tends to carry carbs, and those in abundance equal chunky thighs."

"They're muscled," she squealed.

"Yeah, sure, keep telling yourself that, sweetheart."

She gritted her teeth and punched the bulkhead, leaving an indent shaped like a fist.

"In truth, you do need to eat more. You may not have noticed it yet. You're losing weight standing there. Your mutations require fuel, and surviving on noodles and grit isn't going to cut it."

"Yes, Chef NOX." She saluted, then strode out of the room and down to the mess for...well, noodles. Real food didn't survive in space unless vacuum sealed. And that shit was expensive. Then again, it was noodles and coffee, or real food and no coffee. Sacrifices had to be made.

She opened a noodle pack, shoved it into the rehydrator, and hit the start button. While it hummed in her ears, along with rhythmic pings, she percolated a single cup of coffee. Better the sound of food cooking than the distant drones within *Jinsei's* engines and life support.

She moaned after the first sip of liquid gold, the kind she'd rob for. The hot coffee—bitter because all sugar they bought went into making grit—slid down her throat and warmed her stomach. Beggars couldn't be fussy. Although, one of those decadent coffees with 'real' whipped cream on top? She snorted. Like cows still existed.

Dad had had a cow once. Found it on some colonized planet. She'd gotten excited at the thought of butter, cheese, milk, and cream, but it turned out to be a he. And a grumpier bull she'd never met. She giggled. And she'd met... She counted on her fingers. One?

Still, Typhus had been a good listener if she fed him for his time. Give and take existed even in the animal world. NOX had suggested they slaughter the bull for its meat. Dad hadn't spoken to him for three days.

"Fornax is in a few days. I'll hit every star and siphon as much sol as possible."

"Good. With Kir and his men on board, we'll need more power."

"Thought so too. It's systematic, hydromatic, why, it's greased—"

She groaned. That damn song, even sung in echo formed such a tune wedgy. Now, she'd whistle the same tune all day. Grabbing the noodles from the rehydrator, she slammed its door and headed to the bridge.

And of course, her moving between compartments, bays, along passages didn't spare her from NOX's overly enthusiastic rendition.

She sank into the pilot chair and prayed Kir arrived sooner. A little human company might be nice.

Chapter Six

FEALTY

Rianus

In the city of Qilaetor

TIEREN GLOWERED AT HIS grandmother, who had him pinned to his seat with a look. She'd heard the gods had spoken to the outcast and had descended on his orderly world with her perfumed robes and silver hair. He couldn't recall when he'd last seen her fly. Rolling his shoulders, he tried to calm the urge to spread his wings and take to the sky. It would free him from what was to be an awkward conversation.

She sipped the foul-smelling tisane, purported to heal her lungs. "Do you want me to travel to the Isles of Eleta at my age?"

She demanded his loyalty, and he swore it each time he saw her. Of his clan, only she and Braon had shown him kindness. He shook his head. "Your sacrifice will not be needed to loosen my tongue, Nona. You have but to ask your questions, and I will answer as best I can."

"Ask?" She snorted. "I need not ask, but alas. Share what the vision showed to you."

He ran a hand over his face, hoping she didn't notice his exhaustion with her sharp gaze. His nights were spent in a lust-filled dream state,

45

frustration the result. He'd suspected he wouldn't be able to communicate with Mick. His days fared no better, a constant battle for his brother's right to remain on the throne. Soon, Braon would start his Trial of Tolend, and Mick would descend from the heavens. Pengfei would arrive within a day to help Braon prepare. Tieren had yet to think of a way to protect his brother without bringing doubt to his ability to rule.

The Trial of Tolend required a squawkling to survive on their own and to return to Qilaetor having killed a rare beast. Fear engulfed his senses in a black cloud, and he sat up, squared his shoulders, and allowed it to sweep through him, like a breeze bringing the sweet fragrance of *jaketta* fruit.

Without Braon, the clan of Fanyell would no longer rule Rianus. The Greeven would not accept Tieren as their ruler, their king, not with his obsidian skin and plumage. He was as cursed as his mother was when she birthed him. If it wasn't for Nona, Father would have exiled Tieren and his mother to the Isles of Eleta.

Instead, Tieren became his brother's guardian, tasked with ensuring his protection at all times. Except, according to the parchments, during the Trial of Tolend. Braon was on his own, and Tieren could do nothing to save him. Assassins sent by the Fanyell enemies would also try their hand. Braon had to survive it all. If he failed, the Fanyell royal line would die with him.

"Tieren, *abucaah*, speak to me."

He grunted. "I am no longer a child, a squawkling, Nona." Pushing himself out of his seat, he covered the distance between them and lowered himself before her. If he had to share, only her ears needed to hear. "Braon will be kidnapped during his Trial."

Her cheeks paled, taking on an ashen hue. "Assalan?"

"You should have mated him, Nona, and saved me from that pain in my ass," he teased, pressing a kiss to her stiff knuckles.

She chortled. "Not for all the gods' feathers."

"It is not Assalan, but an unknown enemy. A female will descend from the heavens and steal Braon when he is in Greeven form." A female? How little that one word portrayed what Mick invoked in him. Those big brown eyes, her pale brown skin so unlike a Greeven's. "By the parchments, I cannot interfere."

"I sense you intend to anyway." Nona frowned. "You may be feared, Tieren, but even you cannot hope to escape judgment for this."

His thoughts exactly. Drawing in a calming breath, he sliced a glance at the closest servant before leaning in to whisper, "she is my *kekaseea*."

Nona gasped, and her four fingers clasping his arm trembled. "For the gods to bless you so, surely the people of Rianus will see there is nothing to fear from someone of your dark coloring."

He smiled. Her faith in their people always amazed him. "They will see me 'saving' Braon during his Trial."

She tightened her fingers on his forearm. Urgency thickened her voice. "Take Pengfei with you. His presence might add weight to your innocence. Do nothing to save your brother. Do everything to capture this female."

Tieren grinned. "We have the same plan. If I can reach Braon before she does."

"Why would she target Braon? Is she an assassin?" Harsh coughs racked Nona's frail shoulders.

"Hush, Nona." Tieren cupped her delicate hand in his. "She is a star traveler, not Greeven, but no less beautiful for her strangeness." He sighed, raising his gaze to the hovering emlo stones illuminating his chambers. Mined in the depths of their oceans, the glowing stones' warm light did nothing to calm his thoughts. "I have pondered her motives, but I cannot understand why Braon."

"Mm, this is most alarming, Tieren." Nona accepted a fresh goblet of tisane a servant rushed forward to offer. "Does Braon know?"

"I cannot warn him, you know this." Tieren allowed the weight of his concern to sink his shoulders. Around his late father's mother, he need not be on his guard.

"She torments you, this female?"

He clenched his jaw against revealing how wicked his dreams had become. "She might not stay with me. I might have to kill her. The future beyond her arrival remains unknown."

"Nona? Tieren?" Braon skipped into Tieren's chambers, his joyful, energetic movements that of a squawkling. Behind him, resplendent in gold and silver armor against white plumage, the Auviphis Order crowded the passage. Chosen from birth to train and protect the heir to the throne, the males lined up, their pikes clasped. Pity they weren't allowed near Braon during the Trial.

"Welcome, little brother." Tieren grabbed Braon's hand and tugged him to the carpet at Nona's feet. He ruffled Braon's bold, white plumage before throwing an arm across his shoulders.

"*Zelet*, Tieren, I am not so little anymore."

"I shall call you the king when you return from your Trial with a monster's head in hand." Tieren forced a chuckle.

Braon huffed. "Few monsters remain on Rianus."

"The gods will provide." Nona patted his shoulder.

"So, I am doomed no matter what I kill." He pinched his pale lips, and darkness circled his blue eyes.

"I ask you to survive and to return to me well, *abucaah*." Nona smiled at Braon and offered her hand, awaiting his assistance to stand. She paused a moment on trembling knees before waddling from the chambers.

"Survive?" Braon frowned at Tieren. "Was your vision of my trial?"

Tieren cursed and stripped off his robe, tossing it across the strewn cushions instead of pooling it on the mosaic floor. He unlaced the back of his boots and tugged them off, arching a brow at Braon, who had yet to disrobe.

Braon grumbled and removed his robe, baring his white, youthful body, all gangly limbs and lean muscle. "I just ate, so wild battusks aren't tempting enough. And no, I don't need more practice, if you're thinking that." Both his dark-gray eyebrows shot up, challenging Tieren.

"I am starving, and yes, you do need the practice." Tieren met his gaze, forcing Braon to note his seriousness. He cupped Braon's nape, pressing his temple to his. "How long will your successor let me or Nona live after they burn your corpse on the burial pyres?"

He leaped back and smirked. "Besides, once you are king, I intend to take a long vacation." Anywhere quiet and alone with his *kekaseea* sounded perfect. Now wasn't the time to mention Mick to Braon.

Tieren summoned his Greeven, allowing the wings to peel from his back and extend. Feathers and fur coated his skin, and claws extended from his fingertips. He roared when his back curved and spasmed. Sparks swirled his vision, blurring before sharpening. The searing agony pulsed for a second before he flapped his wings and threw himself off the non-balustraded platform. To set his true self free, the sensations were as painful as they were liberating.

Joy charged through him when he plummeted toward the craggy rocks beneath the fortress. Waves assaulted the cliffs, spraying his face with a fine mist, their thunder soothing the tension claiming his shoulders.

Ahead in the arena, between three spires, hung ancient devices, gleaming in the pale suns' light. Once used to train flocks of Greeven, they now served as testing grounds. The winds tossed the rings, spun the dials, and swung the pendulums, making it as unpredictable as it was hazardous. Most Greeven had forgotten the ancient ways, but not Tieren. This was where he practiced and honed his fighting and flying skills to better protect Braon. His father had shown him, urged by Nona, and one of Tieren's least favorite memories.

He had found solace here after a day of verbal abuse, in the shadows and away from his royal mentors.

You should have died, darkling.

Gods, you are hideous to look upon.

I shall never call you tsuna.

Those taunts still circled his mind, having clung to his soul like drowned battusks to a rock. He wouldn't fail his father, for he had shown Tieren mercy by not tossing him on these very rocks to die. But he would honor Nona, for her kindness.

Tucking in his arms, his wings cocooning his body, he spiraled through the first ring swinging across the chasm. A drop to the lowest ring whipped the wind through his feathers, tossed his plumage, and watered his eyes, sharper now that he was in Greeven form. The cold metal brushed the tips of his wings as he dipped through. The climb took all his strength, as it was designed to do, forcing him to work at reaching the next ring set high above the spires. The momentum of each swing was guided by the warm sunlight and the frigid sea air.

Braon's grunt from beneath Tieren spurred him on, and he pushed, climbing higher. Then Braon shot past him, his wings tucked in then flicking out as he boosted his speed and strength. Tieren added more energy to his climb, but it was no use, Braon slipped through the ring with agility, plummeting, barrel-rolling into two more rings before landing on the flattened edge of a spire.

Tieren set down beside him, scraping his claws on the smooth stone. Around the platform, the Auviphis guarded, their backs to Braon and Tieren.

He tucked in his wings lest a gust swept him off, then unfurled his face to speak. "Well done, brother."

Braon's feathered chest rose and fell as he sucked in air. He revealed his face to share his wide grin. "I didn't see any battusks. They must have sensed you were coming today, Tieren."

Tieren rolled his shoulders, eager for the hunt. "I'll stay if you want to head home, *tui takaag*."

Braon launched himself skyward, taking the Auviphis with him. Tieren studied the rocks below in search of a gray amphibious rodent. His stomach gurgled. On the far-off beaches, pauszors rested on the warm sands with their bleached bodies the size of small ships. He sighed and spread out his wings, catching a stiff breeze. It carried him off the spire. He circled the shaft, descending to the base where the waves continued their steadfast bombardment.

Perhaps Braon was right, for as the sun rose, not a battusk showed its hide. Crying out at the failure, Tieren returned to his chambers, empty-bellied and his soul dark.

CHAPTER SEVEN

FORNAX

Year: 2364

HR 858c - An uncharted super-earth

Fornax constellation

KIROS FLICKED HIS FINGERS, gesturing to Drys to remain silent. He chose his footsteps with care, unhappy with the softness of the ground beneath his feet. NOX hadn't responded to hails, which meant having to find Mick planetside after a quick scan. True to his word, Eli hadn't dawdled on Eridanus's way station, but the stop and the retaking of the cargo carrier had impacted their race to reach the *Jinsei*.

Lanek had yet to join them. They struggled to find a ship heading this way. There was the possibility of using the cargo carrier once the galactic security or G-sec closed the case and awarded the bounty to S.o.S. For now, it was Drys and himself dealing with the oppressive humidity, the spongy surface, and the cacophonous cries of unknown wildlife.

Palming his blaster, Kiros raised it and slipped into the shadows of a cave. He released a sigh when a cool breeze brought some relief. The whispering blasts of a rifle urged him to travel deeper into a vast cavern. Down below, green flares illuminated a sheer rock wall covered in gray tortoise-shaped lumps. Lining the floor were mobile nets to catch anything falling. A whisper hit a lump, and it plummeted, then another. Kiros grinned. Mick was a good shot.

He traced the trajectory to where Mick sprawled on a ledge. Before Kiros could gain his attention, Mick leaped forward and sprinted toward the wall, blurring as he ran. Kiros focused on the wall, spotting the lump falling too high up and too far away from a net. No way Mick could make it in time, yet there he was, vaulting to grab onto a stalactite to catch the lump in a gloved hand.

"Holy shit," Drys said from beside him. "Who's this lass?"

"Lass?" *That isn't Mick?* Kiros's whipped his head, zooming in on the person dropping from the stalactite to land in a crouch with ease.

Tight cargo breeches encased muscled legs. A sweat-saturated tank top clung to hefty breasts, with a thick braid trailing her. A mask hid half her face. She placed the lumps into cryo-tubes as if two men staring at her wasn't an anomaly. She gathered the flares, extinguishing all but one. Dangling three cryo-tubes from one hand and the rifle thrown across her shoulders, she strolled toward him.

Ice slid down his spine. Heat flushed his face. With his heart roaring in his ears, his nostrils flared while he fought for breath. The sway of her hips, her bouncing breasts, and her determined, confident strides hardened him. Arousal slammed into him, setting his senses ablaze.

"Frig," he said, his voice hoarse. *Who is this woman? Where the hell is Mick? Was she the reason Mick had been resistant to the S.o.S being onboard? Was he protecting her?* Kiros shook his head. *No, that makes no sense. This woman can protect herself.*

"I second that," Drys said, drawing Kiros back to the moment.

"Hello," she said, her voice stifled by the filter-mask. "You made good time."

Kiros didn't know what to say. Mick must have told her about him to make her this familiar, or did she think she could take them on? Drys elbowed past him as he hurried to carry the cryo-tubes. She offered them to Drys without hesitation before striding toward the shuttle. Kiros stared after her, the swinging green flare hanging from her belt flashed over a tight ass. Sucking in a breath, he rushed to catch up. She climbed into the antique shuttle, taking the cryo-tubes from Drys with a mumbled thanks. The rectangular vessel's markings on scarred metal stated the *Jinsei*'s ownership.

"Return to the *Sentry*," Kiros said to Drys. "Wait for docking instructions."

Drys opened his mouth, took one look at his face, and walked off. Kiros didn't watch him go but kept his focus on the woman who sealed the cryo-tubes and loaded them into the drones. Her patience irritated him, spiking the fury coiling and spitting in the pit of his stomach.

"Where's Mick?" he asked.

Her gaze flicked to him, but she said nothing, placing the final cryo-tube into a drone. She leaned past him and pressed the button behind him to close the shuttle door. She perused his face as she waited, a hand gripping her mask.

"NOX, status?" she asked after the door sealed shut and cool air flooded the compartment.

"Air cleansed, Mick," NOX said.

"Thanks. Allow the *Sentry* to dock."

"Mick?" Kiros gripped her upper arms, the heat of her sweat-slicked skin searing his palms. He peered into familiar eyes—a warm brown now framed with pretty lashes.

"Hello, Kiros," she said, tugging her mask off.

"What the frig?" He cupped her cheeks, holding her still to study her face. Those cheekbones, soft cheeks, pouting lips. She smiled, and his breath hitched. *Yes, she's Mick.* He thrust her away from him with a growl. "How dare you lie to me all these years?"

"Dad's decision." She shrugged, dropping into a chair to pilot the shuttle as if their discussion had ended.

"It's been a decade since his funeral. You could've told me."

The shuttle whipped up, forcing Kiros to throw out a hand to steady himself.

"I thought of telling you at our weekly coffee dates."

He refused to feel guilty for not staying in contact with her. It was a two-way street. Although, to be fair, contacting S.o.S wasn't meant to be easy.

"It's not an excuse." He gripped the back of the chair to shift closer to the console and the center of the shuttle for added balance. Instead, it gave him an exquisite view of her cleavage where an odd amulet nestled. A drop of sweat slid from her collarbone to disappear between her heaving breasts. *Friggin hell.* He fixed his gaze on the shuttle's fore vids, determined not to ogle her.

"It happened so long ago, Kiros." She broke through the cloud cover, filling the shuttle with a bright-yellow light before penetrating the atmosphere. The shuddering vessel jarred him. He gritted his teeth against it. "What would you have done if you had a daughter?"

"I sure as hell wouldn't have lied to S.o.S."

She shrugged again. "Dad didn't have your skillsets. Hiding my gender was his only option." She flicked a glance at Kiros and smiled.

Why hadn't he noticed the sensual curl of her plump lips before? Maybe he should have swapped with Lanek. At least he would be balls-deep in a woman instead of lusting after his oldest friend.

"You'd make a wonderful father."

Heat swarmed his chest like trapped insects. Oh, no, he wasn't going to let her sweet talk herself out of this. "You knowingly deceived me, Mick. If that's your friggin name."

"It is...Mick for Mikaela." She docked the shuttle with smooth, practiced movements before jumping up. He didn't step back, instead, he glared at her upturned face. "What bothers you the most, Kir?"

He closed his eyes against the sweetness of the nickname she'd given him. Her hand on his cheek had him scowling at her again.

"S.o.S' reputation is safe if you claim you knew all along. Solomon did." She snatched her hand away and frowned, dimpling her forehead between her dark eyebrows. "Or do you think I can't handle myself?" She bumped him with a hip. He stumbled back, surprised at her audacity. "I can kill any and all of your men, Kiros. Things aren't what...they used to be."

The door slid open, and she hopped out, striding past his gaping men. Drys grinned like an idiot, content to wait and watch the shit show unfold. She headed to a nearby stack of fuel canisters. Striding past them under the watchful gazes of his crew, she climbed into the shuttle to attach the fuel to the drones. Red blurred Kiros's vision, and he slammed the button, closing the door to block out his smirking men.

"I hate how you're dismissive of my anger. I have a right to be…" He threw his hands into the air, vibrating with the urge to punch something.

"Hurt?" she asked, as if he'd been unable to admit that. Yet, she was right. It hurt that she hadn't shared this with him. Like a knife to the gut, burning and wrenching.

"Frig, Mick. It's me, Kir. The guy who sparred with you, who taught you how to use a knife and a rifle. We spent hours talking into the night on my friggin bed."

"I did see you naked once, so that's out of the way." She grinned as if this was a laughing matter.

"No, you didn't." He dropped his gaze, wishing he could see *her* naked now.

"That time a ferila bit your ass. You cried like a babe." She chuckled, her breasts bouncing as she approached him.

"A rat's a rat," he mumbled. "Alien or not."

Resting her hand over his heart—he swore he could feel her heat through his thick chest guard—she dipped her head to meet his eyes. "Come on, Kir. It's me, Mick-the-boy. Does it make a difference I'm not male?" She flicked her hand at her breasts in a dismissive manner. "That I have these?"

"My men will proposition you," he growled. "You complicate the job."

"It's been a while, so a good fuck is in order, and I have news for you, Kir, I could do this job without you." She stepped back.

He released a slow breath, trying to hide how much she affected him. "There will be no fucking my men, Mick. I mean it."

She giggled—a feminine sound that twisted his balls. Leaning back, she picked up a spanner and bent it before dropping it onto his palm. "Try and stop me."

Kiros stared at the deformed metal tool in his hand.

She's augmented? Friggin hell.

CHAPTER EIGHT

UNGRATEFUL

Year: 2364

HR 858c - An uncharted super-earth

Fornax constellation

MICK PACED THE *JINSEI'S* bridge, unable to calm her pounding heart. Rubbing her arms, she tried to erase the feel of Kir's touch. "You, my dear NOX, are an ass." She pointed at the console, blaming NOX for the last hour. "Why the hell didn't you warn me?"

"Don't bother me unless the *Jinsei's* exploding." *Her* voice filled the bridge, and she smacked the mute button. Instead of arguing with her and easing the tension within her, he replayed her words, snatching the wind out of her sails.

"Friggin guests squatting in *my* ship." She screamed. Being here when Kiros and his men arrived would have been a damn sight preferable to facing him alone.

NOX's humming cut off. "What the hell has spiked your blood pressure? You're just lucky your mutations can handle your mood swings."

Sweeping aside the last kernel of patience was an image of her sprawled on a couch with a pants-less A.I. documenting her responses on a yellow legal pad. "Get out. Go bother the soldiers."

Silence descended, and with it came guilt. She dipped her head, resting her chin on her chest as tears burned behind her eyes. NOX wasn't a real person, but she thought of him as a younger brother. She hadn't meant to take her frustrations out on him, and she would explain what she was feeling when she calmed down. Thinking he had her back was a foolish human expectation.

She ran a thumb over the bird embossed on the amulet. Tieren came to mind. The bird's hooked beak reminded her of his nose. It changed his handsome features, making him intriguing. Had he been blessed with a Roman nose, he might have been too devastating for her senses. Dammit, she'd wanted to ask NOX to investigate why the strange jewelry had begun to vibrate.

Seeing Kiros had brought the last weeks' angst and fears to the fore. She longed for him to be like he used to be, not this domineering, irrational alpha male. Hear him roar, the ass.

She would give him time, and the *Jinsei's* size meant not bumping into each other unless he sought her out. Part of her hoped he did. There was something virile about him that had her heart leaping and plummeting, her stomach twisting into knots. He tied her tongue with his stubbornness and the intensity in his eyes. It hadn't been as bad as she'd expected. Seeing him had flooded her body with ecstatic warmth, sending tingles to her extremities.

She knew that feeling, something she'd felt since meeting her imaginary Tieren...lust. That would complicate her relationship with Kiros, and she wouldn't pursue it. Not from her side. Regardless, if this between them meant a thorough bunk-warming, then that was fine too. A mercenary and whatever she was couldn't sail the galaxies together, could they?

More to the point, did she want to?

And what about Tieren? She supposed a physical man was better than...whatever Tieren was. A figment of her overactive hormones? Surely she would have created a man she could speak to, do something with other than mime to or hug? Although, his hugs were awesome.

The console beeped, announcing a comm. Drawing in a shuddering breath, she activated it and grinned. Fentus needed more than the nine guinja she'd deployed minutes ago. Double that for double the payout. She'd expected it, which was why she left her nets. Flicking to the other vid, she analyzed NOX's scan of the planet. The standard protocol was to check for undiscovered species, mapping the universe one xeno creature at a time. She documented them, took a tissue sample for Fentus to research, and in a way, continued her father's work. Two red blips confirmed the existence of unknown creatures. Tapping the vid, she sent the details to the locator and headed to the armory. She'd need more than her rifle, Flint.

Tranq guns wouldn't work since the tranquilizer might kill. She needed to use her excise darts. One shot and a tug on the micro-thin cable would extract a biological sample. This she'd include in the drone with photographic evidence of the creature. Had she killed a few to survive? Yes. Would she kill today if needed? A hard yes. The discovery of a new species came with a decent bonus, and more credits meant extra fuel. The risk of life and limb was worth it.

"NOX, fuel the shuttle. I'm heading down for another batch of guinja, and your scan revealed two new species since our last trip.

Check the recon scanners. If we're still finding creatures, it's not as effective as we need it to be."

"Sure thing, Mick. Fueling now." His voice trailed her, echoing along the bulkheads.

"Keep me patched into the ship's system." She paused to gaze at the bulkhead. "Track and record all their conversations."

"A for acknowledged, oh captain."

"Lock the bridge. Password as usual." She slipped into a small storeroom, housing exo-suits, and other cargo. All the weapons she'd accumulated, modified, and destroyed lay in an embedded safe. Unclipping the daggers, she slid them into her boots and belt sheath. A few grenades disappeared into her pockets. Flint was in the shuttle, so she strapped a charged blaster to her thigh and grabbed the cryo-rifle, Locke, preferring to freeze rather than kill. If the creature reached her, the blaster or dagger would do. Sealing the safe behind her, she strode along the passage, listening for approaching footsteps. Dealing with Kiros now would delay her.

She halted at the top of the ladder to the shuttle bay. Kiros's men milled around, sitting on her crates, leaning against the workbench, and fiddling with her tools.

"Go find the mess hall," she said, swinging onto the ladder to slide down, not using the rungs. Ignoring their open interest, frowns, or stoicism, she entered the shuttle and clipped Locke into the wall mount, alongside Flint. She took a moment to run her finger along its gleaming carbon steel barrel.

"Initiating docking bay lockdown...again." NOX's tinny voice reverberated off the bay's metallic walls.

She faced the men peering at her through the door. "Behind the line, boys."

"Returning planetside?" An older man with gray hair feathering across his shoulders joined his compatriots in the safety zone. She recognized that voice. Drys, wasn't it?

"I need another batch of guinja. If holier-than-thou Kiros asks, tell him where I am." She punched the button, closed the door on their stunned faces, then slid into the pilot seat. Flipping switches on the console, she powered up the shuttle's still-warm engines.

NOX's voice penetrated the shuttle, no doubt booming through the bay, as well. "Bay door opening in 5...4...3...2...1. Step behind the line. Space ain't a merciful mistress."

A glance at the side vids showed the men standing behind the line with a shimmering shield protecting them from the vacuum of space. Wasting no time, she reversed the shuttle and hovered outside the bay door, watching it close. Good, no unexpected deaths to deal with. Punching in commands, she instructed the shuttle to return to its previous location. Guinja first in case the new species injured her. She'd secure those credits, then spend an hour or two hunting.

"Not what you had in mind for me, hey, Dad?" She raised her gaze to the shuttle's ceiling where pipes layered its surface. In all her adventures, she had yet to encounter heaven. Perhaps it was in another dimension? She hoped so, for if anyone deserved a spot there, it was her father. Grabbing a comm device, she popped it into her ear, catching the soldiers in mid-discussion while drowning out the shuttle's hisses and clangs.

Drys chuckled, "he ain't gonna like that she left...without protection."

"Who was that?" asked another man with a nasal voice.

"Mick," Drys said.

"Not the belle of the ball, but I'd fuck her." Nasal-voice sniggered.

She snorted. There would be no fucking unless *she* instigated it.

"She's a no-go zone. Kiros's orders," Drys said.

What the hell? How dare he? She clenched her jaw, pursing her lips as she fought the fury rising to choke her. He had cockblocked his men. It wasn't as if she had many opportunities to get laid, for shit's sake. Especially after her steamy Tieren dreams where his touch invoked so many feelings and sensations yet satisfaction was elusive. The way station Rebirth was near the Phoenix constellation, if the urge persisted. She grimaced. That far out of the main lanes meant unhygienic, diseased-riddled criminals or skinny-assed scientists. Kiros's soldiers looked clean...doable.

She would talk to him about this when she returned. *The asshat.*

The shuttle shuddered as it dove through the atmosphere in a controlled fall under the heat of the setting suns. As planets go, this one wasn't bad. Humans could make a home here, but then this pristine world would know corruption. The shuttle had crushed the vegetation beneath it, and she had captured undeserving creatures for research. Yup, because of her, this planet headed to hell in a handbasket. *Oh, the guilt.*

She chuckled at her silly thoughts, but she could breathe again. Tension eased from her taut muscles. "NOX, record the conversations, but don't patch them through." Their words stole her peace and focus. Perhaps tonight, she'd listen to a few in the safety of her quarters.

"Kiros is super pissed at your departure." NOX tutted, sounding more like he clicked two bolts against each other. "He requested access to the bridge. Mm, not a good idea in his present emotional state. I suspect he's lost his mind."

She coughed to hide her laughter. "Denied, and assign him the quarters next to Dad's." Maybe the proximity to Dad's might make him feel guilty or regret not reaching out to her. "To learn more about human behavior, study them, NOX. Men's reactions are different from women's."

"Oh, that's brilliant. Thanks, Mick."

Laughter erupted out of her without warning. NOX would pester them now with all the questions he had asked her over the last decade. Wicked glee filled her at the prank—a moment of youthful zeal.

The shuttle touched down, and she darted around the small confines, grabbing Flint, empty cryo-tubes, and flares. Punching the button, the door slid open, and she jumped down onto the soft surface. The heat hit her, snatching her breath and beading her skin with sweat. Perhaps farther north or south of her position had favorable weather. She doubted it would deter colonists. Humans were like cockroaches, able to survive or endure the hardiest of environments.

Jabbing the button with an elbow, she shut the door. The steady drips somewhere in the cavern and the trickling of water were soothing. She wished she could stay in its cool confines. It didn't take her long to capture nine guinja. Gathering the nets took less time—a press of the can's lid to retract the net. She tossed the cans inside the drawer, iced the guinja in the tubes, slid them inside the drones, and closed the door.

A trip north was next. She let the shuttle auto-pilot as she slugged back a shot of grit. What she would love is an ice-cold shower, but that would have to wait until she returned to the *Jinsei*. Unless...

"NOX." No response. She scowled, switching through the channels until she came across a boisterous if not a dull version of 'How do you solve a problem like Mikaela.' *Great, now he's improvising.* "NOX."

"What?" His rudeness should irritate her, but it was more relatable than the droning she had endured when she was a child. NOX had humanized so much since then.

"Locate a waterfall or freshwater pond. Scan it for bacteria and other hazardous creatures, and send me the points." A dip in cool waters? She shivered at the delicious thought of it.

"If it's good quality, I'd suggest a replenishment of our stores. With so many on board, it might deplete what we have. Extra water's never a waste."

She cupped her mouth to cover a snort. Like he used the water. There he went again with the proverbial 'we.' "If your scans are clear, take the *Jinsei* planetside. Don't land, though. Let's keep our imprint on this planet to a minimum."

As she waited, she listened to NOX's soprano. "...ever since I was a skinny little slip of a thing..."

Tapping her foot to the tune as the shuttle hurtled to the closest red beep, she sipped a second grit, not needing to dull her senses too much. Who knew how deadly the creature was.

"Water's pure, bacteria minimal, and the temperature in the ponds is in the single digits. Sending points now and navigating the *Jinsei* to a larger source."

The locator beeped, flashing a green dot. NOX had found something close to the second red dot. She grinned, excited to have a full-body bath, one she hadn't had since the funeral. In outer space, water was worth more than gold, adamantine, and platinum combined. There was no wasting it on a bath. Showers were set to three minutes with its waste-off sent to the hydroponics lab where she grew and brewed grit.

The shuttle dipped, landing in the middle of a desert. She grimaced. North wasn't better temperature-wise. Muting NOX's rendition of himself in a bikini sipping martinis, she spun the vids, scanning for a life form. Nothing was visible despite the red dot beeping. Grabbing a cam, she pinned it to her shirt, right between her breasts. What she did henceforth would be viewed by many xeno-zoologists. With Locke in hand, she exited the compartment. Her booted feet sank into the gray sand, and the oppressive heat coated her body like a hot, wet blanket.

The grit's numbing effects faded, granting her enhanced hearing. Nothing but the dry wind assaulted her ears. The overpowering fragrance of baked earth filled her nostrils, familiar yet not. She tugged on a mask and sighed; mint-scented antiseptic—sharp and pungent—dominated her olfactory glands, bringing her some relief.

Raising her face to the bright-yellow sky, she dragged herself up the windward side of the dune, hoping to see what lay beyond it. Endless silver-to-black sand was at her back. Perhaps there was something noteworthy north of her position. An oasis or a camel-like creature? She paused on the crest and sighed. It was breathtaking, but every direction and horizon showed nothing but empty sand, devoid of life.

Sweat drenched her shirt, slick under her breasts, and escaped tendrils from her braid clung to her skin. She tapped her the, but the red dot didn't waiver.

"NOX, scan again. This place's empty."

"....wind comes sweeping through the plain..." He didn't respond, but more red dots popped up, like the beginnings of a nasty rash. She peered at the lifeless sand, then up at the birdless sky. Tugging out a quake grenade, she armed and threw it far. It landed with a plop, then exploded, leaving a small crater, enough to disturb anything buried underneath. One heartbeat, two, but silence reigned.

The sand shifted under her feet. The ground rumbled from a minor tremor. Then, one by one, shuttle-sized creatures popped up—beautiful, iridescent anemones with their fronds filtering the air. Their numbers spread across the sands like a rippling wave.

She shot a glance at the shuddering shuttle, as if a creature lay beneath it. If one of them consumed her shuttle, she'd be stranded. Kiros would have to fetch her, and there was no way she would admit she needed his help, anyone's for that matter. She burst into a run, tumbled down the slope, regained her footing then sprinted. Around her, more anemones appeared, casting shadows and almost touching her with their reaching fronds. She feared for the shuttle more than her life.

When she dove inside it, she screamed, "Launch twenty meters up."

The shuttle shot up just as fronds caressed and cupped the underside of it, tilting it. She slid across the floor, slamming into the metal bulkhead. Fire exploded through her shoulder and chest, pulsing outward. She whimpered. Sucking in sharp breaths, she calmed the panic blurring her vision. She could use her arm, so it wasn't a dislocation. The med pod could look at it later if the mutation didn't heal it. Sprawling onto the floor and this high up, she peeked off the door's edge. The anemones looked like water, reflecting and absorbing light.

With efficient movements, she attached an excise dart to Flint. She fired at the closest creature and retracted the cable. Inside the glass vile was a pool of iridescent liquid the consistency of mercury. Removing the dart, she attached a tracker to the rifle and fired again. The device would cling to the surface of the creature and monitor it. When she next flew past this planet, she'd retrieve what data it had gathered and send it to Fentus.

Placing the excise dart in its transport canister, she punched in the details and images from her chest cam for the machine to etch into the glass. Then freezing it, she slid it inside one of the cryo-tubes. She peered at the ocean of creatures below and smiled at what lay ahead for her. A bath.

Chapter Nine

HELPLESS
Year: 2364
On board the Jinsei
HR 858c - An uncharted super-earth
Fornax constellation

WORDS WERE IMPOSSIBLE, SO furious was Kiros. With blurred vision and an inability to inhale, he struggled to find calm amid his faltering heartbeat and dampened hearing. As A.I.'s go, NOX had to retire. His primary function should be the safety of his owner, but he had a blasé attitude about his tasks that maddened Kiros.

"What do you mean she's not on board?"

"A doubled order for guinja sent Mick planetside. Also, my scans revealed two new species. She samples and tags them for research. *My way of continuing Dad's work.*"

Her audio recording cinched Kiros's chest tight, and he grunted, fighting the effect of her husky voice on his senses.

"Quit your worrying, Kiros, she's more than capable of handling any situation."

"How the hell would you know?" He ran his hand over his braids, forcing air into his lungs. "I need to head down there, make sure she's fine."

"Probables state you'll endanger her." NOX made a sound that was like metal on gravel; Kiros couldn't tell if it was a grunt or a laugh.

A vid screen on the wall fluttered to life, and an image unfolded of creatures on a desert floor. He placed a hand on either side of the screen and stiffened his shoulders. His fingers curled into fists at her being in danger, as he'd expected. Helplessness washed over him like a wet blanket draped over his back. He shivered. She pumped her arms, sprinting between these creatures. Screaming commands, she threw herself into the shuttle.

A surge of fury-laced energy tore through him, constricting every muscle in his body as if he prepared to attack. Her hiss meant she'd injured herself, followed by a close-up of metal and the muted thuds of a rifle firing. She jumped up, and her surroundings came into view as she took care of the biological samples. With a shot of grit in hand, the fore vids showed the shuttle's trajectory to the next destination.

"Send this to my quarters." He rushed there with the expectation that her tasks would be unremarkable or tedious—he might as well be comfortable, sipping tank-made rum.

Tugging off his chest armor, he tossed it on a chair before sprawling on the bed. NOX activated the vid on Kiros's ceiling showing Mick's consumption of more grit and flickering scenes on the shuttles fore vids. She crossed her legs in front of her, and the camera rose and fell with her breathing, telling him where she had pinned it.

As the shuttle touched down with the fore vids revealing forests covered in snow, she unfolded her legs. "Friggin hell, NOX, are you trying to kill me? Or are we testing my limitations again?"

"Seems I can't please you today," NOX huffed. "It's cold, no bacteria, and no creatures like you asked."

"I'll freeze my ass off, you worthless machine."

"I doubt that, Mick. Quit being such a drama queen. Your core temperature runs hotter than in humans. You'll be fine."

Hotter than a human when she's human? Kiros arched a brow at that revealing titbit. Augmentations didn't alter the individual at a molecular level.

She swore under her breath, too low for Kiros to discern the words. When she tugged off her boots and tossed them to the side, along with her pants, he realized her intentions. His heart leaped to choke him, and he stilled, frozen in stunned anticipation. The cam fell with fabric layering the bottom of the vid where it landed, giving him a partial view of the pond. Mist hovered above its surface as a slim calf, sculpted thigh, the curve of a backside, and the dip in her waist came into view. In a blur of movement, she dived in, disappearing for the longest, nerve-wrenching, heart-twisting moment before surfacing a little off-visual.

"Shit, it's freezing."

Not him, he was on fire. Flames engulfed his trembling body and settled in his crotch. He was hard and horny, and she had revealed nothing but an ass cheek. The urge to grab another drink warred with his need not to blink and miss a moment.

But this was young-Mick, not some tart he could fuck and walk away from. There would be no dalliance with her, and he would keep to the law he had passed down to his crew. Adjusting his pants around his hard-on, he slid off the bed to pour a dram of rum, needing the alcohol to burn common sense into him.

There was no fucking Thomas's daughter. It felt like a violation of his old friend's trust. Then again, boy-Mick had never looked like this.

Splashing from the vid tightened Kiros's grip on the metal cup, but he didn't peek, not needing to see, to know how unlike a boy she was.

"That wasn't too bad. My senses switched between friggin-cold to this-is-nice. If we had time to spare, I might have lingered." Zips, fasteners, grunts, and huffs peppered her words.

"Told you so," NOX sang.

The shuttle powered up, and once more, she sipped grit, tapping a tune on the console. "I am a model major general..."

NOX's tinny voice broke into song, "...*very* model of a modern..."

Kiros sprawled on the bed again, balancing the cup on his chest, with one arm thrown behind his head.

"Thanks, wise ass." She threw back the grit and poured another. "What's the weather like where we're heading?"

"Cold."

"Just friggin great. Remind me to restock the shuttle's grit, and what's the status on my last batch?"

Kiros frowned. Why her addiction to grit? Why the need to make more? He understood that she traveled for months alone, and perhaps that explained the necessity to brew moonshine, still, there were nicer alcohols she could craft. He hated the taste of grit, as if soil resided in his mouth. No matter how much he drank of it, his taste-buds refused to endure it.

"Another four days before it's ready. We're running low on sugar and yeast."

"Shit. I'll restock when next we hit a station. And I'll get laid too. Stupid asshat." She grumbled the last.

Kiros grinned. Ah, so she'd heard of his restriction and wasn't happy about it if he judged her stomping foot and pounding fist. *Good.*

"Status of cryo-pens? Might as well restock those too." Her hand flew past the cam, accompanied by a groan.

NOX sighed, or his equivalent of it. "Or learn how to sleep despite your mutation."

Mutation? What the frig did NOX mean by that?

"Like I haven't tried?" Once again, she was up and out of the shuttle, pale blue ice in all directions.

Kiros flicked off the vid and bolted from the bed.

Pacing eased the tension rippling through his body but not the lust driving him. "NOX, how is she not human?" He stopped and arched his back, raising his face to the ceiling.

"An incident with a hokou male. Her DNA has been altering since then."

Kiros froze in mid-step. "Altering? As in continual changes? In what way?"

"Increased strength, speed, heightened senses, and her body heals without aid from most injuries. Super-human, you could say."

Frig. Kiros sat on the closest crate, his limbs heavy and sluggish. "Is it slowing, NOX?"

"No, it's changing her internal organs. I've analyzed all known data on the hokou species. I've discovered that this particular male was ill or drugged."

"She's dying, isn't she?" Ice drenched Kiros's face, and something squeezed his heart so hard, he feared it would crack a rib.

"That's Mick's assumption, as well. I've run trials on her blood samples, and nothing seems to affect the conversion rate. I'm not a fortune reader or well enough skilled in probables and statistics. I can't foresee in what state the mutation will leave her nor whether it'll kill her."

Kiros was unable to speak, and if he could, there was nothing to say. She could take care of herself now, but not before she was bitten, when she'd needed him the most. "NOX, the incident, how did the creature attack?"

"Bit her shoulder. She has no scars from the event to prove it happened."

No scars? "Is that when you noticed she can heal?"

"Hell, yes. Kind of makes the pod redundant." He chuckled—two bolts rubbing together. "She's heading back to the *Jinsei*. ETA ten minutes."

Kiros grunted, jumping to his feet. It was time he had a heart-to-heart with his old friend, Mick.

Chapter Ten

CONFRONTATION

Year: 2364

HR 858c - An uncharted super-earth

Fornax constellation

MICK'S INSTINCTS PRICKED HER skin, and she leaped back, dodging a swinging white tentacle. It faded, turning invisible. A ten-limbed creature skittered across the snow. Spiraling flakes showed its passing. Whatever the frig this was, it had attacked her the moment the shuttle door opened. Barbs lanced across her torso, arm, and shoulder. Fiery rashes followed, and her skin bubbled as if scorched. A scream lodged in her throat. All her super-sensitized nerves burst into life and bombarded her mind.

The pitter-patter of suckers across the shuttle's roof silenced her chaotic mind and drove her to unclip the pistols from the bulkhead. She loaded incendiary rounds, then dropped to the floor, resting her back against the farthest corner to the door. And waited.

The cold seeped in, blowing snow across the floor and her boots. The mutation kept her from feeling it for longer than a second, like it had at the pond. Through the howling wind, she caught the scraping of suckers along the metal before they curled around the edge of the door. One pale blue tentacle, then another until a bulbous head with innumerable eyes peered at her. It stilled, analyzing, its focus shifting around the compartment.

Icy tongues licked her spine and tensed her shoulders. She drew in a deep breath and held it captive. As the creature descended inch-by-inch, then dipped inside the shuttle, she released a controlled sigh and fired.

The first bullet struck. The alien octopus jerked back, and a high-pitched scream pierced her eardrums. It charged her. Whimpering at the pumping of her blood dominating her hearing, she emptied the pistols, dropped them, and snatched the daggers, holding them in front of her. Bright yellow exploded where the bullets embedded, splattering chunks of the creature's flesh.

It slithered along the floor, coming to a twitching halt a whisper from the first dagger's blade. Limp tentacles bumped her boots, and lifeless eyes stared at her. They were solid black. Interesting, considering how easily it faded in and out of sight.

Sucking in sharp breaths, she tried to still her thumping heart. It had slowed when her life was in danger. Only now, post-attack, did it speed ahead with adrenaline pulsing along her veins. She clambered to her feet, sheathed the daggers, and nudged the creature's body with a boot. Now she had a dead alien octopus in the shuttle, and its sticky white blood covered her. It drenched her clothing and splattered or pooled across every surface in the shuttle. She could kick the creature out, or she could freeze it. Fentus would pay more for it, even if it was dead.

None of the cryo-tubes on board the shuttle were large enough. She'd have to drone it from the *Jinsei*. Taking out the chain net, she bolted the thing to the bulkhead, reducing the chance of a surprise resurrection while she piloted the shuttle. Before closing the door, she scanned the bright, white horizon. Ripples like drops in a pond were so large that, if she couldn't see far, she wouldn't have noticed the movement beneath the surface.

She punched the button, and the door closed. Collapsing into the seat, she commanded the shuttle to return to the *Jinsei*, then leaned back to assess her wounds. The blistering had spread, giving off additional heat. She hissed when she ran a fingertip over her shoulder, where its darts had shredded her T-shirt.

"Why the frig did this have to happen with Kiros on board?" She grimaced when she wiped the sweat and white blood off her brow. "NOX, power up the med pod."

"Why? Your readings are normal."

"Check my pain markers." Sitting still stung her skin with fiery sparks, registering pain now that adrenaline no longer overwhelmed her senses.

"Oh, dear, I see we have a slight problem. And here I thought the pod was redundant." NOX tutted. "Powering it now."

"Don't inform Kiros of this. I don't need a damn lecture. I'd like to see how he'd have handled a friggin ambush."

"Too late, Mick. I told him you were ten minutes out."

"Shit." She slammed back grit after grit as the shuttle passed through the atmosphere into outer space. From yellow skies to dark blue, the shift was as beautiful as it was painstakingly slow. The bay door opened when she neared. She took control, docking the shuttle with practiced ease.

Having clenched her teeth for the last three minutes against the unceasing agony spreading across her skin, she leaped out of the shuttle and slammed the button, locking the door behind her.

Kiros's pilot and mechanic gathered around her, firing questions at her. She spared them but a glance. *Pod, now,* roared through her thoughts. She sprinted along the walkways and tunnels before throwing herself into the opened pod. The glass bubble trapped her inside, and a fine white mist cooled her skin. She moaned, then hurried to peel off the remnants of her T-shirt to better aid the healing.

Kiros strode into the med bay, anger and perhaps fear contorted his handsome features. "What did I friggin tell you, NOX?" He splayed his fingers on the glass and stared at her. "What happened?"

"Just a run-in with a pissed-off creature. Its darts contain venom or acid. I can't say for sure yet." Her bra strap, as shredded as the T-shirt, sagged one breast, but there was no way on her God-given *Jinsei* would she hide herself or the state of undress. *Frig him.* After what she'd endured, she wasn't in the mood to play the virgin.

NOX grated his circuits to sound like he cleared his throat. "Your mutation is fighting it."

"I call bullshit," she said through gritted teeth. The rashes are spreading." Another spray of white mist cooled her wounds again. Her nipples pebbled before heat flushed her skin. Once the mist faded, the burning revived, still there but reduced.

NOX hacked a cough, his version of a laugh. "Rather that than what it was doing to your organs."

"This isn't funny," Kiros roared at the bulkhead before meeting her gaze. "How often does this happen, Mick? Endangering yourself?"

"Not often. Hello, Kiros, in pain here and not giving a frig how you feel, so you can quit with the I-care attitude."

The pod injected something into her neck. Cold flames rushed along her veins, and she screamed, arching off the base. Within an instant, the fire along her skin ceased. A sweet lassitude softened her muscles and dulled her senses. She wiggled her ass to find a comfortable position, smiling at Kiros. He had beautiful eyes. Then her smile evaporated as her mutation worked the pain medication from her system. She had but a moment of bliss, of silence, of feeling warm and loved.

"NOX told me what happened, why you're mutated." He pressed his other palm to the glass. His scar from her first dagger lesson marred his skin. Had he once thought of her when he looked at it? Judging by the number of times he reached out to her, she would hazard a no.

Heaviness slowed her heartbeat, dark with sadness and longing. He'd never thought of her, thought of contacting her, thought of meeting her for a whisky. That said how he felt about her—nothing, a blip, a memory. She couldn't trust his concern, not now, not ever.

"Accidents happen. Like I said, I can take care of myself. Spare me your pretense. You don't care, Kiros. This is what I am now, this is how I'm surviving, without Dad, you, or any other damn person. All I have is this ship and NOX." She rose onto her elbows to meet his gaze. "If you plan on questioning everything I do, I suggest you board your ship and get the frig off mine."

Where his palms rested on the glass, he curled them into fists. His face twisted with fury. Like she gave a frig about his opinion.

Darkness shrouded his eyes. "I kill folks with less respect."

She blinked at him, then laughed. It might be the pain talking, but shit, that was funny.

"NOX, set a course for Cetus, and mark Kiros and his men as a risk to our safety." She smirked. "If I give the command, jettison their ship and any men in the bay."

Tapping the blue circle holograph above the glass tinted the pod and granted her peace. Kiros thumped the glass, which garbled his words when he yelled.

"One cryo-pen, please, NOX. Sing me a song as I drift off, and wake me when the pod has done all it can." Another injection flooded her blood with ice, and she smiled, falling asleep to NOX belting out, *'Something has changed within me.'*

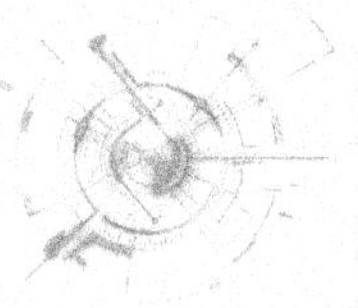

THE POD OPENED ON a whisper, and the influx of cool air and droning noises woke her. She stretched, arched her back, and moaned. If the damn things weren't so expensive fuel-wise, she'd use it to sleep in. Somehow, it had drowned out the ship's echoes, clicks, hums, and hisses. No air had brushed along her skin like the phantom caress of a lost lover.

A quick stroke of her torso, arm, and shoulder confirmed the pod had healed her. Or her mutation had. She wouldn't know for sure until she spoke to NOX.

Antiseptic spray lingered in the air along with the burned-steak ozone stench she was used to. There was also a hint of Kiros's masculine scent. With a sigh, she climbed out of the pod and strode to her quarters. She winced with every thump of her boots on the metal grating. In a clean bra and tank, she hurried to the shuttle while sticking a finger through the tears in her pants. *Frig.* She needed new clothes stat.

Kiros and his three men sat on crates. With an easy camaraderie, no doubt earned through combat, they cleaned their weapons and bantered among themselves. Silence descended when she strode between them to punch the code on the shuttle door.

"Don't mind me, boys. As you were." She leaped into the compartment and unclipped the chain net. Grabbing the creature by a tentacle, she dragged it out and left it on the ramp. In the corner of the bay sat the large cryo-tubes. She rested her hands on her hips, uncaring that she smeared more of its white blood on her ruined cargo pants. They were beyond salvation and would soon see the incinerator.

"Need help?" Drys paused beside her. He, too, studied the tubes stacked six high.

She arched a brow at him. "Thanks, but I've got this."

With a vault up, she hooked her fingers over the highest ledge. She hung there for a moment, smirked at Drys below, then braced herself on the side of the bay. With a backward yank, the tube slid off the stack. All below dove out of its way. She smothered a chuckle, pushed off the bay's wall, and somersaulted down to land in a crouch. Her arm muscles and shoulders burned at the abuse, but she was trying to make a point. She wasn't a damsel in need of aid.

As if it weighed nothing, she placed the tube alongside the creature. She tossed it in, taking the time to tuck in its tentacles. On a glass disc, she programmed the feed, then slid it into its slot on the closest and largest drone. It took a moment to clip the cryo-tube inside. When the letters lit, confirming the seal locked, she lifted the drone into a torpedo-like tube and latched the hatch. The last points entered were still valid. She punched the red button and sent the drone to Fentus.

With that task done, decontamination remained. She unraveled the hose, opened the nozzle, and sprayed the inside of the shuttle and the ramp. The desterilization mixture would drain through the grated flooring.

While the shuttle air-dried, she gave her observers a two-fingered salute and marched to her quarters. The final task to end a dismal day would be a thorough shower. Instead of being able to do so in peace, Kiros trailed her.

Chapter Eleven

STUMPED

Year: 2364

HR 858c - An uncharted super-earth

En route to Tau Ceti

MICK FRUSTRATED KIROS WITH her blasé attitude, disrespect, and friggin beauty. He ran after her, needing to air his grievances. Was he a creep to have drooled over her in the med pod? A large part of him had hated seeing her in pain, but a tiny kernel of shame had taken the time to admire.

Her words had lanced through him, tainting his cherished memories. He *had* neglected her and was the first to admit it. But frig, her strength and tone dripping with authority had fired a burning lust, and he was still semi-erect. He hardened at the mere thought of her speaking to him like that again.

Shit, he was as undecided as if she had concussed him.

"Wait outside." She closed the door to her quarters in his face.

Gritting his teeth, he leaned on the buzzer. When she didn't open the door, he took turns pounding on the scarred metal or pressing the buzzer until, at last, her image appeared in the small vid. Water rippled over her face, plastering her hair to her head.

"So friggin help me, Kir. I'm covered in blood. Could you give me a damn minute to wash it off?" Droplets clung to her eyelashes, and at that moment, he ached to be in the shower with her.

Swallowing the groan, he met her gaze. "As long as you promise to speak to me."

"Hydroponics. Five minutes."

The vid clicked off, but he didn't move. Instead, he pressed his temple to the cold metal of the bulkhead, running a sanity check.

"I've never seen you like this." Drys leaned against the same bulkhead. "What's with you and Mick?"

Kiros was in no mood to hash out his feelings or endure an inquisition. "It's complicated."

"So it seems. Just fuck her, and get it out of your system."

Kiros growled and pounded his temple on the metal. "At your age, one of your past femme fatales must have taught you that you don't bring sex into a friendship."

"Friends?" Drys scoffed. "Kiros, you've never mentioned Mick in all the years I've known you. That ain't a friendship."

"History, then." Kiros pushed off and faced the older man, one he thought of as the father he'd never had. Solomon had served in a similar capacity, except for the whole do-something-wrong-and-die thing hovering over Kiros's head.

Drys faced the passage. "I doubt you'll see her again, especially after you steal the quarry right from under her."

Kiros grimaced. "Good point."

"Having second thoughts?" Drys whipped out a dagger to clean a fingernail.

"Nope. It's a shit ton of credits." Kiros ran his palm over his face, trying to erase images of pounding into the only woman on board. "It's a good plan, Drys. Catch a ride, use her resources, and steal the prize."

"Well, the way you're acting, you'd swear *she* was the prize." Drys twirled the dagger before focusing on the next finger.

"Are you blind as well as old?" Kiros flicked a thumb at the door. "Have you seen her?"

"So what? You can find more amenable partners at the next way station." Drys grinned, pocketed the knife then thumped Kiros on his back. "I have eyes, my son. It's her you want. Like I said, just do her."

Kiros shuddered, imagining pinning her to a hydroponics tank and burying himself in her. His cock twitched in eagerness. "I'll think about it." He snorted. Like he could stop daydreaming, needing, aching?

"And best rescind the order to leave her alone. By the looks of things, she can fend off our men."

"That's not why—" Kiros clenched his jaw shut. The thought of his men touching her tainted his vision red.

"Whoa, calm your horses. You can't fuck her with that order in place, Kiros, even if you're the current Solomon. These men would stab you in the back over a misunderstanding. Let's not give them a reason to distrust you."

Shit. He thumped his temple on the metal again. "Fine." He tapped commands on the holographics embedded in his arm. "Order rescinded."

Drys laughed, rubbing his hands together with glee. "Let the games begin."

Kiros glared, not appreciating his humor. "This isn't funny."

"Sure it is. You'll have to win her fair and square." Drys sauntered off, whistling a jaunty tune.

"Dammit," Kiros muttered.

Mick's door swished open, and a waft of soap-scented air hit him. "Ah, you're still here." She pressed a palm to his chest. It took all his control to hide his shiver.

With a shove, she pushed past him, striding down the corridor. He scurried after her, feeling like a puppy and losing control the more he chased her.

"I need to check on my space spinach. Running out of grit isn't an option."

He struggled to keep his gaze on her shoulders when the swirl and sway of her ass was too tempting. "Why not make something better?"

"It's all I can afford, Kir."

He loved and hated her calling him by that nickname. It reminded him that he had acted like her big brother, which was incongruent with the wicked thoughts plaguing him now. He loved the familiarity, though. They did have history, and he did feel some sort of obligation to Thomas, some level of affection for her. Still, the shape of her ass, and the swing of her unbound hair across her back... His fingers twitched to curl themselves into that mass and tug while he fucked her from behind.

The stench of soil, organics, and the tang of alcohol hit him when he followed her into the lab. Spinach in various stages of growth lined the bulkheads, some spilling out of pots hanging from the ceiling. Green sludge in the tanks bubbled and gurgled.

"What do you want to say?" She tapped on the tanks, read the holographic statuses, and made small adjustments before spritzing water over the hanging spinach.

It took a second for him to recall what he meant to rant over. "You needless endanger yourself."

"Like I said before, which I doubt you heard as hardheaded as you can be, why do you care?"

Her serenity in the face of his suffering shot blazing fury through him, and he gripped her upper arms, forcing her to meet his gaze. This close, his nostrils flared at her feminine fragrance.

"I wasn't there for you when you needed me. I get that. But I'm here now. What would Thomas say about the risks you take?"

She sucked in a sharp breath, pain darkening her brown eyes.

Something twisted his insides into a tight knot. If he didn't know better, he would say it was guilt. "Sorry, Mick, I didn't mean..." He tugged and curled her into his arms, tucking her face into the curve of his neck. His body trembled at the proximity, but he ignored it, meaning to offer comfort.

She wrapped her arms around him and squeezed, cinching his lungs. He tried to speak, to tell her to loosen her grip, but then she nuzzled his neck, and all thoughts of breathing abandoned him.

Physical contact felt so good, and with her curves pressing his hard edges, it was bliss. Tingles rippled across his skin, making him fully erect. If she shifted her hips, rubbed across him in any way, he would pin her to a tank and fuck her hard.

She pulled away, despite his tight grip, and warm, grit-saturated air rushed into his lungs.

"Thanks, Kir. A physical hug is rare and appreciated."

He frowned. Physical implied she'd had virtual or otherwise hugs. Was that even possible? What did that even mean?

Leaning her ass against a tank, she offered him a small smile. "I need the credits. The *Jinsei* is a thirsty beast, but I can't bear to trade it in for something smaller and more economical. It was Dad's, y'know."

The twisted knot tightened, forming a ball of tension he didn't know how to unravel. And here he was, planning to betray her.

"Sure, I endanger myself, but I heal well." She gestured to her shoulder and arm where that blue creature had hurt her.

Before he could stop himself, he nudged her fingers aside and stroked her smooth skin. Goosebumps skittered where he touched. He paused and arched a brow.

She shook her head. "Symptoms of the mutation. Hypersensitivity to everything."

His mind went there. "Orgasms?"

"Worsens it, as earth-shattering as they are." She tried to shrug. "I mean, the euphoria is incredible, like witnessing a supernova. Just the aftermath…" She trembled, slipping from under his fingers to break away. "Human contact, a dual-edged sword."

"Well, I'm here. As many hugs as you need."

She smirked. "I don't want hugs, Kir. I'd appreciate a sparring partner. You up for it?"

He grinned. "Hell, yeah. Can you remember everything I taught you?" He gestured to the door and trailed her, grateful to have resisted temptation thus far.

"A little." She didn't say anything more en route to the gym.

He was content to watch her ass sway. The lights flickered on when she entered, and in the already illuminated corner was Wyatt on the weights, his head tilted as he listened to an audiobook on his earbuds. He paused mid-bicep curl.

"Hey, Wyatt," Kiros greeted, not sure he liked the man watching him with Mick.

She stopped in the center of the mat and raised her fists in front of her face. "Come on, show me what you've got."

There was a wicked gleam in her gaze that fired Kiros's blood. He chuckled and lunged for her. She sidestepped him with ease, her weight on her front foot and her balance good. Each miss added tension to his shoulders, and his attacks became desperate.

"Stand still," he roared, wiping the sweat dripping off his chin with the roll of his shoulder.

"Fine." She spread her legs but kept her hands raised.

He lunged again. She caught his wrist. He blinked at her from the floor, stunned to go from standing to sprawling. "What the frig?" His back throbbed from having hit the mat, and he couldn't recall how he landed there. "I didn't teach you that."

He pinched his lips, not willing to admit defeat. She thrust out a hand. He gripped it, finding himself airborne a second later.

"Told you, faster reflexes, more strength. At some point, the mutation will kill me, or I deteriorate into an old woman. Time will tell." Her shrug was stiff.

Slapping his thighs and ass, he watched her. "Have you told anyone? I mean, a scientist or a doctor?"

She gave him a pointed look. "Are you insane? Why don't I just drone myself to Fentus?" Falling into a semi-passive stance, she flicked her fingers at him. "I'm what the Followers are looking for, Kir. A mutated life form they can exploit for spiritual gain."

When he ducked her fist, the brush of air across his cheek told him he had dodged it by no more than a hair. Shocked that he had, he almost didn't swing his elbow back. It hit her between the shoulders, but she rolled forward, a gasp the only indication he'd connected. Not hesitating and giving her a chance to retaliate, he tackled her and straddled her hips, pinning her hands by her ears.

She smiled, and her brown eyes turned molten, enticing him with their warmth. "It's so good to spar."

This was too easy, having seen her out in the field. A slithering suspicion crept into his mind. "Mick, are you going easy on me?"

Her breasts shook as she laughed. There wasn't a trickle of sweat at her temple, and no moisture dewed her lip, proving his instinct correct.

Her fingers tightening on his biceps should have warned him. Flat on his back, he stared at her, their positions switched. By no means was he a lightweight, but he'd seen her leap heights and carry heavy objects no unaugmented human could.

A shiver rippled goosebumps along her skin, and her nipples pebbled in the dry-as-a-bone tank. She tilted her head to the ceiling and closed her eyes on a sigh. "Air recycling changed direction. Can you feel it?"

He thrust his pelvis up, trying to dislodge her, but she used her knees, squeezing him until he stopped. She layered her torso over his and rested her temple on his chin. Releasing his hands, she swept his braids off his face and ran her fingertips from brow to jaw. He gripped her hips, appreciating how they filled his palms. She may be mutated, but to his aroused body, she was all woman.

He ran his gaze over her familiar face. Those big brown eyes with their eagerness and hero-worship, now had fluttering eyelashes and a slight tilt, too seductive for his control. Her adorable nose was like a short ski slope. The plumpness of her lips fascinated him, more so when she smiled. Those pouting lips should have revealed her gender, yet he'd seen only what Thomas, Solomon, and Mick had taught him to. Running his palms up her back, he rested them between her shoulder blades, needing her closer.

"It's wonderful to see you, Kir, and I'm sorry I lied about being a boy."

Air whooshed out of his lungs, easing the residual hurt. Warmth pulsed from his heart outward, but dread settled in his stomach like a night after too much drinking.

"I had a little crush on you." Within his embrace, she wiggled to drag her nails down his chest.

"What?" He struggled to focus on her words, and if she was as experienced as she claimed, she would soon encounter a certain stiffness. Wait, crush, as in she liked him?

"Silly, I know." She kissed his chin and vaulted off him before offering a hand. He blinked at it, his body still registering the soft, hot brush of her lips. "Like you would fuck an old friend? Y'know, go for the sweet spot?"

His gaze dipped, lingering on the curve of her neck, the rise and fall of her tank-encased breasts, and lower, to her taut stomach and the juncture of her thighs. Yes, she was right to call it the sweet spot. Restraint tore a shudder from him.

"I need a shower." A cold one, if he had his way.

"Thanks for this, Kir," she called when he stomped off, more miserable than he could remember feeling.

Chapter Twelve

THE SHADOWS AND FOG shifted, revealing portions of Mick's face contorted in pain or fury. This dream was different. Tieren knew it the moment fire spread across his shoulder, arm, and torso. He arched off the bed on a silent scream of uncontrollable agony, cold burning his neck. This torment wasn't his. She needed him. Helplessness stiffened every sinew and muscle in his body. He squeezed his eyes shut, struggling with the impossible urge to aid her. The pain dissipated, but shivers rippled along his skin, and an intense, aching need consumed his core. He was hard and hot for no reason.

Throwing his legs off the bed, he rested his elbows on his knees and cupped his face. He didn't like her in pain, nor did he like that she was aroused. The thought of her with another male grated him. He punched the bed before pushing himself off it to pace.

What he should be asking is how could he feel her emotions or her presence like a fluttering wing at the back of his mind? How could they interact in the dream world?

Pengfei had arrived at sunset, confirming time was running out for Braon. A solution to their problems still eluded Tieren.

Though it was still night, he needed answers. Spinning on his bare heel, he marched to the old shaman's chambers a few levels below his own. Oh, he was a fool. On the Isles of Eleta, Pengfei had enquired, but Tieren had silenced him, not yet willing to accept his fate.

Large wooden doors opened, and Pengfei leaned against one, waiting for Tieren to stride along the mosaic-tiled corridor toward him. The emlo stones illuminated his path and the knowing gleam in Pengfei's eyes.

"Welcome, *tsuna*." He swung the door wide, then caught and closed it behind Tieren. "You could have taken the time to dress."

Tieren jerked, then relaxed at Pengfei's teasing smile. "My apologies for my state of undress."

He gestured to his loose leggings hanging low from his hips to cinch in at the ankles. Rubbing his bare chest, he shrugged at still wearing his dowo and fell into restless pacing in front of the cushions Pengfei sat on. The old male should be happy he was wearing something. The cloth brushing his legs heightened his senses after the vivid bond he had shared with his *kekaseea*.

"Troubled?" Pengfei arched a brow, as if he didn't know what bothered Tieren.

Regardless of what Pengfei knew, sharing the sensual side didn't sit well with Tieren. "I suffered from her injuries. How is this possible?"

Pengfei's eyes widened. "She is drawing closer." He poured a goblet of *jaketta* wine and offered it to Tieren. "Such a strong connection isn't unheard of. It bodes well."

Tieren's shoulders drooped when the wine's warmth burned through the knot in his stomach. "Does it when I might have to kill her?" He closed his eyes and relived their first meeting.

The darkness of her eyes was so like his. Her skin wasn't the pale-gray-white of the Greeven, but not dark either. He didn't have to imagine sliding his palm over her softer skin, gripping her hip, dipping into the indent of her waist, and cupping a breast. Each longing brought images to mind as if he relived a memory, and renewed heat as familiar as an old friend blasted his body. She fascinated him with this mix of pain and pleasure. But the inability to communicate frustrated the *Gawen* out of him.

Pengfei snorted, drawing Tieren to the moment. "You'll know soon enough."

"Did you see my vision as well?" He frowned, having never heard of such an occurrence.

Pengfei sipped from his goblet and wiggled his fingers as he chose a morsel of meat from the platter on the dead-emlo stone table. "Sometimes the gods share the visions, but not with you. I received snippets along with instructions, Tieren, which is why I agreed to visit Qilae-tor."

Tieren scowled. "I don't like that we might have contradicting visions."

"Mine has to do with ensuring Braon reigns, *atsuna*. Assalan must never seize power. The gods are most concerned. I have tasks to set into motion within the next lunar."

Pengfei lowered his gaze, hiding his expression and ending the discussion. The rest Tieren was not meant to know.

"Tell me what you have seen. Do you receive fleeting glimpses or sensations?" Pengfei licked a finger before wiping it on a cloth draped over his knee.

"We met face to face, and as real as you before me. I could hold her, run my hand over her skin. Other nights, I experience sensations, images so detailed, as if they were memories." Tieren rolled his shoulders to minimize the effect she had on his body and mind, then lowered himself to the cushions.

"Mm, it is intriguing that the gods bolster your connection or continue to bless you with glimpses of the future." He met Tieren's gaze. "Only in your dreams?"

"Or during the transition from sleep to wakefulness." Not sure if he should reveal more, Tieren hesitated, running a finger over the rim of the goblet. "I sense her presence in my mind. How much can she glean from me, like secrets and memories?"

"I can't say. Each mating is different. We shall discover more when she arrives."

Tieren pursed his lips, unhappy with waiting. "She cannot speak Greeven."

"Communication might be your greatest hurdle." Pengfei grinned. Tieren gritted his teeth, as if he hadn't figured that out on his own. "But attraction cares nothing for such matters."

Tieren snorted. She invoked passionate responses in him, nothing so insignificant as attraction.

"The halls whisper of your challenge tomorrow. Beware, *atsuna*, you may not be king, but you are still a threat. You train in the old ways. Uphold the ancients' honor. Most cannot hope to defeat you without treachery."

"Assalan does not frighten me, Pengfei." He smirked over the rim of his cup. "And I am always on guard."

Pengfei's eyes darkened. "Your upbringing wasn't as it should be, yet the lessons you learned will stand you in good stead."

"We are all intimidated at some point in their lives. Some more than others." Tieren shouldn't have to discuss his tormentors nor how much he'd prayed to the gods to save him from them. Pushing his goblet across the table, he rose to his feet and gestured to the platform, with a powerful need to spread his wings and breathe in cool air.

"Care for a soar?"

A slow smile spread Pengfei's cheeks, and he rose, flicking off his robes. "Oh, to soar like a squawkling." As he shimmied out of his dowo, he pranced naked to the platform's edge and tossed Tieren a beaming grin. Talons curled from his fingernails, and snowy feathers and fur rippled from his back. With a shake of his tail, he squawked, calling Tieren to follow, then leaped off.

Chuckling, Tieren peeled off his dowo and padded on bare feet while summoning his inner Greeven. The wind tousled his hair as it formed feathers, and his vision sharpened on a swooping Pengfei, his white coat glistening in the moonlight.

Hours later, back in his dowo, Tieren sat on the edge of the platform to his chambers, watching the suns rise. The sweet scent of dew hung in the air, but on the cliffs, the rings touched by the sunlight swung into life. Servants scurried along the rocky paths, carrying objects meant for comfort. He growled. Their integrity had fallen far to risk a life over a cushion. The blame for lost lives rested on his shoulders for agreeing to this farcical challenge. His ancestors would have pecked the challenger's eyes out. He should. His people couldn't hate him more than they did.

"*Atsuna*, have you not rested?" Meilo hurried in carrying a bowl of steaming water.

"A little. I met with Pengfei while you were drooling on your wife's breast." Tieren rose, hanging his toes off the edge. To plummet and to soar were the greatest senses of freedom. That was what he truly longed for. To be free of all this: the pressures placed on him by his father, Braon's reliance, Nona's trust. He raised his gaze to the stars fading as the suns attacked their meager light. What must it be like up there?

His *kekaseea* would arrive in a gray box, but could it carry him away from Rianus?

He curled his fingers into his palms. The sharp bite of his fingernails snapped him back to reality. It was foolish thinking. He was who he was meant to be. A darkling prince not fit to rule but good enough to protect those worthier than him.

Striding toward the dead-emlo plinth, he dipped his fingers into the steaming water and splashed his face with too much force, drenching his plumage.

Meilo sniggered. "Drowned battusk."

Tieren chuckled, flicking water at his friend before studying his reflection in the mirror. He resembled his father, but the darkness in his eyes spoke of suffering. His smile faded, and he turned away, wondering how Mick saw him. Whether she liked the look of him mattered not. The ancient magic that melded their souls was as powerful as the crossing between Qilaetor and the Isles of Eleta.

"What weapons has Assalan chosen?" Meilo spread Tieren's armor across the bed. In tarnished steel, it rippled in the light, from gray to silver, and as close as the royal armorers could match Tieren's dark plumage. Still, he stood out, as he always had.

"Does it matter? He will use treachery to win since losing to me would bring him great shame." Tieren stroked his breastplate. The weight of it would slow his reactions. "Has Imsal arrived yet?"

"I expected him at dawn." Meilo gestured to the levels below. "Isn't it foolish to test out new armor now? What if it fails and Assalan manages to impale you?"

Tieren grinned. "I have seen him eat; impaling anything with a fork is a trial."

"Laugh if you must, Tieren. I'm serious. Braon cannot afford to lose you."

"I shall not die this day, Meilo. The gods have shown me my future."

Meilo's stiff shoulders slumped, and he smiled. "True. I shall send a servant to help Imsal carry." He whipped open a door and spoke to the guards as shadowed as Tieren. All the servants, warriors, and guards were. If Tieren had wanted to, he had the numbers for an all-out rebellion. But all the blood spilled would be on his hands.

Meilo's concern didn't echo in Tieren's heart. He didn't doubt his ability to best Assalan, and doing so would showcase the new armor. The court, and 'General' Assalan in particular, had rejected Imsal's ideas, claiming improvements to the standard armor were unnecessary. They weren't at war and preferred to spend their coin elsewhere. True, the Drueen had been quiet, their skirmishes fewer. Still, to assume such a warrior nation wouldn't take up arms again was foolish, short-sighted, and dangerous. The Greeven outnumbered them, but the Drueen, with wider wingspans, more strength in their bulkier bodies, and teeth-laden jaws should not be underestimated. Many a Greeven would die. And for what? Gold mines?

Tieren found Ismal's designs intriguing and had worked with the armorer to perfect them, testing the metal's ability to defend him. That was another reason why he had accepted Assalan's challenge.

"Imsal's at the fortress gates." Meilo frowned. "Why did you not say you sent guards?"

"Trust no one, Meilo."

He gaped and splayed his fingers across his chest. "Not even me? And the guards guarding him?"

Tieren snorted. "Someone with power or the desire for it, those you must be wary of." His guards had shared in his persecution. Most darklings born were sent to him, no matter the gender, and he raised them in the abandoned barracks in the underground labyrinth beneath Qilaetor. The shunned had formed the family he had always longed for, yet he'd had to remain aloof. He was still a prince, and they were to him what Braon was, his duty.

He hadn't visited in a while and would do so this day.

"Ambassador Sugard has requested your presence for the History of Rianus class he is giving." Meilo winced. "Sounds as dull." He dabbed Tieren's chest where water had dribbled. "Lord Karlez would like to discuss the farming techniques employed in the south, stating they are flaunting traditions."

A lecture on history he could endure, even if it was Sugard's veiled attempt to remind Tieren how long the Sugards had once ruled Rianus. Tieren grimaced. It had been ages since he last walked the hallowed halls for the privileged few born without blemish. Nona had ensured Tieren received personal tutelage, for which he was grateful. He rubbed his chest, soothing the ache forming. Leaving Rianus meant abandoning her to the *Gawen's* fickleness.

Imsal waddled through the open door, overburdened with bundles of dark metal. Sweat drenched his brow. He huffed, his old knees creaking when he lowered the armor to the floor.

"Did my guards not help you carry, Imsal?" Tieren glowered at his hovering males.

They bowed and shut the door. Knowing how stubborn Imsal could be, Tieren couldn't fault his males for failing to follow orders. He faced the aging armorer, who flicked out the breastplate like it weighed no more than a tunic.

"Come now, *atsuna*, let's get it on you." He arched a brow at Tieren's dowo.

Tieren stripped to summon his Greeven. With ruffled feathers, he dipped his head so that Imsal could slip the breastplate over his plumage.

He braced his body for the weight of normal armor, but it didn't come. Not only was the metal light, but it gave off a comforting warmth. Rows of scales rippled as he shuffled from taloned foot to foot.

"Stand still, *atsuna*," Imsal tutted and reached around him to tie on the tail guards.

Tieren raised his wings to aid him. The standard armor affected his ability to fly, to alter direction, to feel the wind in his wings. Imsal's armor was as light as...well, a feather.

Stains of various shades marred his threadbare tunic. The stench of stale *jaketta* wine assailed Tieren when Imsal leaned closer to tighten the buckles. His weakness for wine was why no one respected him. Tieren didn't see it as something to judge the male for. There were events in his past he needed to forget. People dealt with things in various ways. No one was perfect all the time, and anyone who claimed so deceived themselves.

Tugging on Tieren's wings, Imsal clipped the back brace to the tip caps, holding the wing guards in place.

He stumbled back, with a proud grin splitting his swarthy cheeks. "Well, how does it feel?"

Tieren willed his beak to recede. "Good, light, movable."

"Yes, but will it protect you?" Meilo held Tieren's folded dowo as if he expected to hand it to him at any moment.

"Shall we test it?" Tieren chuckled. "I thought you abhorred all forms of violence." He waddled to the edge of his platform. "Come, Meilo, meet me in the labyrinth. Let us spar like we used to." He launched himself skyward and flapped his wings, hovering. "Don't make me wait."

Allowing his Greeven to consume his face, he squawked a taunt and dove, chaffing his laughter. The thrill of the fight blasted his blood with energetic fire. Meilo sparring harkened to their younger days, and getting him to fight was a gift, a reliving of cherished memories.

Tieren would prefer to spar with a friend than battle Assalan, but some choices weren't his to make.

Chapter Thirteen

PURSUED

Year: 2364

En route to Cetus via Sculptor

THE MAN IN THE corner thumped the dumbbell down and rose, rubbing a towel across his sweat-drenched face before looping it around his neck. "Thank you." Chocolate-brown dreadlocks bounced as he strode toward her. His sweatpants hung low on his hips, exposing a sexy quadrant of dark skin and even darker hair. "It's not often I see Kiros taken down. He's such a strong bastard."

Mick shrugged, flicking through the training programs while trying not to focus on the damp T-shirt-covered chest inches from her. Dreamy Tieren had her on a permanent simmer. Kir had tipped the scales, and now, she ached like a dog on heat. "He used to kick my ass every time." What had Kir called him? Wayne? No, Wyatt.

"I couldn't help but eavesdrop, even through my audiobook." Wyatt gestured to the buds plugged into his ears. "If you can feel the change in airflow, your mutation has heightened your senses. Do you struggle to sleep? To focus?"

She didn't answer. Why should she? This mutation was hers to deal with, and too many people knowing about it endangered her. The soldiers under Solomon's banner were strangers to her. Any of them could betray her to the Followers, Fentus, or another science research company. She grimaced, imagining waking up trapped inside a drone.

"Here." He unclipped his buds and raised them to her ears, hesitating as if waiting for her permission.

Curious, she nodded. He brushed her hair back to press the buds into her ears. A shiver rippled from her neck to her toes when his touch lingered. He dragged his fingers from her shoulder to her forearm and tapped her implant to life, startling a kaleidoscope of holographic letters. Layering his arm along hers, he transferred something. A buzz rippled along her arm, and she waited with her wrist exposed. He selected the holographic green arrow, and a soft shush flooded her ears.

She gasped. It drowned out everything, even her heartbeat and the blood rushing along her veins. Yanking out an earbud, she flinched at the usual bombardment from the universe and the *Jinsei*.

He smiled. "White noise dampens sounds. You could try sonic silence, but with your mutated hearing, you might pick up the minor audio peaks."

She beamed, stumped as to how to show her gratitude. With this, she didn't need cryo-pens or grit. "Thank you."

She tugged out the other earbud, but he wrapped his long fingers around her hand.

"Keep them. I have spares." Sauntering off, his long strides added a swagger to his tight ass. "I received the rescind." He tapped his wrist. "You're back on the menu." He ran an admiring gaze from her legs to her breasts before snagging her gaze. "You have my deets. We can meet for a coffee." He grinned, humor brightening his green eyes. "Your treat."

Was he asking her on a date? At the possibility, excitement swept through her, sparking goosebumps to life. No man had ever dated her, not when trips across the galaxies took weeks to months. Nurturing long-distance relationships was impossible unless the man joined her on the *Jinsei*. And there was no way she'd invite him aboard after one drink or fuck. So, no, dating wasn't something she'd ever experienced.

"I'd love that. I can meet you in the mess in an hour?"

He tapped the door frame and winked. "See you then."

She didn't rush to her quarters to choose a sexy outfit because she didn't own one. Glancing at her tank and camo pants slumped her shoulders. Hell, she wouldn't know how to fluff her hair or apply cosmetics she didn't have. What he saw was what he'd get. She sniffed her armpit and winced. Okay, maybe a quick shower might be in order.

A cold, mocking laughter tore through her. "You're the only woman on the damn ship, Mick, how you look or smell is inconsequential." Tapping the green arrow to play the white noise, she worked through fighting stances, from floor to standing, attacks from behind, in front, the side, and still, not a drop of sweat dampened her skin. She rubbed her furrowed brow, searching for a layer of moisture, and found nothing.

"NOX, full bio scan, please." Her voice warbled, and she hurried to clear it. She wasn't about to lose her shit now. Too little too late after the friggin horse had bolted. "Do it now, and give me the results within the hour."

"You say that like it's quick. What's the matter? Feeling off? Experiencing any side effects?"

She gritted her teeth, expecting his next questions to be "how does it make you feel?" or "any tingling in your extremities?" Silly NOX playing the doctor, but there was no one else she could turn to.

"Could the creature's acid mingle with the hokou's blood?" The current mutation might not fight off a new mutation, or it could merge into something more potent or lethal. Well, the truth was out. The universe was trying to kill her.

"The hokou was ages ago. I doubt its venom is still in you."

"Um, NOX, Hector bit me the day he died." *Frig.* She'd forgotten to mention it.

"What?" A grinding whirred. "Checking the vids. What the hell, Mick? Were you ever going to tell me?"

"It healed," she muttered. Though, at the time, discussing further mutations hadn't been on her mind. Grieving had. She winced at that memory and cupped the amulet hanging around her neck.

"From now on, I'm damned well going to monitor you twenty-four-friggin-seven." He huffed like a puff of air escaping. "In light of this *new* information, it's still not possible. That was weeks ago, and any residual hokou venom would've worked out of your system. You did struggle to heal this time, though." Metal grated gravel when NOX laughed. "Your mutated blood won if there was some sort of molecular battle."

"Shit." She bit her lip at the idea of her saliva turning into acid. And would it restrict itself to her saliva, or would her blood burn through whatever it splattered on? "Are there traces of the new creature remaining in my system, and if so, what's it doing to me?" There would be no fucking for her until she had the results.

"Lemme see. The pod bolstered the hokou's healing." NOX hummed as if deep in thought. "And modulated your body's temperature since your fever rose to an alarming high. Certainly non-human tolerance levels here."

She growled, wishing she could smack something. What the frig had NOX been doing while she was in the med pod? Spinning on her heels, she bolted for the punching bag to throw a few pummels. "Didn't you monitor me?" She glared at the ceiling. "I'm your priority, you useless bucket of bolts."

She was doomed to die with NOX as her only ally. Images flooded her tormented mind, of her drooling and spasming on the floor with NOX commenting that perhaps the mutation *was* killing her. Visiting a proper doctor might not be a bad idea.

"Of course, I monitored you, but I happen to be piloting, running diagnostics, scanning planets, babysitting our guests, and fending off a pissed-off Kiros. What were you doing?"

Arching her brow at his unexpected defensiveness, she coughed to hide a laugh. "Have you been pestering the men with your endless questions?" She had tried for years to get him to argue with her. Less than a week with a few men and he sounded like a petulant teenager.

"Their answers have been most enlightening." NOX's tone took on an eager quality, and hours loomed ahead of him regaling her on his findings.

"Why didn't you tell me you're swamped, NOX? I bet you haven't had the time to find new show tunes. If I handle Kiros from here on, would that free you up for your favorite pastime?" She added a wicked sweetness to her voice, and had NOX been human, he would've been suspicious of her motives.

"That's thoughtful of you, Mick, but I've indeed found new show tunes. Would you like to hear them?"

She grinned. *Gotcha.* "Of course, I'd love to hear you sing as soon as you have the results." *Carrot dangled. Oh, poor NOX still had much to learn.*

"Yes, the results need to be a priority. I'll get right on it, Mick."

"Thank you, NOX." She walked away, shaking her head. One would think after decades with her that he would've mastered the idiosyncrasies of a woman's mind.

On the bridge, she accessed the route NOX had mapped to reach Cetus. The *Jinsei* would skim the suns, storing sol power. Once at capacity, NOX would switch the fuel tanks off until the *Jinsei* drained the sol stored. Dad had used sol to warm and light the menagerie, but after his death, Mick had rerouted most of the cells to power the *Jinsei*. As expensive modifications go, it had saved her ass more times than she could count.

The route arced the Phoenix constellation, a stop off at Rebirth, a way station on the cusp of the Sculptor galaxy, then onward to Cetus. She was looking forward to a change of scenery. Rebirth was nicer than most way stations if she stayed out of the lower levels. It was home to science groups intent on studying the ongoing high rate of star formation within Sculptor. The products available, though more expensive, would be of better quality. The food was recognizable and palatable despite the mining companies owning levels below the scientists' hallowed viewing decks. Endless funding made all the difference.

Locking the bridge behind her, she skipped along the narrow corridor, slid down the ladder, and slipped inside the mess to find Wyatt at a table with two cups. He flashed a smile and gestured to the bench in front of him.

Drys flicked a worrying glance at them, then dipped his head, focusing on the antique paperback in his hand. She had read a few of Dad's when she was younger. They remained untouched in his quarters.

"I was hoping you'd be early." Wyatt offered her another charming smile.

"Why?" She balanced her elbow on the table and rested her chin on her palm, content to watch Wyatt pour coffee from the automatic dispenser. He had taken a shower, his dreadlocks were still damp, and a spicy cologne engulfed her when he sat again. Heat burned her cheeks, which was odd since exercising hadn't spiked her temperature. Yet another oddity she needed to mention to Dr. NOX.

The thought that Wyatt had gone to this much effort for her was what flustered her.

Most of her hookups had lasted five minutes in a dark alleyway. Giving pleasure hadn't been a priority for the men. Studying Wyatt's sharp jaw and hazel eyes fluttered her heartbeat. He would be slow, methodical, and his focus intense. She didn't doubt she'd scream his name more than once.

The problem was, he didn't fire her blood like Tieren or Kir did, but Wyatt was the safer option.

"Lanek's en route." Kir burst into the mess and froze. His gaze sliced between her and Wyatt, then to the mug Wyatt held out to her. "Said he snagged a lift with a courier ship and will meet us at Rebirth." Kir splayed his fingers on the table and nudged his head at Wyatt. "Go calibrate the *Sentry's* canons."

Wyatt gripped his mug. "But—"

Kir growled in warning. Wyatt jerked, and darkness settled in his hazel eyes as he rose to his feet.

She caught his hand for a squeeze. "Raincheck?"

A slow smile dimpled his cheeks. "Anytime, Mick."

"Call me Mikaela."

His cheeks darkened, but when Kir growled again, Wyatt stormed off.

"What the frig was that?" She glowered at Kir. "And if I catch a whiff of a lie, I'll bust your nose." Narrowing her focus, she listened to his rapid heartbeat and rough breathing. Shit, Kiros was too pissed for her to track a lie. She ought to break his nose anyway.

His nostrils flared, but she raised her chin, meeting his glare with her own. A pulse ticked at his clenched jaw, and he folded his arms across his chest, conveying he wasn't about to explain himself. He was being such a dumbass.

She titled her head to the bulkhead. "NOX, who am I?"

"You know who you are." Something thumped, like he'd dropped a set of weights. "Shit, is it the muta—"

"Humor me, NOX." She resisted the urge to roll her eyes, not with Kir's gaze on her.

"Oh, okay." NOX cleared his non-existent throat, sounding more like sandpaper over stone. "You're Mikaela 'Mick' Danvers, daughter of—"

"Thank you for confirming my identity." She arched a brow at Kir, delighted when he pursed his lips. "Do I have siblings, NOX? Family of any sort?"

"No records indicate relations—"

"What? No, that can't be right. Nothing that states Kiros Caldwell is my brother?" She gasped in mock horror, pressing four stiff fingers to her gaping mouth. "Imagine that. No relation, so get the frig out of my business, Kir. Keep pushing me, and I'll fuck Wyatt in front of your men."

She winced. Shit, now Kir might treat Wyatt worse than he had a moment ago. Her presence was splitting his team apart. They relied on each other, more brothers than teammates. She focused on the ceiling, fighting the burning agony of a migraine building behind her eyes.

"This was a bad idea, Kir. We'll head our separate ways from Rebirth." She slipped around him, ignoring his slack jaw.

"Don't I have a say?"

She spun on him, almost slamming into his chest. "I'm not Mick-the-boy, Kir, and you're not my protector." Pinching the bridge of her nose, she accepted the pounding migraine as her penance. Exhaustion gathered the pain and streaked fire down her spine. Despite the few hours of rest in the pod, she yearned to sleep for days.

"How about we move to another bay and keep out of your hair?"

Laughter bubbled up her throat and bent her over. Tears pooled on her eyelashes and stifled her humor. She hurried to catch them with her fingertips, not sure what they would do if she let them fall.

"If you kept out of my hair, we wouldn't be having this conversation. I can't afford to power up another bay." Dizziness assailed her, and she threw out a hand, slamming the palm on the metal bulkhead, denting it. Kir reached for her, but she stumbled out of his reach. "I'm tired. We can talk about this later."

Nausea coiled in the pit of her stomach, which made no sense. She was fine a moment ago. A throbbing pain arced outward from her right breast. *What the frig?*

"NOX, power the pod." She squeezed the words through clenched teeth, as another wave of pain exploded across her hip. Gripping it, she staggered.

"Mick?" Kir's voice came from behind her. The bastard had trailed her.

"Not now." Silence met her scream.

But typical of him, he didn't stay quiet. "What's happening, NOX?"

Gathering the last of her energy, she punched him in the nose. The crack resounded in the passage, along with his roar. "I'm not warning you again."

This time when she hobbled to the pod, he didn't follow.

Chapter Fourteen

Tieren winced when Meilo swung a flail. Before he staggered under its weight, the spiked metal ball scraped the scales of Imsal's new armor. The flour bags had exploded on impact, dusting him, Meilo, and the straw-lined floor in green. The sword lay on the hay barrel untouched. That skill wasn't one Meilo had mastered, but he believed a flail was an easy weapon to wield. So far, he had sunk it in the stone wall and missed embedding it in Imsal's shin.

"Why didn't you summon me, fair *tsuna*?" Ghilian chuckled from where he leaned a shoulder against a stone pillar. Dust layered his face and traveled garments. "At this rate, you'll be late for the challenge."

Tieren grinned, striding forward to wrap his fingers around his friend's neck to press his temple to his. He released him and threw an arm across his cloaked shoulders. "Ghilian, it's good to see you. What news from the south?"

"What news, he says, when I return to this challenge-non-sense?" Ghilian tilted and studied Tieren. He grimaced. "There's more?"

"Oh, so much more." Sweet joy bubbled up Tieren's throat, and he raised his face to the stone ceiling for a good laugh. "Meilo will fill you in. Now, save your brother from himself and help us test this armor. You're right, being late would weaken my standing. I'd like to be on the spire when Assalan swaggers into the arena."

Meilo offered the ungainly weapon to Ghilian. "You can't possibly know how to—"

Ghilian grabbed the shaft and swung, sending the spiked ball spinning.

Meilo leaped away with a cry, then circled the room to settle beside Imsal.

"I see this design withstood the bags. Are you hoping it will hold against spikes and swords?" Ghilian withdrew his sword when he released the flail, sending it flying toward Tieren.

He was too distracted and didn't dodge in time. The ball hit his chest as Ghilian swung his blade down onto Tieren's wing guard. The ball and sword bounced off the armor. Fire burned in Tieren's chest, then pulsed outward. For a second, his left arm tingled before going numb.

"Good that it deflected the initial strikes. Now dance for me." Ghilian thrust and parried.

Tieren did his best to dodge each attack, with scraping noises announcing when he failed.

"Your movements are spry. How light is it, Imsal?" Ghilian ran a palm over the layered scales. "I even like the color."

"Its weight is a quarter of the standard armor." Imsal tugged on his knotted beard. "I found a way to heat the metal, to mold it, to hammer it thinner than ever before."

Without warning, Ghilian barreled toward Tieren to knock him over.

"Don't you dare hurt Tieren." A squawkling clambered over the hay barrels and threw herself in front of Tieren. He roared a warning and wrapped his wings around her, curving his body to take the brunt of Ghilian's charge. Nausea coiled in his stomach, as fear burst to life, overriding the bruising his wings took when Ghilian bounced off.

"Hali, what were you thinking?" Tieren tucked his head to meet her dark gaze. She clung to him, with her spindly arms gripping his knees.

"*Atsuna*, you are to be protected. Everyone says so."

He chuckled and unfolded his wings, uncaring that Ghilian sprawled on the straw with a chagrined smile. "Beaten by a squawk-ling, Ghilian?"

"One I should train. I can't decide if she is courageous or foolish." He leaped to his feet and dusted off his dowo.

Hali huffed and raised her chin. "I don't need your training, Ghilian men Senatt. I have been practicing on my own."

Tieren caught her swinging punch while tucking his wings away. The armor shifted under the change and thunked as it hit the floor. He flicked his shoulders to dislodge the wing guards, lest they slid down and hurt her. Imsal hurried to catch them.

"It is good that you are eager, young one. Still, you should learn from those who have come before you. Knowledge opens doors, and with each door you walk through, you will grow stronger." He hefted her into his arms and grinned at Ghilian over the dark crown of her head. "Best add Hali to your ranks."

"I agree." Ghilian scooped her out of Tieren's arms to toss her into the air before catching her and kissing her temple. "Now, Hali, where is your keeper?"

She shuddered and burrowed into his arms. "I snuck away. She wants to bathe me."

"Oh, no, that *is* horrifying." Tieren pursed his lips to hold back another laugh. "I need to bathe too. Come, you and I shall visit the pools together." He held out his hand, and she leaped across to him. "Ghilian, send her keeper to me."

Tieren took on his Greeven form and launched himself skyward, trusting Imsal and Meilo to follow. He landed on the rough platform below the arena and lowered Hali's feet to the floor. She was too young to fly, thank the gods, because when she did, she would be more than a handful.

"*Atsuna.*" A servant scurried forward to offer him a robe while ushering Hali into the caves.

Tieren shed his Greeven form and slipped into the robe. He didn't have long before the challenge started, but a quick dip to ease the child's fears would be time wisely spent.

"*Atsuna*, I did not expect to see you here." Fresaie ruffled her brilliant white plumage, which glowed in the morning light. Too beautiful for modesty, she sashayed toward him while accepting an offered robe. In slipping it on, she took her time, tilting a hip and extending a leg or arm to best display her assets.

Before the *Gawen's* revelation on the Isles of Eleta, he would have admired her with open interest. It was as if the muddy scales were stripped from him. Her blue eyes narrowed, as if she calculated her actions versus his responses. Choosing him as a mate wasn't on her agenda, not when her father would end their union before their soul ties formed. Her interest lay in rebelling, in dipping her talons in the dark side.

Oh, she found him arousing. Of that, he had no doubt, with her sweet, musky scent confirming her desire. Things had changed. *He* had changed. Now, only dark eyes and hair lured and tormented him. Fresaie paled in comparison.

With his arms filled with Tieren's new armor, Meilo landed on the platform. He tossed a withering look at Fresaie.

"Just a quick dip before I prepare for the challenge." Tieren forced a polite smile and turned to leave her, but she leaped in front of him.

He had once thought her beautiful, with long flowing plumage and warm-white skin. When she found her pleasure, her eyes lightened to ice blue. Would his *kekaseea's* eye color alter? His breath caught. Memories flooded him, events he had yet to experience. He hardened, throbbing and aching.

Ignoring Fresaie and her gasps of outrage, he strode along a tunnel filled with steam and warmth. A servant gestured to an arched opening carved into the rock. He slipped inside and chuckled at Hali splashing in a nearby pool. Separated by thin sheets of murky rock, he disrobed and slid into the bubbling, heated water. A groan tore from him when his bruised muscles relaxed. He sank deeper, rested his head on the smooth rocky edge, and stared into the tendrils of steam, imagining recognizable shapes forming.

He trusted Meilo to fetch him when it was time, so he closed his eyes and let the lapping water lull him.

CHAPTER FIFTEEN

TIEREN GATHERED HER IN his arms, and warmth curled around her. Thick locks of hair flopped across his temple and flicked upward, reminding her of a cockatoo's crest. When she buried her fingers in the dark depths, it was like digging into melted wax. His eyelashes fluttered on a hushed groan, and when he focused on her again, the cognac in his eyes brightened to gold.

"*Kekaseea.*" Rough, electrifying, and deep was his voice when he clicked the word in his strange language.

As naked as the first time she met him, he shifted and nestled between her thighs. His fingers gripping her hips sparked a different heat from the coiled knot in her stomach to her aching core. He drew in a long breath, as if he relished a fragrance carried on a breeze. "I love when your body yearns for me."

Whatever he said sounded sexy, rasping across her senses. If only she could understand him. *Frig.* She needed to follow up with NOX.

With Kir and the S.o.S. on board, finding the meaning of *kekaseea* had slipped her mind.

She stared at her fingers sliding over his biceps to curl around his shoulders. Those were *her* hands, and his skin hot velvet, as if she recalled the memory of it.

Fire burned in her right breast, building to consume her senses and focus. She pulled away, glancing at her chest. In a blink, Tieren's heat left her as he dissolved. She cried out, sitting up and bumping her head on the inside of the pod.

"NOX?" She rubbed her smarting temple for a second before the sting vanished.

"You rang?" His droll tone had her rolling her eyes.

"Why's my chest on fire?" Seconds later, white foam drenched her. She squealed, thumping the pod's glass like it was to blame for her wet state. "Burning agony, idiot."

Gravel rolled over metal in his version of a chuckle. "Nothing on the scans indicate a physical or biological reason for a fiery chest."

"Dumbass is making the rounds. It must be contagious."

He ignored her grumbling. "I have the results. Seems your mutation leaped ahead."

"Shit, my saliva's acidic?" She moaned, fighting the sting of tears. No more kissing for her ever.

"No, accordi—"

"Oh, well, then what's the mutation leap mean?" She tapped the glass, flicking through the results in search of some sort of explanation. Waiting for NOX would kill her before the mutations did, that was for friggin sure. "How will it impact me?"

"If you let me finish…" He puffed, his version of a huff. "It slowed the hokou mutation. Other than that, I can't predict how it impacts your existing strength, healing, and speed."

"So, take it easy?" She frowned, scooted off the pod, and pulled open a drawer. Scalpels glimmered in the harsh artificial light. She chose one at random.

"What are you doing?" Kiros hovered at the door. A white strip across his nose and a black eye proved she was a woman of her word.

She gasped, having not heard him approach. Tears welled at the thought that she'd lost her 'powers,' leaving her vulnerable and unable to stand on her own. She'd come to rely on the mutations to keep her safe and alive.

But she needed Kiros, or at least someone she could trust, to be her friend. "Kir."

He stilled, and his expression softened into one of familiar affection.

Gripping the scalpel, she sliced her palm. Pain burned outward, pulsing along the cut's edge. She swallowed a scream.

"Mick." He bolted across the med-bay, snatching a bandage from the open drawer to press to her palm he cupped in his.

"I must know if I can still heal." She rested her other hand on his chest and gently pushed him.

He released her and lifted the roll of bandage off her palm. The wound, though smeared with blood, had begun to knit together. Cold horror slithered down her spine at the blue tendrils like jagged tattoos shooting under her skin. It was surreal, watching herself heal and feeling no pain after the initial burn. Her skin prickled though, like a thousand fire ants crawled across the wound.

"Frig." When the cut sealed, the tattoos faded.

"What's happening to you?" Kir waved the bandage stained red and blue, then tossed it into a bio-hazard disposal unit.

"I...don't know, Kir." She dropped the scalpel onto the counter and shuddered at what she had to do. "I'll see someone on Rebirth. It has departments of scientists, right?"

He paused and captured her palm in his again to trail a fingertip across it. Now *that* she felt. "Fentus?"

She shrugged. "They would be my best bet." Snatching her hand back, she pressed a finger to her lips to silence him. She tilted her head to listen. The familiar and dreaded hum of the *Jinsei* reached her, along with Drys down in the cargo bay teasing Wyatt about *their* date.

Okay, so she still had her supernatural hearing. Check. Healing, check...well, kind of. She threw her arms around Kir and lifted him a meter off the floor. He oofed when she dropped him. Strength, check. She couldn't test her speed on board, but she'd do that at the first opportunity.

Grinning at finding herself semi-normal, she hugged Kir, who gaped at her like she had lost her mind.

"Mick?" Concern lilted his voice.

She leaned back to cup his cheek. "I'm an anomaly, Kir, and I don't know how to deal with it."

He settled his ass against the counter while tugging her between his splayed legs and into his arms. "Under the circumstances, you're handling it well."

"Right." She pushed off his chest, reminding him that she hadn't forgotten his earlier display of dumbassery. "NOX, scan me each morning and compile all your findings for Fentus. Any imagery you have, add that. If they're going to figure out what's happening to me, they'll need as much information as we can give them." She faced Kir. "I owe Wyatt a thank you, so will you please give me a little space?"

He frowned, folding his arms across his chest. "Why?"

Resting a pointed look on him, she sauntered out of the med-bay and scampered along the passages to the bay. Gripping the railing, she scanned the area until she found Wyatt sprawled across a crate, tapping his foot to something he was listening to.

He sat up when he spotted her.

"Wyatt, my quarters."

He flicked a nervous yet furious look at Kiros, but when Wyatt met her gaze, he smiled.

"Mick." Kir's growl was low. The dumbass had followed her. He was becoming predictable.

"You forced this, Kir. My quarters is the one place on *Jinsei* I'm guaranteed privacy." She pointed at him and lowered her voice. "If you bully Wyatt, overburden him with pointless tasks, dock his share, or even taunt him, I will bust your nose again." Spinning away, she took two steps, then paused. "NOX, continue to monitor all conversations and flag those where Wyatt's mentioned."

"Acknowledged."

Outside Dad's quarters, she hesitated, chewing a torn thumbnail while staring at his keypad. Other than the port, he had a stash of liquor, the real deal, accumulated over many years. All she needed to do was stroll in and slip a bottle out of the cabinet. Easy. She'd done this before, the day Emma and Hector had died.

Her churning gut fluttered her heartbeat, and she stood there, sucking in deep breaths. Well, trying to. She was a badass, taking on wild creatures, Solomon of S.o.S, and yet, entering Dad's quarters tested her mettle every friggin time.

Slamming her palm on the keypad cracked it, but the swish of the door opening drew her full attention. The smell hit her first, prickling her eyes at the familiarity. Dad and his silly candles, as it warded off extinct mosquitoes. He'd said the medicinal scent calmed him, helped him focus. A sharp spicy note was his cologne, something he hadn't changed in all the years she'd known him. Chosen by her mother, or so he claimed.

Gripping the doorframe, her body fought her mind's unwillingness to enter. "Get in there, Mick."

She stumbled forward and stopped. Everything was as she'd left it. His bed was pristine, untouched, representing his absence. Dragging her gaze to his desk, his journal took centerstage with completed journals lining his bookshelf. He had distrusted electronic journals and only used them when he needed to communicate something of importance. The rest were his daily thoughts. She couldn't bring herself to read them.

One bookshelf had a glass door, displaying his bottles of brandy, whisky, and Ganymede wine. But when she tried to open the door, the glass flickered.

She chuckled. "Holographic glass? Now, that's surprising, Dad." Sliding bottles aside, she considered the contents. The brandy looked the fullest. She grabbed it then held it up to the light to swirl the amber liquid. Before she could second guess her choice, she darted out of the room. The door closing behind her released the tension gripping her shoulders, and she pressed her temple to Dad's door before heading to her quarters.

Wyatt leaned against the bulkhead with his legs crossed at the ankles. "This is dangerous. Kiros is pissed."

She huffed and opened the door, then yanked Wyatt inside. "Right, two things." She gestured to a chair and placed the bottle in front of him.

After a quick search for two cups, she opened the bottle and poured a large splash into each cup. She downed hers, and as the heated, smooth, and spicy liquor hit her throat and belly, she moaned. "Wow. I'm used to grit. This is—"

"Amazing?" Wyatt grinned, swirling his cup before taking another sip. "Okay, what are the three things?"

"One; thank you again for the earbuds." She refilled their cups but nursed hers this time. With the amulet clasped in her hand, she stroked the bird. The pad of her thumb unerringly found the hooked beak. She peered at the bird. Did it look like Tieren? No, it was just a muscular bird, nothing more. Still... She frowned. Not once in her dreams had she been wearing the amulet when she never removed it, not even to shower.

"And the second?"

She released the amulet, letting it nestle in her cleavage. A now-familiar hum took up residence in her chest. "Sex."

He jerked back, surprise dropping his chin. His cheeks darkened, and he shifted on his chair, clearing his throat as he fidgeted. "You're so bold, Mikaela."

"Shall I flirt, beat about the bush?" She laughed. "No, I can't be anything other than what I am. Wyatt, fucking you will hurt S.o.S, won't it?"

He stilled and sipped his brandy in silence. "It might."

"That's not my intention." She studied him, the way his dreadlocks swayed around him, the deep intensity in his eyes, his hero-like nose, and wide mouth. He was attractive, and had he been anything but an S.o.S member, she would've liked to keep him.

"I get it." He drained his cup and shook it, asking for a refill. "But no sex doesn't mean we can't be friends."

She smiled, offering him a slight shake of her head. "The perception that we're lovers will worsen the way Kiros treats you."

"Then he isn't the man I thought he was."

She refilled their cups, savoring the silence of the *Jinsei's* engines, the soft thumping of her and Wyatt's hearts, and the subtleness of his cologne. "I won't lie though, if he asks."

"Neither will I." Wyatt laughed and raised his cup in a salute. "In fact, I can't wait for him to do so."

CHAPTER SIXTEEN

MEILO HEFTED HALI ONTO his shoulder as Tieren launched himself skyward, swooping to brush his feathers across the outstretched hands of the crowds gathered in the morning sunlight. The sight of pale and dark faces cheering him flooded his chest with warm hope. This was what Rianus should be like; Greevens united in joy and sorrow.

He landed on a spire and waited, legs spread and wings splayed out. With nothing but the armor on, he stood tall. His people knew him not to be ostentatious, unlike the procession that meandered up the hill toward the arena. Purple and gold blinded him, and he snorted at the waste of gold. Drums thundered and echoed off the craggy walls, growing louder as the procession crawled closer. By the time they reached the center, the sun would be mid-sky and beating down on them all.

Typical of Assalan to make everyone wait for him, as if only his time mattered. Hungry and sunburned squawklings fluttered around their parents, unable to harness their endless energy. So like Hali. Tieren smiled, raised his beak to the sky, and closed his eyes, drawing in slow, deliberate breaths. His hearts calmed, as the roar of the crowds and the thumping of the drums faded.

A cool breeze fluffed his feathers, rejuvenating his energy and enthusiasm. Assalan hoped to destroy Tieren's standing in their people's eyes, as if he feared Tieren's influence. The Labyrinth had to expand its walls for more and more abandoned darklings. He would love for Assalan to show him how his influence had altered the fear and hatred of the pure Greeven.

With his gold beads gleaming in his silver hair, Assalan descended and landed in clanking armor. The weight of it almost brought him to his knees. He had to halt a sprawl with the tips of his wings touching the rock. Sunlight glimmered off every surface of his golden armor. Claw knuckles added extra reach to his talons, and tiny blades sheathed in his wings mimicked the coverts of his feathers.

Bringing additional weapons into an arena was in bad form. Set in deep holes along the platform's edge was a choice of weapons—evenly balanced to show no partiality. Only the warrior's skill mattered.

"*Tsuna* Tieren, I adore your armor, is it made of cloth?" Assalan gestured to Ismal's dark armor catching little of the sunlight.

Ignoring the bombastic fool, Tieren vaulted to swoop through the swinging rings. Gasps and pleas for more trailed his flight, and he landed on the arena on light feet. He curled in his wings, and with his four-fingered talons, pulled a spear from the wall. Serrated teeth from a pauszor spiraled up the shaft toward the steel spearhead. He thumped the rock, announcing the commencement of the challenge.

The crowds stamped with each call to battle he made until Assalan had no choice but to join him.

He kept the spear relaxed but ready, waiting for Assalan to make the first move. By now, his archers would be in place, prepared to hinder Tieren's ability to fight. The smug smile on Assalan's exposed face confirmed his plans. His males would wait until Tieren was at his weakest.

His frown deepened as the sun crossed the sky. Assalan had yet to attack. What was the point of this exhibition, of his challenge, if not to fight? Even though Meilo thought him mad, Tieren had his reasons for agreeing. Perhaps he'd misunderstood Assalan's motivations?

The crowd grew impatient. At last, Assalan raised his hand in an extravagant gesture before withdrawing a sibatu sickle sword from a hole. Roars and cries encouraged his swaggering. Tieren's focus was on the old general's missing talons which implied either a valiant battle or a lack of skill. Tieren would find out soon enough.

With each lunge and parry, the crowds applauded, while droplets of sweat dewed on Assalan's temple. The new armor didn't hinder Tieren's movements as he dodged every offense Assalan launched. At least Tieren's opponent wasn't smirking anymore, with his clenched lips and jutting jaw. When his ancient bones and stringy muscles trembled, then he would signal the archers.

Tieren flicked a gaze from one cliff face to another and almost missed Assalan's sword thrust. Cocooning himself by pulling his wings around him, the sword bounced off the wing guards as Ghilian had tested earlier.

Not hesitating, Tieren parted his wings and swept his talons across Assalan, scoring his armor but not halting the onslaught. Leaping back, he spun the spear, keeping Assalan at bay while he considered how to end this.

He had made his point. Imsal's armor was better, lighter, and worth the treasury's investment. And against the renowned General Assalan, a male who had survived the Great Siege of the Drusoht, Tieren had stood, unharmed and unbested.

Assalan's breathing was ragged, his sword tip rested on the stone, and his wings drooped under the weight of his armor while Tieren hadn't drawn a sweat. Assalan stumbled to a knee, held the sickle sword in front of him, and cupped his shoulder with his two-taloned hand.

The crowd gasped before silence fell.

Assalan's gesture was an ancient show of respect, but the glint of sunlight off metal caught Tieren's gaze as an arrow hurtled toward him. He had a decision to make; turn into the arrow's path and play the martyr, proving Assalan's duplicitousness, or dodge the arrow by stepping into the reach of Assalan's blade.

He opted for the former, leaping and spinning, whipping out his wings to brush his wing guards across Assalan's exposed face. Angling his chest into the path of the arrow, he risked a lethal wound. But he misjudged, and the arrow bounced off the armor.

Landing with his knuckles on the ground, silence reigned for a second before the crowds exploded into an uproar, demanding justice. Blood dribbled from the wound across Assalan's temple, and his eyes darkened with fury.

"You..." Assalan bolted and pulled his daggers from his wing guards, firing them in quick succession.

Tieren chuckled and flicked his wings in front of him, trusting Imsal's armor. One by one, the daggers skittered across the stone. "Your true character has been revealed, Assalan. Such an event was a matter of time."

Greeven descended and formed a ring, with their heels on the edge of the arena. The Auviphis extended their shields in one move. The thump of their pikes on the rock silenced the crowds.

Assalan threw back his head and laughed like a madman. He spun in a circle, his wings spread out wide. "Do you concede, dark *tsuna*?"

Braon, Ambassador Sugard, and Cousin Karlez landed around Tieren, exposing their faces as soon as they curled in their wings.

Tieren frowned at their arrival. "What are you doing, *Tsuna* Braon?" He had assured his brother that he was more than capable of handling Assalan.

Yet, Braon didn't respond but stepped aside as a pale Greeven descended, touching down with grace and beauty.

With her plumage ruffling in the wind, Nona dipped her regal head in greeting before her face appeared. "It is as I suspected, Assalan. You were a sore loser so many years ago, and it does my hearts no good to discover that your selfishness has worsened."

He flashed his charming smile, even as his gaze darted from Braon to Sugard. "Of what do you refer, fair Petey?"

She harrumphed and rippled her wings, tucking them behind her. "Your archers have been executed. For someone so well-versed in strategy, you didn't once stumble upon my spies." Her serene smile brightened her features when she faced the crowd. "As per our ancient law, what say you? How should Assalan be judged for his foul play?"

Like a wave splashing across the coarse sand, the crowds turned their backs on the arena, raising an arm or a wing. Tieren stilled. Such a judgment was too harsh, but he couldn't gainsay their decision. It was their law, and one he, as the wronged opponent, must mete out.

"Petey..." Assalan pleaded with Nona as he must have done when she'd chosen another suitor so many decades ago.

"Rianus has decided, Assalan." She lifted her chin, and with a slight nod to an Auviphis, Tieren was offered a jeweled sibatu.

"No, I beg of you." Assalan stumbled back but bounced off the circle of guards. "Kill me, please."

"General Assalan, I, Dowager Queen of Rianus, hereby banish you." She lowered her voice. "Strip him."

The Auviphis crowded Assalan and tore off his armor. With talons on his shoulders, they forced him to kneel while extending his wings.

Nona was unbreakable in her resolve. "As a general, you know the penalty of treachery. *Tsuna* Tieren, please proceed."

Tieren gritted his teeth, forcing his muscles to obey him. "For my part, I am sorry, Assalan." With two quick swings of the sibatu, he severed Assalan's wings.

His roar echoed off the rock walls and spires as his blood splashed across the arena and his severed wings. Gathering them against his body, he crumpled, curling into a ball, sobbing and whimpering.

As a few Auviphis escorted Nona away, the crowd roared their approval, with their cheers fading. The challenge was over, and they began to meander down the hill or took to flight.

Tieren lingered, noting Sugard and Kulez's smug expressions. Bile rose to choke him, and he tossed the sibatu, uncaring where it landed.

No Greeven deserved the loss of their wings. There were other punishments Nona could have forced as the reigning royal.

"Send a healer to me." He glared at Kulez, his expectation clear. When his cousin hesitated, Tieren shoved his face in front of him. "Now, cousin, or so help me, you shall join Assalan."

Kulez paled and vaulted, rushing to do as commanded. Tieren snorted. Had his cousin known him a little better, he would have realized Tieren was bluffing.

"You show him kindness?" Sugard spat at Assalan's incoherent form. "He would not have given you the same consideration."

"A *tsuna* must be merciful when it is right to do so." Tieren glared the ambassador into silence. Meilo and Ghilian landed on the arena, just as Sugard took off. "Take the general to the Labyrinth."

"But—" Meilo clicked his mouth shut.

Tieren raised his face to the sky, as darkness the color of his skin stained his soul. This was not how he had hoped this challenge would end, but it seemed as if his grandmother had other plans.

Braon wrapped his talons over Tieren's shoulder before throwing a wing around him. "She's old but not powerless."

Tieren dipped his head, rubbing at the pain burning in his chest. The armor prevented him from connecting with his feathers, his skin, and perhaps easing the burden of guilt. "I didn't suspect, little brother."

"You cannot anticipate everything, Tieren. Was it not you who said this, that a true ruler must adapt?"

Tieren met Braon's blue gaze. "Throwing my words at me? That's a low blow."

"I'll see to Assalan's care." Braon pulled away and smiled. "Try to find peace in this."

Braon and the Auviphis launched skyward, then plummeted to the Labyrinth's entrance.

Tieren withdrew his Greeven form and let Imsal's armor slip to the smooth arena platform. Settling on the edge, he caught a passing breeze, letting it run its fingers through his plumage. His arms ached, not from any exertion, but from the need to hold his *kekaseea*.

And as the wind tossed the golden rings and swung them high above the abandoned spectator stands, his hearts screamed that only she could offer him comfort now.

CHAPTER SEVENTEEN

REBIRTH

Year: 2364

The way station, Rebirth.

MICK STEPPED OFF THE ramp onto the pristine white floor of Rebirth's docking bays. She paused while the station scanned her, killing any hazardous and unknown bacteria layering her skin and clothes. It didn't help her feel cleaner; only a bath could do that.

A glass-domed ceiling cocooned the causeways yet granted a full view of the Sculptor or Grus galaxies as the station spun. Colors, from the stalls, crowds, and holo boards, contrasted with the white structures housing labs, offices, and apartments, looking more like a child's painting than a high-class research station. A sweet, metallic fragrance perfumed the recycled air, better than the *Jinsei*. With a dreamy smile, she inhaled, filling her lungs.

Not that she minded, Kiros and his men had disembarked first, scattering on their personal missions. More of his men would arrive, and if she had her way, this was where she and S.o.S. would split. She'd be alone, and for once, she preferred it.

Security officers in deep gray uniforms were stationed every twenty meters, their gazes vigilant with their hands on their multi-phasers clasped to their chests.

Yet here she stood, in dirty black boots that had once been brown. Flecks of dust skimmed off them while she gaped like a tourist. The last time she'd been on Rebirth was with Dad.

"Mikaela Danvers?" A bald man paused in front of her. His shimmering, pearlescent, silver tunic fell to his knees, under which were tight white leggings and tiny gunmetal-gray slippers donned his feet. He didn't have the look of a scientist.

Arching a brow at him, she nodded.

Two men closed the distance behind him. She stiffened her shoulders, preparing to defend herself.

The bald man smiled. "Do not be alarmed. They are here for my protection. I am Cason Themis, and I come on behalf of Elizabeth Danvers."

Mick frowned, granting the man her full attention. "You knew my mom?"

"Correction. I *know* your mom. It has taken her many years to track you down." Cason held out a data crystal on his unblemished palm. "She sends this."

Mick shuddered, as a familiar pain clawed its way up from her childhood. "Mom's dead." She swerved around the man and stomped off. *How dare he.* Gritting her teeth, she spun and faced him. "Do you do this often? Torment people with crystals from dead loved ones? Are you sick or something?"

"It's true. Watch the crystal. It has her details if you wish to contact her." He offered the crystal again. "She goes by Selira Myers now."

And she changed her name? Mick reeled, throwing out a hand to catch the railing. It dented under her fingers, but she ignored that. Instead, she pinched the bridge of her nose to fight off the dizziness spinning her vision.

"I'm staying at the Regent if you wish to talk."

She scowled and caught his wrist with as gentle a touch as she could muster. "How did you find me?"

"An intercepted Fentus drone." He grinned, exposing perfect white teeth. "Don't worry, we sent it onward, but it told us where you'd been. We tracked your trajectory and hoped to meet you here."

She peered at the coding embedded in the glass. "If this Selira's my mom, why now?"

His polite smile was that of a server dealing with a problematic customer. "Any questions of a personal nature should be answered on the crystal."

"Then why do I need your location to talk?" The more the man spoke, the more Mick distrusted him.

"I am to communicate your unanswered questions." He bowed and trailed his men, gliding away as graceful as a holo-dancer.

She slipped the crystal into her pocket. "NOX, did you get that?"

"Yup, running a scan now."

She stomped down the causeway, uncaring about the dust trailing her. A stop-off at Fentus was her first point of call. A bath might be on the cards, then a trip to one of the miner bars in the lower levels to find a little...affection. In the last few days, with Kiros stalking her and Wyatt befriending her, she'd decided to not fuck either and kick S.o.S off her ship.

Dodging the children running between their parents' legs, tourists, travelers, merchants, and security, she paused outside one of the holo windows where a splash of red caught her eye. Strips of cloth criss-crossed and molded the A.I. on the dais. The off-shoulder and asymmetry of the hem swishing around the metallic knees added to the sheer femininity of the garment. The lighting flickered, and a hologram painted the A.I.'s features with Mick's. She stared at a replica of herself in the dress.

"Shit." She spun to enter the shop but stopped herself in time. "You don't need that dress, Mick, you need pants, shirts, and for the love of the galaxies, a bra. As pretty as that dress is, it's a waste of credits." Lecturing herself wasn't helping, so she gritted her teeth and dragged herself away from temptation. Fentus, a bath, a good fuck, and in that order, with no dress-shopping on the friggin list.

The crowded causeway split around her like a boulder in a stream. No doubt, avoiding her glowering self. Except for two security men who stepped into her path. She almost brushed them aside but, instead, drew in a calming breath. Forcing a smile, she read their name tags, checked the safety on their phasers, and listened in on the voice in their earpieces muttering about ordering lunch.

"ID?" Sec. Moore ran his gaze over her face, no doubt scanning her. The glow in his retinae announced his augmentation—standard for security. His partner, Sec. Ramirez, his gaze was a little more admiring. He had a clean look about him. She pouted, hoping to catch his interest. Then snorted at her pathetic efforts, like she had any skill in enticing a man.

Patience poured off them as they waited for her to identify herself. She blurted, "Mikaela Danvers."

Moore nodded. "Voice recognition confirmed. Enjoy your stay."

"Thank you." She paused, expecting them to go about their business, but Ramirez hesitated. When she folded her arms across her chest, his dark gaze shifted to her cleavage straining the cleanest, unstained tank top she owned.

"My shift ends in an hour."

She jerked, then ran another assessing gaze over his uniform molding a body worth knowing. "Just like that?"

"I like the look of you." He grinned, and the bright white of his smile against his toffee-colored skin sent a frisson of lust through her.

"I can make myself available." She offered her arm for his details, and he swiped his over it.

"I'll see you at the Lumina Sky Bar." When he sauntered off, there was a definite swagger to his hips. She stared after him for a few minutes before recalling she had to find the Fentus labs.

Spinning on a heel, she stormed into the boutique and bought the damn dress, along with the items of clothing she needed. Since she was splurging, she added an extra pair of boots. Hers had seen better days, but then again, what of hers hadn't? On other stations, her choices were limited. Here, she bought everything in black, hoping the color would hide the wear-and-tear better.

Calling a transparent pod, she settled into a metallic seat and gave it her destination. It whirred as it climbed the station, stopping with the barest of jerks on the third level from the top. Labs at this height meant the company must be doing well. She liked to think Fentus was successful due to her samples. It helped to assuage any lingering guilt when she had to kill the creatures to survive.

"Welcome to Fentus." An A.I. smiled, her lips curling with gentle precision.

Mick had never seen anything more lifelike. "I'm Mikaela Danvers. Summon the top scientist here on Rebirth."

The A.I. paused, and her eyes glowed with her eyelashes fluttering. "Dr. Nielson will be with you shortly." She gestured to the white couch which looked like soft leather made by a real cow.

Mick glanced at her stained cargo pants and shook her head. All she needed to do was ruin one of these chairs.

"Not *the* Mikaela Danvers?" A gray-haired man strolled into the reception area with his white cloak flapping. He had a kind face, even if his nose was a little too bulbous. "Here on Rebirth?" He beamed, snatching her free hand for a vigorous shake.

She frowned. *The* Mikaela? He spoke as if she was someone famous. Huh, she would settle for rich. "Um, hello."

"Your samples are making breakthroughs. I'm sorry, I can see you weren't aware of how much your work is valued." He waited, still gripping her hand.

"Thanks?" Darting a glance at the unblinking A.I., Mick pointed at the door he had come through. "Can we go somewhere private?"

Now that she was here, on the cusp of revealing her mutations, it sped up her heartbeat. With the quiet hum of the spinning station, the whirring of the A.I.'s mechanics, and Nielson's excited breathing, adrenaline rushed along her veins. Wild, fanged, acid-spitting creatures didn't scare her, but a man in a white lab coat did.

"Of course. Coffee?"

She shook her head and trailed him into a small meeting room with a view of Grus far in the distance. Colossal mining ships traveled to and from Grus, yet they looked like dirt specs against the magnitude of the galaxy they siphoned gases from.

"What do you wish to discuss?" Nielson slumped into a chair and rested an elbow on the table, smiling at her as if she'd brought him the secret to alchemy.

Drawing in a deep breath, she blurted her first thoughts. "You'll need to take a sample of my blood. I can have my A.I. send you the tests he has run, any vid footage of my...abilities."

"Abilities?" Nielson ran an assessing gaze over her.

"I was bitten by a mutated hokou...twice. Much has happened since then, but I fear, I am either dying or becoming superhuman. I need an expert opinion *and* your discretion, of course." Mick grimaced. "I hunt creatures like me. I..." She bit her lip at the tests she would no doubt have to endure or how they might treat her like an experiment.

"I see." Nielson pushed to his feet. "Let me grab a few things."

Unable to remain seated, she turned to admire the view. He hadn't doubted her, hadn't asked her to prove it...yet. Perhaps she should, just to ensure he understood the severity of her situation.

Before she could glance at the time, Nielson returned, carrying a white tray.

She assumed the chair he had vacated and offered her neck. Had she been her human self, she would have felt a pinch, but now, the cold of the syringe sent a shiver through her seconds before fire burned along her veins. She rolled her lips to swallow a moan.

He gasped at the blue swirling through the vial of her blood. "Blue?"

Instead of explaining, she activated her holo and showed him what footage she had of the acid-spitting, tentacled alien-octopus she'd taken on. "I sent it to Fentus, unnamed."

He gripped her arm to watch the vid, his eyes growing wider.

"This is why I'm worried. It affected my hokou mutation's ability to heal me."

"H...heal?" He arched his brow, then slumped into a chair.

Slicing the scalpel across her palm set her senses alight, but despite the pain, she held out her hand. He dabbed at the cut with a tissue then sucked in a sharp breath at the blue tattoos knitting her skin closed.

"Tell me, what are your symptoms?"

Sighing, she ticked them off on her fingertips. "The footage and test results will be evidence enough. I'm here for the remainder of the station's cycle." She rose, indicating the end of the session. "I have a mission in the Cetus constellation but can return here when I'm done."

"A mission?"

"Yes, as you must know, finding samples for Fentus is only part of my services. I do have other clients."

Nielson frowned. "Why not work for Fentus permanently? You do such amazing work that I can't see why we don't fund you full-time." He smiled. "Let me speak to my superior."

Hope blossomed, filling her chest with a deep longing. She gritted her teeth behind a polite smile. "I have an appointment in twenty minutes, can you recommend a hotel?"

He jerked back, shaking his head and tossing his gray hair wild. "Hotel? Oh, no, as a visiting dignitary, you're entitled to the use of our suites. Free of charge."

Nothing in the universe was free. "But I'm not—"

"Which will mean I'll know where to find you once I've spoken to my superior." He gestured to the passage.

She led the way, casting a glance at the A.I. smiling at no one. Gathering her parcels, Mick trailed him out of the labs and onto a pod. It shot upward to the top floor. When she disembarked, a glowing blue sign for Lumina Sky Bar pointed to the right, but Nielson led her left, pausing outside a white door with pristine gold lettering.

He punched codes into the keypad to the right of the door. "Place your hand."

She did so, and the door slid open to a white apartment.

"Until later, Ms. Danvers." He snatched her hand for another vigorous shake before hurrying away, leaving her to fend for herself.

CHAPTER EIGHTEEN

WHAT'S A GIRL GOTTA DO?

Year: 2364

The way station, Rebirth.

SINCE TIME WAS RUNNING out, Mick crept inside, gasping at the crisp lines, the minimal design of the furniture, and the breathless view of the Grus, Phoenix, and Sculptor galaxies. Resting her packages on the marble floor, she ran a fingertip across the white counter before disappearing into the bedroom. A massive bathtub rested in one corner, and she squealed, climbing into it and splaying her arms along the sides.

Perhaps later she would succumb to a bath, but all she had time for was a shower. She did so now, peeling off her clothes and dumping them down the incinerator tube.

Tiny ampules of shampoo and body lotion lined an alcove built into the shower, and she helped herself. A sniff assured her the fragrance shouldn't be too overwhelming with hints of artificial citrus and jasmine.

When she ended the shower, a white light scanned her, drying her for the most part. She scooped a towel off the heated rail and buried her face in it. The fragrance of sun-dried cloth greeted her, hushing her groan before she rubbed her face and hair.

Excitement tingled her skin, whether it was because of a possible passionate night or a permanent position at Fentus, she couldn't say.

Padding on bare feet into the living room, she pulled on her new underwear, then slipped the dress from the bag, stepping into it and clipping it into place. Despite her reflection on the mirrored surface of the front door confirming she looked exactly like the holo had predicted, she fidgeted at the sight of her exposed legs. Tugging on her hem didn't magically extend the length to cover her knees.

The crisscross of the top half of the dress hugged her torso and thrust her breasts up, enhancing her cleavage where the amulet nestled. Her tank tops were as revealing, so that wasn't something new. Running her palms along her thighs, she stared at her reflection. This, meeting a man for a little action, was she being a fool? Was she that desperate for human touch?

Would she do Kiros or Wyatt instead of a stranger?

Shoving her face an inch from the mirror, she tapped the crow's feet around her eyes with her ring finger. "In a heartbeat, but that's not an option for you, Mikaela. Grab your balls, girl." She arched a brow in challenge. "If you want this."

She did, if only to prove to herself that she wasn't falling for an imaginary Tieren or that Kiros hadn't gotten to her.

Twisting to ensure the back of the dress hid the bra strap, she admired the length of her hair, the tips of which reached her ass. Time for a cut, it seemed. A search of the bedroom blessed her with a brush, and something in the shampoo she had used, helped ease the knots. After a quick braiding, she tugged on the calve-high boots. They were a little more luxurious than her old ones but might protect her from future acid-spitting creatures. Therefore, a justifiable expense.

After a few inhales and exhales, she left the apartment, waiting for the door to close behind her before trotting along the wide passage to the bar. The new boots pinched her while they adjusted to the dimensions of her feet. By tomorrow, they would fit perfectly. For now, she did her best to hide a wince.

Pausing at the entrance of the bar, she admired the booths in plush black pleather, the richness of the garments the customers wore, and the vibrant and bubbling drinks carried by the A.I. servers. The air was as enticing, intense with smoky notes, adding to the seductive ambiance along with low-hanging lights creating mini havens around each booth. Against the one wall were floor-to-ceiling windows like a mural of the galaxies surrounding the station.

Ramirez, in dark blue pants and a crisp button-up shirt, waved from the booth by a window. She smiled and navigated the A.I. servers and customers to reach him.

When he leaped to his feet, standing tall and so gallant, she saw why she accepted his invitation. Dark hair peeked out of the V of his shirt almost too tight for his shoulders, and his brown hair flopped across his brow, looking damp as if he too had showered. *Mm, clean was good.*

"You're even more beautiful in that dress." With a pulse ticking at his jaw, he ran a lingering gaze over her body. His reaction to her eased a little of her discomfort. She relaxed her shoulders and allowed lust to take center stage.

"Thank you." Sliding into the booth exposed her thighs, and she fought the urge to pull the strips of red cloth into place. He watched her, his gaze unblinking, then when she cleared her throat, he joined her, bringing with him the masculine fragrance of his skin merged with a spicy cologne.

"How long are you staying on Rebirth?"

She wished she could be honest and say two hours, a night, but she didn't know the precise time. "Not long. I need to chart a planet in Cetus."

"Are you an archaeologist?" He flicked his fingers at an A.I. and arched a brow at Mick, asking her what she would like.

"Orange juice, please." It had been so long since she'd been in such a place. Who was she kidding? How about never? And since this was a sexual encounter with a handsome man, there was no need to pretend otherwise.

When the A.I. glided away, she didn't bother to respond to his polite interest in her career choices. She reached across to stroke his wrist. "What did you have planned?"

A slow, sensual smile crawled across his plump lips. "My place."

"Or mine." What would Nielson say if he knew she used his "suite" for sex? She laughed, hoping his hero worship would diminish a little. Now that had been unexpected.

Ramirez frowned. "Yours? I thought you said—"

"A friend offered me a place to dress." She sipped the orange juice as soon as the A.I. placed the glass on the table. The tart tang of freshly squeezed oranges hit her in the back of her throat. How much would this sinful decadence cost her? More than her boots?

She savored each drop, licking her lips on a hum of pleasure, aware he ogled her.

"Like orange juice, huh?"

"It's been a while." Lowering her gaze to his lips, running it along his jaw then dipping to the column of his neck and the opening of his shirt, she sighed.

He downed his whisky, and stood, offering her his hand.

She accepted it, pausing in her new boots when he swiped the paypoint built into the table's surface.

He layered her hand on his forearm and escorted her out of the bar, but as soon as they strolled along the passage, he pulled her against his side with his arm around her shoulders.

"Are you sure?"

She smiled. It was sweet of him to ask. "Traveling between planets is a lonely business."

He nuzzled her neck, running his lips along her earlobe. The warmth of his breath and the softness of his lips summoned a shiver. "I watched you march along the causeway. The sway of your hips, and the bounce of your breasts, fired my blood."

A message vibrated up his arm, and he tapped it, flashing her an apologetic smile. "Comes with being a security officer."

Outside the suite, she paused with her hand on the panel. When the door slid open, he gestured for her to enter first, his gallantry surprising, again. Her hips sashayed like she was an experienced concubine. She chuckled at her silly thoughts.

"She's better than your usual choices."

A female voice froze Mick. A woman in a security uniform with the nametag 'Carlton' smiled as she closed the door behind her. With her dark hair pinned on top of her head and her deep-brown exotic eyes, she was a stunner.

"I'm not into threesomes." Sure, Mick needed affection, but this was a little too much for her.

The woman laughed. "They all say that. Listen, sweet cheeks, this is a jacking. Gimme your credits."

"Well, that's silly, since I know who you are." Mick gestured to their badges. She settled her gaze on Ramirez with his ass resting against the counter and his focus on the suite, as if he searched for valuables. So much for a night of sex. Sighing, she faced Carlton. "You have a choice to make. Leave now, and I won't hurt you."

Carlton snorted, resting a hand on her phaser. "Careful, you might break a fingernail."

Mick laughed, then bolted, grabbing her by the throat for a gentle squeeze. Preternatural speed, check. "I can kill you before you *think* of drawing your phaser."

Carlton's eyes bugged, as she gasped and gurgled.

Ramirez lunged for her, but Mick kicked him back, sending him skidding across the kitchen island. Carlton moaned in protest, tugging at Mick's grip.

"Did you not think this through?" Mick arched a brow then headbutted her and tossed her slumped body to the side.

Ramirez roared, charging at her like a Spanish bull provoked by her red dress. She used his momentum, dodged his behemoth plow, and guided him head-first into the wall. A nasty crunch marked his broken nose. He smeared blood as he slithered to the floor.

"Oh, that's going to hurt in the morning." With a sigh at her ruined evening, she leaned on the red buzzer on the door panel.

"Rebirth Security." A man with soft blond hair answered her hail.

She battered her eyelashes. "Officer, please, I need your help. I'm in suite seven, and two people tried to jack me."

His face drew near, bringing his bold blue eyes and a furrowed brow into focus. "Are you all right, miss?"

"I... I managed to surprise them, but I don't know how long they'll remain unconscious. Please, send someone big and strong like yourself." She dipped her head to hide the wince at her poor acting skills. Any security officer worth his salt would notice the finger-shaped bruises on Carlton's throat and wonder how little old her could take down big, hulking Ramirez.

"Open your front door. My men are en route."

"Oh, thank you *so* much." She hung up and opened the door, before pouring a glass of the suite's fine vodka. Leaping onto the island, she rested her ass on the edge, swinging her legs while she sipped from the glass. Back and forth, she tossed the idea of calling Nielson, to vet who she was and that she had a right to be here.

"Miss?" One of the four men peeking through the door pressed two fingers to his helmet in greeting.

"Hi." She finger waved, downed the vodka, then scooted off the island. "I was on a date with Ramirez, then she jumped us."

"Carlton? Ramirez?" Salute Man skulked in and dropped to his haunches in front of Carlton to check for a pulse. Mick caught a glimpse of his name tag, Laurie.

"The sec vids confirm her story." Tennison grunted when he flipped Ramirez over. The other two men guarded the door.

"Dr. Nielson verifies Mikaela Danvers as the occupant. He's en route," a man at the door peeked in to say before resuming position. She didn't catch his nametag.

"Shit, and all I wanted was a little action." She huffed.

Tennison and Laurie flicked glances at her. She poured another splash of vodka into her glass, relishing the droning silence it granted her. Still, this close, Laurie's heartbeat jumped at her words, and his breathing shuddered. Mm, maybe her night wasn't a complete waste.

"Ms. Danvers, are you all right?" Nielson, in his lab coat, lurched into the suite, wringing his hands as if he was to blame for this.

"I'm fine, Doc."

His breath whooshed out of him. "Good. Officers, Ms. Danvers is an important employee at Fentus and deserves your utmost care."

A slow smile spread, and she bounced on her heels, ignoring her pinching boots. "I am?"

Nielson beamed at her. "Approved by Fentus. All future endeavors will be at our cost. It's Fentus protocol that all ships are up to code. I'm sure your A.I. can handle things." He shuddered as if he abhorred violence, stepped over the bodies, and slipped out of the suite. "I'll call you as soon as we have the test results." And with a tentative wave, he was gone.

"We'll place a man at the door, Ms. Danvers," Tennison said before dragging Ramirez out. One of the men from the passage darted in to throw Carlton over his shoulder, and with a nod at Laurie, left.

"If you need me, Ms. Danvers, I'll be right over here." Laurie gestured to the door.

She waited until only he remained. "And your name is?"

"Duncan Laurie, miss."

"Mick, please." She smiled. "Do you need to guard me from there, or can you do it with me riding you?"

His breath hitched, and he stilled, blinking at her. Then with a growl, he whipped off his visor and crowded her. Soft blond hair tumbled across his temple, and desire swirled in his blue eyes.

"Utmost care Dr. Nielson said." He caught her wrist and tugged her into his arms, his touch gentle even though his actions were forceful. Curling his fingers around her neck, he teased his lips across hers. Warm and soft, the feel of them spurred her desire.

She hummed, liking the zing of electricity rushing along her nerve endings. His nostrils flared as if he too relished the chemistry between them. He ran the tip of his tongue along her lips, asking to enter. She obliged. Heat bolstering the spicy flavor of a man assaulted her when he swept his tongue inside her mouth. He groaned, curling his arms around her to cup her ass. With a grunt, he lifted her, his fingers kneading where they touched.

She couldn't breathe and didn't care, kissing him back with an explosive need. This was what she wanted, something hot, steamy, and passionate. He clomped his way to the bedroom in his anti-gravitational boots without removing his lips and tongue from hers.

Tossing her onto the bed drew a girlish squeal from her, and she laughed, rising onto her elbows to watch him undress. Each discarded garment revealed pale skin rippling with muscle. Broad shoulders, bulging biceps, and pecs that bunched and released as he hopped on each leg to tug off his boots. His pants were next, and with a sharp grating noise, the Velcro released, parting the flap to reveal a fine layer of blond hair leading toward a rather large...package.

He caught her heel and tugged her closer to the edge of the bed, where he unbuckled each boot, tossing them aside. Then, gliding his hands along her calves, he spread her thighs, catching the fabric of her dress with his seeking fingers.

A grin split his cheeks and dimpled one. "You're so beautiful."

She wanted to tell him she didn't need him to blow air up her ass. All she expected from him was a hard fuck and maybe a cuddle afterward. Still, it was kind of him to offer sweet nothings.

Unclipping her dress, she peeled it off, rewarding him with her matching underwear—his lucky day. He stilled with his gaze running over her, lingering while he nibbled on that plump bottom lip of his.

Frig, he was sexy.

With his knee dipping the bed beside her hip, he crawled across her, forcing her to lie back. Swooping in for another kiss, he tormented her nipples through her bra, and when his bare palms grazed her skin, she moaned, closing her eyes against the sensations bombarding her. The vodka's numbing effects had worn off. His and her heartbeats danced and merged before breaking rhythm. The whirr of the gravitational drives droned in the background, and his torn breathing dominated the air between them.

She didn't care, not wanting to end this because she was losing her sanity.

Clawing his back, she pleaded for more of his touch, and as his fingers dipped inside her panties, she cried out. Intense spikes of pleasure pounded her senses.

With a gentle shove, she created enough space to shimmy out of her panties then crawled over him, taking control. The poor man wasn't out of his pants yet. She didn't care, tugging his erection free, she wrapped her fingers around it and pumped, delighted by his groans and twitching fingers.

"Protection," he gritted out, digging into his back pocket.

She hurried to help him then positioned the head of his cock at her entrance, rubbing it across her nub. His sexy mouth parted on a gasp, and with a wicked smile, she impaled herself, an inch at a time.

"Witch," he said, grinning.

She stopped listening, focusing on the feel of him inside her, as every nerve ending sparked to life, forming connections like interwoven galaxies. Gyrating her hips, she slid forward, unable to stem her whimpering or gasps when she repeated the process.

"Mick?" Kiros's voice reached her through her arm.

She shook her head, angling her hips for another glide along Duncan's delicious length. "Frig off, Kir." Bowing her back, she caught Duncan's hands and cupped them to her breasts. He moaned, then licked his lips while tweaking her nipples.

Her amulet vibrated, warming her skin where it rested on her chest. She palmed it, but when her fingers caressed its edges, Duncan's features morphed into Tieren's. Those cognac eyes swirled with deep emotion. She traced his hawk-like nose and plunged her hands into his hair.

"*Kekaseea*," he rasped in his thick accent.

"Please, I need you." Her words brought a sweet smile to his sensual mouth.

Fire, ice, sparks, and need, lambasted her body, and as she rode him, undulating her hips, her peppered breathing trailed her actions. The hokou mutation stayed true to its effect, and she endured each experience with a thousand times more intensity. Too much tingling heat assaulted her, and she struggled to think.

When Tieren flipped her onto her back, she sighed, grateful to him for taking control and pounding into her harder, faster than she could manage in her dazed state. His sweat-slicked obsidian skin touched hers. The subtle fragrance of exotic soap and masculinity filled her nostrils, drowning out the ozone stench and her vanilla shampoo.

A surge of electricity bolted between her chest and core. Her nub rubbed against his pelvis with each thrust. The fiery yearning climbed, intensified until all that mattered was reaching the pinnacle.

It arrived without further fanfare, slamming into her, so exquisite, breathtaking, shriveling her nipples and sending shivers down her neck, over her shoulders, and along her spine. She screamed his name, writhing under him as he continued to pound, in and out.

Then with a roar, he froze, pinning his hips to her thighs as if he rode something infinite, before shuddering, and with a grunt, collapsed on top of her.

Squeezing her eyes shut, she sucked in sharp breaths, holding herself still while her body electrified and pulsed with energy, striking each neuron. This was the bad part, where everything sensitized, bringing her to the edge of madness. With an awe-inspiring orgasm came a burning, throbbing, and an unbearable bombardment on her senses.

"Who's Tieren?"

Gasping, she flicked her eyes open and settled on Duncan, his pale skin blinding. She had expected to see Tieren's darkness. *Frig, whose name did I scream?* "I... I don't know."

She smothered a wince. What could she say? Sorry? He's a figment of her imagination? Instead, she pulled Duncan into her arms for a cuddle, willing to endure his body against her hypersensitive skin if it meant she didn't have to face what Tieren invoked in her. Because if she did, she'd have to admit she'd lost her mind.

Chapter Nineteen

THE LOSER

Year: 2364

The way station, Rebirth.

PACING DIDN'T EASE THE tension in Kiros's shoulders after he had long ago chased Drys away with his distracting sniggers. Calling Mick had left Kiros bereft, with sounds of a good fucking in the background. She'd done it, gone and shared the sweet nectar between her legs with Wyatt. If he set foot in the bay now, Kiros would kill him.

And worse, this was Kiros's friggin' fault. As stubborn as Mick was, she *would* thwart him to prove a point. *Frig, it hurt.* He rubbed his chest above his heart, frowning at the agony pulsing outward.

With shopping bags dangling from her fingers, the woman meandering along the causeway in a vibrant red dress was by no means his Mick. Nothing was familiar; not the vibrancy of her skin, the way the dress clung to her curves, or the sway of her hips twirling the fabric around her knees.

She strolled up the ramp, a soft smile teasing her lips while her eyes carried a far-off expression, as if she was lost in a dream world.

"What the frig are you wearing?" He gritted his teeth. Not what he wanted to lead with, but important to him, nonetheless. He would like to fuck her in it and out of it.

She paused, knitting her brows together as if puzzled by his question. "Clothing."

He wanted to grab her shoulders and shake her. "I don't tolerate smartass comments from my men, Mick."

She shook her head as if to clear her thoughts. "Why the frig are you still on the *Jinsei*?" When she tried to stomp past him, he caught her elbow. Her gaze flicked between his fingers touching her and his face, as if she debated removing his hand from his body. "Fine, it's a dress."

Despite the danger his instincts were screaming he was in, he persevered, "I know what the frig it is, why's it on you?"

"It's only recently been on me, off me, and on me again." She smirked, but her cheeks flushed a mesmerizing peach color. "And if you release me, it will soon be off me."

Off her? His breath hitched, and he shuddered, imagining peeling it off her body to nuzzle the soft swell of a breast. With a guttural growl he couldn't halt, he grabbed her shoulders and spun her, slamming her against the bulkhead. He slashed his mouth across hers and used his body to pin her in place.

The softness of her beneath him, the lingering taste of vodka on her tongue, and the sweetness of vanilla clinging to her skin fueled the fire coursing through his blood. She didn't stink of sex, although, that might have tainted his vision red.

Then he was airborne, flying backward. Fire lanced across his back when he slammed into the passage's bulkhead and slumped to the floor. He groaned, righting himself with a wince. "Frig, Mick, you cracked a rib."

In that red dress, as she strolled toward him, she'd never looked more beautiful. Despite the throbbing agony her toss had inflicted, another part of him ached more.

"Get the frig off the *Jinsei*, Kir. I'm not asking you again."

Everything within him demanded he not leave. "How about if I pay for a bay?"

"Pay?" She laughed. "Now you want to pay when riding on my bill was your stupid idea?"

Guilt lowered his gaze. He wrapped his arm across his torso and clambered to his feet. "Mick, please."

She threw out her hands in a decisive gesture. "We will never fuck, Kir. Not only will it destroy our friendship, but I don't want to end up on the bad side of the Soldiers of Solomon." Arching both brows, she threw a thumb at the pedestrian door. "NOX, where is the *Sentry*?"

"It's out for refuel, Mick."

She raised her face to the ceiling. "Good, and Kir's crew?"

"On shore leave."

A brittle smile split her cheeks. "It was great seeing you, Kir."

"No, I'm not going anywhere. Power up the end bay, Mick, and accept my credits." He took a stumbling step forward, wincing when his magnetic boot connected with the grates, jarring his injury. "You need them, and we're heading to the same destination. Mick, please, one last favor for S.o.S."

He was a fool. They didn't need to hitch a ride, and he sure as frig didn't need to be out of pocket for this stupidity. But, if he had any chance with her, being on the *Jinsei* was the logical choice. And his original plan to steal the *Jinsei* was still on the cards.

She hesitated, and with that small victory, he grabbed for another. "To Cetus and back, Mick, then we can split ways." He dipped to meet her gaze. "I promise."

Her shoulders slumped an inch before she squared them. "NOX, research average cost to berth a ship and power up the farthest bay. Kiros, pay whatever NOX says is due, and if he doesn't, NOX, eject him."

Sashaying past him, she paused before peeking over her shoulder at him. "I'll allow it for Dad and Solomon, but then we're even."

She was so stubborn, so...aggravating, yet he'd never felt so alive, as if fire burned along his veins. That one taste of her hadn't been enough, even if it had cost him a ton of credits and a cracked rib.

Clasping his torso, he stomped down the passage and ramp, not slowing until he waited for the pod to take him to the levels below. "Frig."

A Miner's Hopper was what he needed. Something potent and topped with foam. The white of the upper level faded to grays and dull browns. Sweat, stale recycled protein meals, and ozone replaced the sweet, purified air. Bidirectional streams of people filled the narrow confines of the lower levels, amid flickering lighting and dangling conduits. He threw himself into the mix, keeping his arm in front to ensure no jacking of his credits by accidental touch. Hacking was easy for those desperate enough to learn the weaknesses of the banking systems.

He peeled off to slip inside the Odyssey, dodging feminine hands seeking a little action *and* payment. As hard as he was, he wasn't looking to lose more credits.

"Solomon," Drys roared above the din, silencing conversation but not the tinny high-pitched voice singing in the background.

"Solomon," he nodded at Drys, Lanek, and Seth, and wincing, settled on a steel barstool mounted to the metal-paneled floor. Drys shoved a tankard into his hand, filled to the brim with foam-topped beer. But his eyes twinkled. The crazy bastard had a sixth sense for when Kiros frigged up.

Wyatt fiddled with his buds, for once not buried in his ears. Empty tankards littered the table, and his glazed eyes proclaimed he'd been there the entire time. So, who the hell had Mick fucked?

"Glad you could make it." Kiros raised his tankard to Seth and Lanek. "Got us a berth on *Jinsei*, farthest from the bridge."

"I hear she's a stunner." Lanek grinned, revealing his charm in his bright smile. "Was wondering about the don't-touch then your rescinding it. Decided to go for her sweet spot?"

Kiros grunted, clasping his torso again. "I tried. I think she busted a rib."

"Frig." Seth choked on his beer. "We're S.o.S, we don't tolerate that bullshit."

"The Danvers and Solomon Burger have history, man." Drys raised his fingers to order more Miner's Hoppers for the crew. "For me, I'm enjoying the show."

"Yeah, so you said." Lanek frowned, his gray eyes narrowing. "When do I get to meet this woman?"

Wyatt curled his fingers into a fist where it rested on his thigh. "If you're lucky, never."

"So, why we still sticking with her then?" Seth arched a brow before downing his beer.

Kiros's thoughts exactly. Sure, the *Jinsei* was huge, able to grow S.o.S. beyond Burger's wildest dreams. But as Mick had said, the ship was costly to run. Kiros's chest throbbed. Pain clouded his mind. He should be done with her. Gripping his knees, he settled his gaze on Seth. "Can you hack the *Jinsei*? NOX isn't state-of-the-art A.I., so it should be easy."

"What are you planning?" Drys straightened, his brow furrowing even as a wicked smile teased his lips.

"I say we take the *Jinsei* and abandon her on whatever habitable planet she lands on." Kiros smothered a wince when everything within him rebelled against this plan. Yet as he sat there among men who'd saved his life countless times, he questioned his loyalty to a woman who didn't feel the same. Besides, it wasn't as if she was utilizing the *Jinsei's* capabilities. It was wasted on her. And he wasn't dropping her on a dead planet. Dragon shifters meant Tau Ceti had life. She could survive with her mutations.

"Well, with a few modifications, the *Jinsei* could serve our purposes." Lanek nodded.

"And we can grow S.o.S with space to spare." Drys thumped Kiros on the shoulder, excitement twinkling in his eyes.

"Solomon?" Kiros focused on Wyatt, the one man who could ruin this for S.o.S.

"I like her, but you're my family. You've never steered us wrong before, and besides, there are plenty of other women."

Kiros grinned and took a beer from the A.I. server. To friggin hell to Solomon Burger and the Danvers. "To the *Jinsei*." He raised his tankard in a toast. His men chorused, and tension eased from his shoulders. He was back in control.

Chapter Twenty

IT BEGINS
Year: 2364
The planet Tau Ceti, aka Rianus

SWEAT DRENCHED TIEREN'S BODY, and he kicked off his furs. Splaying out his limbs, he stared at the ceiling, dazed and hard as rock. Her husky voice screaming his name echoed in his ears. His skin rippled as a shiver tore through him. Flipping his legs over the side of the bed, he rested his elbows on his knees and cradled his head.

It was getting worse.

Pengfei had said it was distance related. The closer she drew, the more unbearable the sensations and the dreams would become. He growled and pushed off the bed, shedding his soiled dowo. Padding naked to the platform, he caught the top molding with his fingertips and stretched, sighing when a stray breeze cooled his heated body. It ruffled his unbound plumage, reminiscent of her running her fingers through it and scraping her nails across his scalp.

Face-to-face encounters had diminished. In part, gratitude warmed his chest. After all these sensual dreams, seeing her naked before him would test his honed instincts. And when they did mate, he didn't want it to be in a partial dream world.

In two days, Braon would leave for his trial. She would arrive and either end Tieren's torment or cast him into eternal turmoil. He didn't want to kill her, not with the way his body throbbed and his hearts beat erratically. She was his, and he wanted nothing more than to cherish her.

Mick.

The suns had yet to rise. Grimacing, he spun on his heel to throw on a tunic and dowo. Hopping on each foot, he tugged on his boots, then thrust his doors open. He stormed out of his chambers. His guards jolted, falling into step behind him when he scampered down the stairs many levels below.

The Labyrinth was beginning to stir. Bakeries glowed from their stone ovens, and the sweet aroma of cinnamon filled the warm air. The steady clang of blacksmiths busy at their craft set the wake-up call to those needing it. As he strode along the narrow, interlacing corridors, he passed archways carved into the fortress' bedrock. Splintered wooden doors barred entry. He twisted and turned, passing stacked barrels and woven baskets.

Carvings marred the walls, telling tales and history, lest anyone forgot. He ran his fingers over a row, smiling at the snippet he caught in passing. Lights flickered through small windows as people started their day. Left, left, and right, to the umber door at the end of the path. He knocked once, nodded at his guards when they took their places alongside the door, and entered the home.

"Good morning, *atsuna.*" Ghilian's sister skipped to his side for a brief hug before spinning away to gather bowls off a shelf carved into the wall. Ten years his junior, she had plagued her brothers and Tieren, insisting she could also protect her home. Her strong arguments had led Tieren to change Labyrinth tradition and train anyone willing to learn.

"Rassin, I didn't know you returned. How is your grandfather doing?"

"He is well, just lonely." She flashed a charming smile, flicking her beaded braids off her face while she laid the table.

Burrowed in one corner, Ghilian slept on. And in another, their mother, Zabbica, knelt in prayer. Three people lived in such a small space. Meilo and his wife had moved into a small room of their own. Tieren shifted on the bench, wishing he could share the chambers he had been blessed with. Yet, if there was a place he was welcome and treated like family, it was here.

Rising, he leaned out the door and summoned a guard. "Send for my morning meal."

As he stared after the disappearing male, he searched the passages for Meilo. No doubt he would head up to Tieren's chambers to wake him.

"I cannot wait for your meal to arrive." Rassin tugged him to the bench, and with a hand on his shoulder, pushed him to sit. "Here, eat this for now." She placed a bowl of cold meats and fresh fruit. "It's not much, great *Tsuna* Tieren, but you are welcome to our meager fare."

She giggled as she dodged his grasping hands, setting other bowls out as Zabbica slid onto a chair opposite Tieren.

"Morning, *atsuna*. How are you doing, *abucaah*?" Her kind eyes, like her children's, warmed when she smiled at him. Not many spoke to him with such familiarity.

"All is well."

"You lie?" She tutted, swiping gray-streaked black hair off her cheek. "Why spare my feelings? I pray for you regardless of good or bad news."

Tieren chuckled, shaking his head as he picked a sliver of meat and bit into it. "In two days, my life changes. Whether it is good, I do not know."

"Change is always good. It's how you deal with it that determines the consequences." Peace surrounded her while she nibbled on her meal.

"*Moma*, your tisane." Rassin placed a steaming cup of tea beside Zabbica, then dropped a kiss on her temple. "And for you, *atsuna*?"

"Please." How he should deal with change was to accept his *kekaseea*, welcome her. Killing her couldn't bode well for his realm. Besides, the gods had revealed her arrival to him for a purpose. Still, she would steal his brother. She had to pay for that.

"You are troubled." Zabbica cradled her cup, pressing it to her chin as she studied him. "You're not resting." She tapped her chest. "Trust your hearts to lead you. Not a second of worrying can make you taller, stronger, richer, or live longer."

"Moma, leave the poor male be." Ghilian flicked his furs back and clambered to his feet. He rubbed his belly on a yawn before stretching until his fingers brushed the stone ceiling. "What he needs is action."

Action. Tieren stilled and tilted his head, waiting for Ghilian to elaborate.

"I say we scout out the place in your vision. If need be, we lay a few traps. If we catch her before she takes Prince Braon, then she'll be nothing more than a lost traveler."

Tieren gaped, disbelieving that he hadn't thought of such a simple solution.

"Leave the traps. They take too long to set, and who or what they trap cannot be controlled." Meilo stumbled in under the weight of a basket. "Your meal, *atsuna*." He grunted when he shoved it onto the worn table. "The traps could also be construed as you helping Braon." He twirled Rassin in a quick dance before leaving the house.

Tieren gestured to Rassin to dig into the basket. She did with glee. A sweet smile curled her plump lips. With her dark hair braided and her obsidian skin, she could have been his sister by birth. Nevertheless, she was his to protect by friendship. As were all those seeking shelter in the Labyrinth.

"Do you need anything?" He faced Ghilian, who'd dried his face and was yanking on dowo. "Have the donations arrived from our sponsors?"

"I visited each one, being as transparent as positive. It would not do for our enemies to believe you seek to overthrow Braon." Ghilian pulled a tunic on, muffling his words. He dropped onto the bench opposite Tieren. "A few wagons trailed me home. Most of it was food, which is ideal. Winter is on the horizon."

"The storerooms are almost too full," Zabbica said between sips, smiling with her eyes as she watched and listened.

"Any issues with managing the Labyrinth?" Guilt settled like a thick blanket across Tieren's shoulders. He should have been the one to visit the farms, to negotiate with the land barons, yet these people needed someone dedicated to their needs. With protecting Braon, he had his hands full.

"No complaints." Ghilian shoved food into his mouth, then spoke around it. "Will you make it to Rassin's mating ceremony?"

Rassin stilled, then released a breath on a whoosh. She forced a smile as she slid a tisane in front of Tieren. He yanked her onto his lap for a quick tickle before releasing her. She bounced away with a giggle.

"I will try to be there, little Rassin." With his *kekaseea* landing, Braon's trial and kidnapping, Tieren couldn't promise more than that.

"I know you will." Rassin spun on Ghilian, resting her hands on her hips. "Besides, *atsuna* gave me a beautiful dagger to gift my husband." She patted Tieren's shoulder. "If Tieren says he will try, then that is good enough for me. Stop pressuring him, big brother."

Ghilian threw his hands in the air. "I only ask for the elders; they wish to see him."

"And drinking each other under the table like the last mating ceremony wasn't what you planned to do?" She wagged her finger before pouring Ghilian a tisane too.

Tieren chuckled, dipped his nose in his cup, and inhaled. The aromas of honey and herbs rose to tantalize. He took a sip and sighed when the heated liquid soothed his throat and warmed his belly.

"Drink up, *atsuna*. We need to speak to Pengfei. That old male will want to travel with us, I have no doubt." Ghilian thumped Tieren on the back, almost spilling his tisane.

He sighed. Sometimes familiarity had its downside. Rising, he popped another sliver of meat into his mouth, pressed a kiss to Zabbica's temple, and followed Ghilian out the door. Deeper into the bowels of the Labyrinth they meandered until Ghilian paused outside a door. He opened it, and in Tieren strolled, pausing beside Meilo, who tended to a shivering Assalan.

"How fare's he?" Tieren whispered when Meilo pressed a finger to his lips.

"His fever hasn't broken yet. Moma will come by later to check on him. Her healing touch has brought many back from the brink of death." Meilo wrung out a cloth and dabbed Assalan's sweat-drenched forehead.

The guilt-laden blanket returned, and tears pressed behind Tieren's eyes. He had done this. "I—"

"It is our law as ancient and unfathomable as those metal rings you swoop through." Meilo's calm stare settled the unease churning in Tieren's gut. "To not have meted out punishment was to appear weak."

"Some rules need to be broken," Tieren growled.

"Some things take longer to change." Meilo dabbed Assalan's temple again.

Tieren left, his hearts not lightened by the visit. Had Assalan's fever broken, then perhaps he would have found solace in that. Ashamed, dewinged, the once-proud general would find no welcome above the Labyrinth.

Leaving Tieren to mull over his thoughts, Ghilian spoke not a word while they climbed the levels.

Pengfei's door was open with carry-alls piled on the tiled passage. He stepped out when Tieren approached. "You are right on time."

"I thought you wanted to stay, to ensure Braon sets off with your blessing."

"These are not just for me." Pengfei gestured to the carry-alls. "I had Meilo pack these yesterday. He and your grandmother will pretend you are not well, the stress of Braon's impending trials keeping you to your bed."

"I have never been ill a day in—"

"The Auviphis will guard your brother." Ghilian gathered two carry-alls, slinging them over his shoulder. "Your grandmother has been planning this since you revealed your vision to her."

"What?" Tieren gasped. He continued to underestimate her cunning.

Pengfei dropped his chin to his chest. "We all understand the importance of him succeeding, *Tsuna* Tieren."

"Very well." He gritted those words out when it wasn't well at all.

"I was most alarmed when she summoned me." Pengfei gathered the last carry-all and gestured to Tieren to lead the way to the docks. Tieren's guards fell in behind them.

"And you knew about this?" Tieren glared at Ghilian. This morning he had thought the male was brilliant for his suggestion. Now, Tieren saw who was behind it all. He would've liked to have bid Nona farewell. "Give me my carry-all." He flicked his fingers until Ghilian caved and passed it over. "To the docks, then a day's travel to the mainland, and up the Lower Mountains of Bircier."

"Something like that." Ghilian grinned, an energetic bounce to his gait.

Tieren wished he could be as carefree, but in two days, he would learn what manner of male he was.

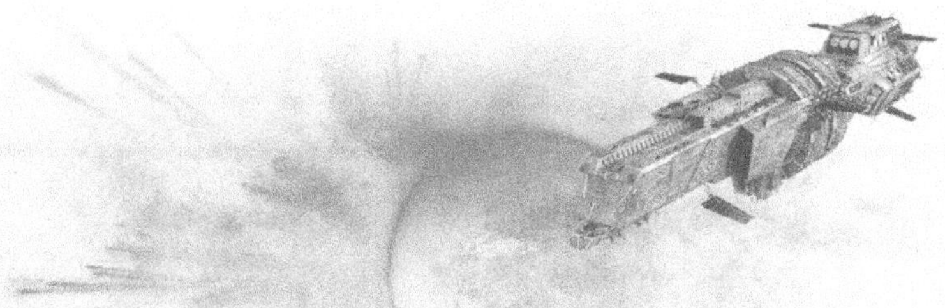

Chapter Twenty-One

UPGRADES

Year: 2364

From the way station, Rebirth, to Cetus.

"So, LET ME GET this straight, NOX. Fentus filled *all* our fuel tanks?" On the bridge, Mick tapped the console, disbelieving the readings. She couldn't recall a time when all eight tanks were full, not even when Dad was alive and flush with credits. Sure, they'd gathered enough sol, but for quick bursts of speed, nothing beat pure fuel.

"Food and water stores too. They had techs roaming the *Jinsei*. I monitored them, ensuring this wasn't a ploy. They upgraded everything to within an inch of its life."

She frowned, the relief easing from her shoulders slithered down her spine to tighten her gut. Nothing in life was free.

"State-of-the-art security too." NOX's chuckle was warm and inviting.

She jerked and turned in a slow circle to grip the bulkhead, angling her head to listen.

"What the frig, NOX." She gaped. "Laugh again, cos you sound like a human."

"Well, duh. Which part of upgrade everything didn't you get?"

She winced. "I see sarcasm and snark were part and parcel of this?"

"I've been working on that, but they've made some improvements. Those bastards nearly took my show tunes. I almost busted a nut."

Giggling, she slumped into her chair, checking the flight path NOX had mapped. "Anything else I need to know?"

"I don't trust our mercenary friends. Babe, they're planning something."

She mouthed the word 'babe' before laughing. The upgraded NOX was far more entertaining. Perhaps the newer him could test out the A.I. suit without destroying something on it. She'd schedule a sparring session.

"Has Kiros paid?" She sighed, agreeing with NOX. "I don't know why he was so desperate to stay with us. Sex is off the table, and there's no other benefit unless they're after something too big to fit in the *Sentry*."

"They'll need the *Jinsei* for that. Knowing you like I do, he can take it from your cold corpse."

"A little melodramatic, but yes." She rested her heels on the console and watched the fore vids as NOX communicated with flight control.

"Well, I tightened security. And I'm feeling trigger-happy today. Let those punks try anything, and I'll jettison their asses."

She grinned, loving his gung-ho attitude even though she had no intention of killing anyone if she didn't have to. "Making enemies of S.o.S isn't a good idea."

"Not if we kill them all, Mick. They started this."

"Which of your settings did Fentus upgrade? I wasn't aware a Nano Omnipresent X-class had 'bloodthirsty' as a feature."

"Ha-ha, very funny, smarty pants."

She grimaced. Not the best nickname, but still, mildly amusing.

"My prime directive is to protect you, even from those claiming friendship." Something tapped-tapped as if he rippled his imaginary fingers on a surface then he cleared his throat. "Wanna discuss your mother?"

Ice drenched her face, and she groaned. "I incinerated the crystal. You didn't happen to—"

"Sorry, babe. I couldn't get a reading on it. Besides, for all we know, that crystal carried a virus. A sick me isn't a pretty thing."

"Yeah, you're probably right. I mean, Mom still alive?" Her heart twinged, but she shoved that hope aside. "If it's important, they'll find me again." She stroked the amulet, tracing the bird's beak with a fingertip. It hummed, as if it offered comfort. "What do you make of this? I found it in Dad's quarters."

"I analyzed it when he first brought it onboard. Common metallic elements, yet somehow, it retains heat." NOX chuckled again. "If I was the suspicious sort, I would've tossed it out an airlock. But it seemed harmless at the time. Now that it reacts to you like a tuning fork, I'm having doubts."

"You, doubting?" She couldn't resist teasing him, finding his new humanlike qualities endearing. Many times, she had longed for this sort of banter. And all it had taken was the sale of her soul.

As sweet as the deal was with Fentus, something about it bothered her. They honored every contract, never once quibbling about credits owed. Perhaps she needed to find out what they did with the samples she sent them. For someone claiming to feel no guilt, it slithered into her mind, altering her thoughts. Innumerable drones had delivered guinja to the closest Fentus labs. They were a harmless species, more in line with tortoises, but those on Prime Earth had offered no ultimate cure. So, she had no idea why Fentus' repeated interest.

"What about *kekaseea*? Any luck there?"

"Ancient texts of unknown origin mentioned *kekas*, meaning bond or union. *Kekaseea* could be a derivative, but I can't be certain. On a separate matter, Fentus repaired the reconnaissance equipment, upgraded a few parts, and recalibrated your canons, as if I haven't been doing that once a week." He huffed.

Pouring a shot of grit, she threw it back, then leaped to her feet. "An A.I. is never too proud to admit when he needs help."

"I am not—" Silence reigned for a full minute. "Fine, point made."

She grinned and poured another drink. With the buzzing in her ears softening, she carried Wyatt's earbuds everywhere instead of relying on grit for peace.

"How long before we can leave?" Energy shook her leg, and her magnetic boot activated and deactivated with each twitch.

"Fentus paid for this berth 'till tomorrow morning. I've sent S.o.S the departure times. Failure to board on time is on them. And yes, Kiros paid."

She jerked back, almost spilling the grit. "I'm surprised." She dragged a wrist across her mouth, muffling a laugh. "I didn't tell him we're not that desperate for credits after Fentus' offer. I figured, if he was serious about coming with and willing to put his money behind it, then fine. Extra credits wouldn't go amiss."

She downed the grit, left the glass on the console, then paused in the doorway with her hand on the ridged edge. "Put on the suit tomorrow. Let's test your upgrades."

He gasped. "Have I died? I take it you've forgiven me for the arm-incident?"

"Aye-aye, my sweet NOX. And maybe, we should invest in a decent suit, one of those fancy ones."

"As long as I get to choose the apps and the limb extensions."

"Proper hands, please. And I choose the skin. You might as well be pleasing to look at." She tapped her fingers. "I'm off for a nap. Wake me if S.o.S try anything. NOX, I mean it."

"Got ya, honey buns."

Chuckling at NOX's new vernacular, she strolled to her quarters, stopping along the way to gather her purchases. Overall, the day was a fruitful one. Undoing the dress, she tossed it and her new clothing into the laundry closest, then dropped onto the bed to unbuckle the boots. Throwing herself onto the bed, she squealed and thrashed her limbs, messing her linen. It had been a red-letter day; one she had needed for so long.

Rolling over, she hooked the earbuds off the side shelf with a pinkie, then plugged in each one. With a wriggle of her ass, she searched for a comfortable position before activating the sound. She stroked a thumb over the amulet's engravings and allowed the white noise to drown out her enhanced hearing.

Maybe she wouldn't kill Wyatt when she annihilated S.o.S.

She smiled.

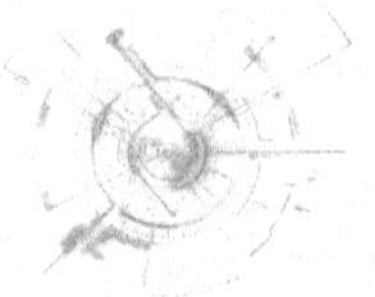

Year: 2364
S.o.S. in their new bay.
En route to Cetus.

"WHAT THE FRIG DO you mean you can't hack it?" Kiros scowled at Seth, not liking the way his best hacker's slashing eyebrows dipped.

Sure, they were hungover, but that had never hindered Seth. Maybe they should try this again after a few cups of coffee. This morning was starting out to be a pain.

"I'm friggin serious. No matter what I do, I'm shut out." Seth lowered his voice, casting furtive glances at the bulkheads. With one hand buried in the guts of an access panel, he wiped the sweat off his cheek with the other, careful not to get moisture on his anti-static glove.

"NOX." Kiros arched his back to address the ceiling—his gaze trailing the pipes and ducting.

"Kiros." Seth gaped. "You can't ask an A.I. for help to hack itself."

"Why not?" Lanek jumped onto a crate while tearing into a protein bar.

"Yes?" NOX's tone sounded imperious.

Kiros shook his head, clearing his mind. He must have imagined it. "Did anything strange happen yesterday?"

"Strange? On the *Jinsei* with a doubly mutated woman soon to be on her menstrual cycle? Mm? Lemme think." A bolt of white light shot out of the panel, accompanied by a squealing Seth leaping out of the way. "And no, you can't hack me. Permission denied."

Kiros gaped. NOX sounded off, not to mention he'd whispered the word 'idiot.' "So, Mick getting laid wasn't...unusual?"

"Nope, and good for her." NOX chuckled as a human man would standing alongside Kiros. Ice chilled his neck, and he threw a wide-eyed glare at Seth. "If that's all you require, oh-great-leader-of-S.o.S?"

Kiros's vision tainted red. He slammed his palms on the bulkhead, leaning into them. "Connect me to Mick."

"Request denied. Oh, this is so much fun." NOX's giggle was as high-pitched as a girl's. "We're testing the A.I. suit, and she's a little...pinned. I'll let her know you wanna chat. Cheerio."

Cheerio? "NOX?" Silence fell while Kiros waited. "NOX!" Nothing, no response, and no explanation for his weird behavior.

"He's been upgraded. That's all it is." Seth shoved his singed fingers under his armpit.

"Yeah, but where would Mick get the credits to afford it?" Kiros leaned his ass on the crate beside Lanek, stealing his half-eaten protein, as well. The berth payment wasn't enough, so something else had to have landed in her lap. "Shit, without NOX, we'll never figure this out."

"I have a buddy on Rebirth. Maybe he can access the security feeds?"

Kiros studied Seth's eager expression. "Do it. We can't take over the *Jinsei* if we don't find a weakness. We're trapped here. Friggin hell, and we have two days until we reach Cetus."

Seth tapped his holographic keys, his head lowered when he thumped along the grated floor to the *Sentry*. Their section of the *Jinsei* came with new quarters, much smaller than the one he had but bigger than the space on the *Sentry*. She hadn't shown her face when he and his men had retrieved their belongings. They should have taken the *Jinsei* then. Now, the door separating their bay from the rest of the ship wouldn't budge. Hence the trapped feeling prickling his skin.

Being at the tail end of the ship wasn't a good position either. If need be, Mick could detach this section, since its design catered for decompartmentalization during research missions. The *Jinsei* could function without this bay.

Frig. What the hell had he gotten himself into? And deep within his psyche, Solomon Burger was laughing at him.

CHAPTER TWENTY-TWO

PREPARATION

Year: 2364

The planet Tau Ceti, aka Rianus

En route to the Forest of Iliana

"MAP OUT WHAT YOUR vision revealed." Pengfei unraveled parchment onto the table, shifting cups and bowls to the edges to keep it from curling. The sea was calm today, but still, a gentle sway did make drawing difficult.

Tieren accepted the offered charcoal and sketched out what he could remember. As a marker, the most recognizable was the pond with its narrow waterfall. He marked an 'X' where her box would land and a 'B' for Braon from where she'd take him.

"I know this area well." Pengfei tapped 'Leito's Ponds' with a forefinger before dragging a path north to the pier. "We'll dock here with the procession, send Braon off in good faith, then I'll tarry."

Tieren circled the mountain icon for Qilaetor. "Let everyone's ships depart first. As the trial's overseer, none should question you remaining behind."

Pengfei beamed. "Exactly."

"We'll have to hike it. Can't have Braon or anyone else spotting us." Ghilian peeled an ersik fruit with an eating dagger, then popped the pink sliver into his mouth.

"What time did she arrive?" Pengfei focused on Tieren, waiting for him to recall the vision.

The way the sunlight had fallen upon her delicate features... Tieren rubbed his chest. "Sunrise or sunset."

"Mm." Pengfei twisted his lips in thought. "Was Braon sleeping?"

Tieren grinned at his brilliance.

The older male nodded. "Good, so in two dawns."

His timeline didn't make sense. Tieren had planned to meet her in less time than that. "One."

"The ships arrive tomorrow, yours among them, then the farewell feast will last hours. The procession will escort Braon, full-bellied and drunk, to the mid-mark, leaving him to journey onward. He will rest beside the pond, which is where she will find him on the second day."

"You have the right of it, Pengfei." Scowling, Tieren offered his back while he poured a glass of *jaketta*. *Zelet.* Longing to meet her sooner wouldn't hasten time.

"Today, we will mark the trees when we scout the path. I shall plod up the hill, looking as if I inspect the route. You two meander through the forest. If I spot you, I'll let you know. Not once must Braon sense you are near."

"We'll carry supplies and bury them." Tieren couldn't underestimate his *kekaseea*. She would capture an almost-adult Greeven as if he weighed nothing more than a battusk. Excitement sparked along Tieren's skin, and shivers rippled through him. Soon. Perhaps, with her near him, he could find rest instead of her image tormenting him.

"...weapons should be taken with. Bebbayaya do roam these woods."

Tieren zoned in on Ghilian's words. "If Braon could kill one, it would end his trial on a high note and solidify his reign."

Pengfei's mouth pulled down, adding to the seriousness of his expression. "It's a bebbayaya, *atsuna.* I wouldn't wish such an encounter on my enemy."

"True, Pengfei, but as legends go, they're fierce and worthy opponents."

Ghilian scratched his chin with his eating dagger, his gaze far away. "If we stumble upon one, we should urge it in Braon's direction."

Tieren was of two minds; protect his brother or have him beat this trial with the best results.

"If we wound it before chasing it toward Braon?" Pengfei's brow furrowed.

Ghilian said nothing, licked the *ersik* juice off his fingers, wiped the dagger on his dowo, and sheathed it in his boot.

Tieren laughed and threw his arm across Pengfei's shoulders. "Doing so will whisper doubt into Braon's mind. He must believe he won by his wits. This alone will bolster his confidence. He is fit to rule. Nona and I have made sure of this. Only, he lacks belief in himself, his abilities."

Pengfei sighed. "This is why the trials were created." He forced a smile that didn't warm his blue eyes. "I...worry."

Tieren patted his shoulder before offering a cup of wine. "I love that about you, ancient one." Smothering a chuckle, he tossed a glance at Ghilian. "Did we bring his crutches?"

Pengfei spluttered, and his cheeks flushed pink. "I'll have you know—"

Tieren dodged his old friend's swinging arm, laughing at how he didn't spill his wine.

"It's good to hear you laugh, *atsuna*." Ghilian leaned his ass against the table.

"It is." Pengfei thumped Tieren on the arm, then threw back his wine. "I'm off for a nap. Wake me when we dock." He waddled off to collapse onto a pile of colorful pillows in the corner of the tent.

Tieren refilled the cup, then left the tent, eager to watch the fortressed mountain that was Qilaetor grow smaller from the stern of the ship. Rising from the ocean and climbing around the mountain was his home. Variegated rock in blacks, grays, and browns formed houses with platforms spiraling like the petals of mushrooms. Greeven circled the towers, small against the pale-brown sky.

Love for his home swelled within him, and he allowed it free rein to conquer every part of his soul. This was what he fought for. And this far away showed none of the ancestral discrimination. It was a realm he could be proud of, free of bullying, fear, and hatred.

Lost in his thoughts, the lurch of the ship drew him back. His cup was half-drunk. He downed the tepid wine and flicked the droplets into the churning green waves. Gripping the railing, he watched the servants lower the sails and moor the ship to the wooden pier.

Pengfei stumbled out of the tent, grumbling every time Ghilian nudged him from behind. Hanging off Ghilian's shoulder were three satchels. A sword hung from his belt, daggers peeked out of his boots, and a crossbow weighed down his other shoulder. Tieren nipped past them into the tent to arm himself—sliding daggers into his boots and buckling on a sword. Archery wasn't his best skill, so he forewent any bow.

His new armor was with Imsal for minor adjustments, nor did a visiting female justify the use of his old armor.

He joined Ghilian and Pengfei where they waited for the gangplank to be extended. Once it clanked into place, they hurried across, pausing on the gray sand to share the satchels. A worn path led the way to Leito's Ponds. Old pebbles and smoothed stones once formed steps to the sacred pools. Pengfei trudged onward while they veered into the Forest of Iliana surrounding the ponds and the ancient ruins sprinkled throughout the island.

Pulling a dagger from his boot, Tieren marked the gray bark of the first tree, ignoring the dark red sap trickling out. This was the starting point. On they hiked, marking and pausing to check the direction. Not once did they spot Pengfei, and by the time they broke through the forest's edge, sweat beaded Tieren's brow.

"We'll bury the satchels behind that old tree." Ghilian gestured to a breathtaking tree, wider than Tieren was tall and burdened with purple leaves. It must have seen many seasons. Ghilian scampered around the roots in search of a spot to dig.

Circling the clearing, they stopped where her box would land. Two Greeven-lengths forward was Braon's sleeping spot with the pond at his back. Tieren dipped his fingers into the cool water and wriggled them. Iwaki, with their iridescent skins in reds and whites, rose to greet him. When Ghilian knelt beside them, they darted away, hiding between the golden fronds of the water weeds. Tieren splashed his face, rising to dry his chin with his tunic.

"This is the place?" Ghilian spun. "We can watch from behind that boulder."

Tieren studied the area. "It's on the wrong side of the path." After pointing to the same ancient tree as Ghilian's, he spread out his arms. "When the time comes, we'll creep into the forest's shadows. I can take Greeven form to hide us."

Pengfei, clutching his chest and huffing, crested the rise, wheezing as he stumbled. Tieren waited while the old male mopped his forehead.

"Not...a...word." He squeezed the warning through his haggard breathing, bending over the boulder while he fought for air.

Ghilian laughed and hefted Pengfei's satchel off his shoulder. "I'll bury these."

"The path is marked. I assume you didn't spot us?" Tieren rested his ass on the boulder beside Pengfei.

"I didn't." Pengfei patted him on the shoulder. "Once we capture your *kekaseea*, we must abandon Braon to his trial."

Tieren frowned, not liking the word capture, nor that he had to abandon Braon when he was stuck in a box. "But—"

Pengfei glared him into silence. "To do more is to interfere."

"What if she does?" Tieren flicked a gaze to the afternoon sky, fire burning his cheeks. Implying that she would hunt her box meant she wouldn't be a captive, for free her he must.

Pengfei's sigh was long and deep. "Then we let her fight the battles."

Tieren leaped to his feet. No way in this beautiful realm would he leave a female in danger. "What? I cannot—"

"*Tsuna* Tieren," Pengfei pushed off the boulder to grip Tieren by the upper arms. "I understand how torn you are. If we must follow her, then protect her. Do nothing to aid Braon."

Tieren gritted his teeth. She *would* hunt. It had been in the set of her jaw, in the ripple of muscle in her defined yet soft body. He hadn't been able to ask her when he'd revealed he could fight. But she had the confidence of a hunter.

"And you cannot convince her otherwise. You do not speak her tongue and she yours."

"By the *Gawen's* feathers." Tieren paced, willing the fury and helplessness to subside. "There has to be a way to win this, Pengfei."

"Ghilian." Pengfei waved the male over. "Come, leave our garments here. Let us fly back."

Ghilian jogged toward them. "Someone might see—"

"Me returning from examining the area?" Pengfei arched a brow. "I am tired, and tomorrow will be a long day."

Tieren yanked off his tunic, dowo, and boots, shoving them at Ghilian. "We flank Pengfei as if we guard him."

Spinning on a heel, Tieren dove into the pond. The cool water eased the tension tightening his muscles. He waded to the bank while Pengfei and Ghilian stripped. Rising out of the water and wading onto the bank, Tieren jumped to shake off most of the droplets. He summoned his Greeven and threw out his wings to dry himself in the sunlight.

When he took to flight, the suns' rays warmed his feathers. He dipped and weaved, circling the northern pond, assessing the density of the surrounding forest. Pengfei took flight with Ghilian trailing him. Tieren tucked in his wings and spun to catch up.

The brilliant teal of the oceans drew forth a smile. He adored his home, and when his burdens became too much, he needed the reminder of why he fought so hard for the Fanyell line.

He touched down where a naked Pengfei waited on deck. "Find some rest, and prepare yourself to play the overprotective brother. Let all note your presence and departure. No one must suspect you are not on your ship when it sails."

"Sails?" Tieren frowned. "What have you planned, ancient one?"

Pengfei met his gaze for some time. Without a word, he entered the tent and poured a cup of wine. He downed it, then stumbled to the pillows in the corner.

Ghilian hovered nearby. "Meilo packed your finest garments, *atsuna*."

Tieren grunted and pulled on a fresh dowo. "Leave it for now, Ghilian. Let me rest tonight before I need to pretend eagerness for Braon's trial."

"Very well. Would you like an evening meal?"

Tieren glowered.

Ghilian raised his hands in submission and left Tieren alone.

Two sleepless nights remained. Then he would slip in, grab his female, and leave.

He snorted. Nothing worth it was ever easy, and he was a fool to think otherwise.

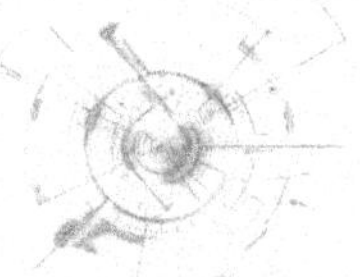

Ships arrived before the suns did, and when Tieren stumbled out of his tent to relieve himself, many watched him do so. Most of the ships were from the common folk wanting to witness the start of Braon's Trial of Tolend. Grunting, he ducked inside his tent and growled when Meilo entered behind him.

"When did you arrive?" He flicked a dismissive wrist. "Never mind." He washed the sleep from his eyes, wishing he could rid himself of the exhaustion as easily. For once, she hadn't disturbed his sleep, but worrying about Braon had.

Allowing Meilo to dress him, Tieren listened with half an ear as Ghilian and Pengfei went over possible outcomes, trying to plan for the worst. Dowo lined with gold thread irritated Tieren's legs, as if the cloth tickled him. His tunic was crisp white with exquisite gold embroidery.

"They'll see me from Qilaetor in this."

"Exactly," Pengfei mumbled with his mouth full of eggloaf.

Tieren lowered himself to the table and filled his bowl from the platters provided. Fruits, sweet breads, cold meats, cheeses, and a steaming tisane would protect his stomach from the amount of wine he needed to consume this day.

Meilo combed Tieren's hair while he ate, and the rhythmic tugging hinted at beadwork.

"Let me guess, gold beads in my braids?" Tieren gritted his teeth, having never dressed like a pompous prince. "Surely people will see through my elaborate attire?"

"When you have never attended a Trial of Tolend, other than your own, of course." Pengfei slathered honey onto bread and bit into it, closing his eyes on a hum.

Time dragged. From the moment Tieren kissed Nona good morning, to when the processions reached the first pond, he played his part, dancing and singing like a drunk troubadour. The distance hadn't taken long yesterday, but no, flocks had to show their support. By the mid-day meal, when they set up pavilions for the dignitaries, Tieren had exhausted himself. His cheeks were stiff and unresponsive.

He slumped at Nona's feet, casting doting gazes at her while stroking the dust-laden hem of her robe.

"What's got into you?" she hissed through a regal smile. When no one was looking, she stamped her slippered foot, trying to dislodge his hand.

He forced a smile as if he was content to be here, drinking with people who despised him. "Pretense." He tugged on her hem. "Need everyone to notice, to see me board the ship and sail for Qilaetor. No one must suspect I remain behind with Pengfei."

While gently stomping on his fidgeting fingers, she toyed with a gold bead in his hair. "Ah. Still, acting like a fool won't deceive everyone."

"All will see me onboard, retching over the side while singing tavern songs no prince should know. I'll stagger into my tent, then in the darkness of night, swim across to Pengfei's ship."

"Swim?" Nona squeaked, her fingers digging into his hair. "Have you lost your mind?"

"It's barely a dip, and I'll keep within the barrier."

She said no more, but her pinched lips conveyed much of what she thought of this idiocy. Her gaze settled on Braon and lingered, with her eyes narrowing. Fresaie's cream skin glowed in a magnificent gold robe. She twirled a lock of brilliant plumage around a delicate finger while clinging to his brother's arm, as if doing so would guarantee her the crown.

Braon laughed and teased, his posture slightly tilted in his drunken state. Sensing Tieren's regard, he dipped his head to him in an almost imperceptible nod, whispered something into Fresaie's ear, and detangled himself from her clutches. He pretended to weave, yet the placement of his feet mimicked a dance.

"Nona," he bowed, then 'fell' forward to kiss her cheek.

"Sit, brother." Tieren tugged on Braon's tunic as resplendent as his. When Braon joined him on the rug, he thumped him on the back and laughed for no reason. *Gawen, how I hate this farce.* Every fiber in his being urged him to rise, take Greeven form, and escape this madness.

"All's well, Tieren." Braon chuckled and slapped his thigh as if Tieren had said something humorous. "Meilo is plying me with watered-down *Jaketta* wine. I'd kill for a tisane, though."

Tieren twitched his fingers at a hovering Meilo, and within minutes, Braon had a tisane in a wine goblet. He sipped, leaning back to shake his head in pleasure.

"When I am king, I'm stealing Meilo." He wagged his finger. "*And* keeping valet, Cerreq."

"It's a pity you had to leave him behind, my prince." Meilo bowed and assumed a position at the pavilion's entrance with a stained tunic. His shoulders sagged. With a muffled moan, he shuffled his feet and straightened his posture, only to slump again. The poor male had worked himself to the brink of collapse.

Tieren clambered to his feet. "Meilo, escort me to my ship. I feel most unwell."

Meilo jerked, then with a timid smile, hurried to offer support. Tieren 'staggered' and belched, leaning most of his weight on his dear friend. Whispers trailed him while he sang his way down the scarred steps to the docks below. All watched him misbehave, and Meilo declared to anyone who asked that the prince wasn't himself.

'Stumbling' across the gangplank, he teetered on the edge, swayed, and caught himself to the gasps and cheers of the flocks.

With wind in our feathers and clouds in our beaks,
chests clad in leather, flying over yon peaks.
We're off on adventures, for glory unbound.
To end in success, each one of us crowned.

Falling into his tent, he let his voice fade when he sprawled onto his pillows. In his day-old garments stinking of sweat and spilled wine, he could do nothing but nap. With how he'd been on his worst behavior, sleep was what he needed. Meilo woke him as the suns set to pretend to vomit over the side. Wiping his mouth on a soiled sleeve, he raised his gaze to Qilaetor.

Many ships had sailed, and only a handful remained. His, Pengfei's, and Nona's made three. The marked sails of the others screamed their ownership; Fresaie, Cousin Karlez, and the unmistakable blue of Ambassador Sugard.

When the lingering warm light touched the green waves, Meilo took up Tieren's song.

Oh, sing me a song of a goblet of wine,

of a prince and a pauszor lost in time.

A battle for love and honor alike,

broke the beast's tooth in a single strike.

Between the suns setting and the moon's rise, Tieren fixed his gaze on Pengfei's ship and dived into the water.

CHAPTER TWENTY-THREE

FLEETING PEACE

Year: 2364

Circling the planet Tau Ceti in the Cetus constellation.

As the *JINSEI* orbited the planet, Mick studied it on the fore vids, checking the readings: oxygen good, carbon emissions low, water pure, resident species primitive. From planet to planet, she often forgot to admire their beauty. Through the dense cinnamon-colored clouds circling the globe, she caught glimpses of green seas and gray continents. She radioed Kiros to get his ass here since she was taking her shuttle. The last two days of peace were bliss, harking to the time before she had allowed S.o.S on board. After today, they would part ways for good.

She prepped the shuttle as was her routine, ensuring she had sufficient ammunition for whatever scenario. The reconnaissance revealed seven intriguing species she could tag and bag which would justify Dr. Nielson's faith in her. Returning to Rebirth with these samples instead of sending drones might win her more favor.

"Where the frig is Kiros, NOX?"

"Loosen those tight panties, Mick, he's on the way."

She grinned, slumped into the chair in front of the console, and poured a glass of grit. "Did you find a suitable specimen for the Followers?"

"Sure did, and it's a beaut. This looks like a tag-em-and-bag-em with no hassle."

She ran a finger along the edge of the glass. "Eager to be rid of our guests?"

"If I have to electrocute Seth one more time, I swear I'll pulse sol through their berth."

She tilted the chair back and laughed. "Dad always said timing's everything. Looks like Dr. Nielson upgraded us when we needed it the most." It still smarted that Kiros would try to hack the *Jinsei*. She couldn't fathom why. She hadn't restricted their food, water, or power, so that wasn't it. NOX had said it was to steal the ship, but that didn't make sense either. The *Jinsei* was a beast to maintain, nothing like the streamlined *Sentry*.

"Permission to enter." Kiros leaned in, peering at her through the shuttle door. Behind him stood his crew—six men to squeeze into her shuttle. Some she didn't know, and they stared with interest, running lewd gazes over her.

She scowled. "What the frig, Kir?"

He met her gaze, then shrugged. "I'm expecting trouble."

"Like I can't handle it?" She shoved her face in his, and he stiffened, not liking her challenging his authority. Like she gave a frig. "I can do this alone, y'know."

"It's a short trip down. Are you for real bitching about a little squeeze?" He charged forward, using his barreled chest and surprise to force her to retreat. Wyatt smiled, giving her a little wave when he slipped past to the pilot seat.

"Fine." She shoved Kir back.

His men piled into the shuttle. Seeing the space diminishing, she slipped Flint's harness over her shoulder and gathered a variety of rounds, shoving them into every pocket. Tapping the implant in her forearm, she whispered to NOX, "Synching."

"We are one," NOX whispered back.

The shuttle door closed. Wyatt powered up the engines.

"Initiating docking bay lockdown." NOX's new masculine voice reverberated through the shuttle, the bay, and along her arm.

A new world appearing on the fore vids was one of the highlights of her job, but broad shoulders hindered her view. She growled, tempted to nudge them out of the way. When she sucked in a calming breath, a miasma of manly smells hit her, not all of them pleasant.

"Bay doors closing."

After NOX's announcement, Wyatt didn't wait as she liked to do to make sure the doors closed without a glitch. He spun the shuttle in a smooth backward arc, then shot forward. His amazing skill didn't affect the passengers. Only Mick noticed with her heightened senses: the hum of the engines, the slight change in gravity, the forward momentum.

A slight tremble rippled through the shuttle as it pierced the atmosphere, yet despite this, what unnerved her was the silence. None of S.o.S spoke or fidgeted, except for a bald man chewing on a matchstick. His brown gaze rested on her and didn't budge.

Her instincts leaped to life under his scrutiny. No expression crossed his somewhat handsome features, but worse than that, his eyes held no life. He had seen much. Things that must have scarred his soul.

She matched his stoicism with her own, meeting his gaze without flinching. Landing was in minutes, and there was no way she'd look away first.

"Directing you to the chosen specimen." The shuttle lurched as NOX took control, implying Wyatt fought him.

"Thank you, NOX." Without breaking eye contact with Tooth-pick-boy, she called out to Kiros. "Listen, I need to sample a few species. I can drop your team off, or you can tag along."

"Going to show me how it's done?" Kir's voice held a teasing note.

"Your choice." She ran a gaze over the Toothpick-boy's smirking face, then flicked her focus away as if he held nothing to fascinate her. His heartbeat leaped, which brought everyone's thumping hearts to her attention. As seasoned fighters, a trip to an uninhabited planet shouldn't flush their bodies with adrenaline. She sniffed, picking up an acrid-sweet scent. And excitement.

She tapped instructions to NOX to be on his guard. Her clamoring instincts agreed with him about the *Jinsei*, about Kiros having another agenda. The little girl in her, who'd worshipped Kir, prayed it wasn't the case. He wouldn't betray her like that.

Wyatt touched the shuttle down, and the door opened, flooding the compartment with fragrant air. Forest was her first thought. S.o.S disembarked, then spread out with their blasters raised. Their stances were military in style. She ignored them, hiking up the hill through the gray-barked trees with purple leaves. Gray soil beneath her feet gave her pause, triggering a sense of déjà vu. Using her preternatural speed, she crested the hill and froze.

A small waterfall tumbled down a striated cliff into a pond. Yellow moss grew on boulders, and the water was a beautiful aquamarine color. Fish-like creatures darted under the surface, flashing reds and whites among the golden water plants. Between her and the pond, curled into a ball was an enormous eagle with its white feathers wrapped around it in slumber.

The binary suns had just risen, so it had yet to awaken. Perfect.

"NOX, is this it?" She kept her voice slow and held her arm close to her mouth.

"There are no dragons on this planet. This is as near as frig is to fuck as we're gonna get."

Chuckling, she sprinted to the shuttle, vaulting the last distance and skidding along the metallic floor on her heels. Grabbing the net gun, she bolted to the crest of the hill where S.o.S gathered.

"No shooting it. I don't care whether it bites your arm off." Kiros hissed those instructions, then pointed two fingers at his men, commanding them to break off in pairs.

She snorted, sashayed past him, took aim, and fired. The chain net thunked as it deployed then draped over the sleeping bird. It jerked and squawked, whipping its wings as it struggled. In a direct line, she strode toward it and gathered the ends of the net.

Its efforts to escape intensified.

"NOX, bring the shuttle closer." Injuring such an exquisite creature wasn't an option.

"Just like that?" Kir grinned, standing beside her with his blaster drawn. "You're no fun, Mick."

Facing her instead of the surrounding forest, S.o.S widened their circle, granting space for the shuttle to land.

"Yup, it's like that." She flipped her bangs out of her face and dragged the massive eagle to the shuttle. "NOX, lower the ramp and scan this bird. I want to know which tranq's viable."

On the shuttle, when she clipped the net in place, the bird stared at her with blue eyes that held intelligence but no fear.

Shaking her head to break its mesmerizing hold on her, she gripped the door's edges. "Kir, let's go."

His men piled in, crowding her closer to the shimmering bird. She blinked, trying to clear her vision. Bones cracked, and its squawks became grunts. Feathers vanished into smooth white limbs. The massive eagle morphed into a young man. Gasping, she knelt beside it...him in disbelief.

Wyatt shot the shuttle up, but she commanded him to halt. He did, hovering it. Frig, he hadn't even closed the shuttle door. Through the legs of the S.o.S, seeing the top of the waterfall made her sigh with relief. They weren't too high up.

"NOX, ignore tranq analysis." She unclipped one corner of the net.

"What's the problem, Mick?" Kir shoved his men aside.

He wouldn't like this. The loss of credits, the time wasted, yet this was the right thing to do. He had to see that. Groaning, she rose to face him, placing a hand on his armored chest. "It's a boy, Kir. We can't hand him over to the Followers."

"We have to, Mick. It's us, or they'll send someone else." He cupped her cheek, resting his thumb on her chin. When he grabbed her hip to usher her out of the way, she thought it was to see for himself.

A humanoid wasn't to be tested on. It violated the Primary, and she wasn't willing to be penalized for this.

Wind at her back whipped her braid, and she cast a glance out of the shuttle to judge the distance down. "We *must* return him, Kir." She studied the boy's pale skin, his white hair lying thick and curling where it met his bare shoulders. Crystal blue eyes watched. Her gaze snagged on his familiar hawk nose.

"No, it can't be," she whispered, then raised pleading eyes to Kir.

He crowded her toward the edge of the shuttle, tilting his head. "If you had spread those thighs for me, sweet Mikaela..."

Puzzled by his unexpected words, she frowned. "What did you say?"

With a shove from him, she tumbled out of the shuttle, flying toward the ground back-first. For a second, she blinked at his beloved face. A scream tore from her as anger burned her eyes, her nose, and along her skin. Flipping in mid-air, she landed feet first, one knee and hand touching the soft purple grass.

The door closed on Kir's grin.

She cursed him as the shuttle shot up. "NOX, take control from Wyatt."

"Done." The shuttle veered left and right until it shot up again. "Sorry, babe, they disabled remote access."

"Friggin hell." She whipped Flint from her shoulder and splayed onto her stomach, taking careful aim. Two shots hit the target, and the shuttle plummeted. Wyatt fought the impending descent, juddering the shuttle. The whine of the engines preceded a thump when it crashed, scattering a kaleidoscope of birds into the sky. It wasn't too far away; she could make it on foot.

"NOX, disable any communication between S.o.S and their ship. Empty their berth into the nearest sun." She gritted her teeth. "No S.o.S will survive to tell the tale."

"Got ya."

She rested her temple on Flint, allowing the sobs to escape. Cold fingers gripped her chest, squeezing her lungs and heart. The agony was on par with Dad dying. Kir had betrayed her. Only fools deserved this kind of treatment, and she was one to have trusted him, to believe friendship and history mattered.

NOX had tried to tell her, and if she prodded the agony engulfing her, she'd known he spoke the truth. Yet she had hoped he was wrong, that Kir was still the man she'd believed him to be.

A shadow fell across her, and she stilled, reaching between the ground and her body to grip the blaster. She rolled over, pulled it from the holster, and aimed.

A naked man leaned over her with obsidian skin, amber eyes, and a hawklike nose her fingers remembered tracing.

Her breath caught. It couldn't be. It was impossible. Here stood her dream man who tormented her with memories she couldn't have formed. She lowered the blaster and raised a trembling hand to his jaw to test the illusion. "Tieren?"

CHAPTER TWENTY-FOUR

Year: 2364

Rianus

In his Greeven form, when Tieren watched the box descend, he could do nothing but flutter his extended wings. Hidden behind the black of his feathers and peering over each shoulder were Pengfei and Ghilian. His hearts thumped to a new rhythm not his own, and he had to remind himself to breathe.

Males in strange garments circled her, hindering Tieren's ability to stop her from reaching Braon. The black things in their hands implied weapons of some sort. These males hadn't been in his vision. He shuffled closer, raising his beak to the air to catch her scent before he saw her, but it was elusive.

Then, she was here, cresting the hill and stepping into the clearing. The suns light kissed her brown hair roped down her back, the swell of her breasts in her tight tunic, the exposed skin at her belly, and her long legs ending in heavy boots.

Fire blazed along his senses as something primal slammed into him. His vision focused, his breath shuddered, and deep within him, a yearning, so much a part of him, unfolded.

"*Kekaseea.*"

Pengfei shushing him exploded heat across Tieren's cheeks.

He glared at the older male. "It's time." Keeping his wings extended, he shuffled forward, placing his feet with care. Pengfei and Ghilian moved with him until they were a leap away from the first male. He had no plumage and chewed on something wooden, making annoying sucking noises.

Braon slept on, too drunk or exhausted to hear the box arrive. Tieren measured the distance between his brother, the box, and the circling males silent on their feet.

"Wake up, Braon." He willed it, watching for a flicker of his white feathers. Instead, a soft snore whispered across the clearing.

The huskiness of Mick's voice drew Tieren's focus, and he studied her interaction with a hulking male. There was a familiarity to their tones, similar to how he spoke with Ghilian. And just like that, she shot a net out of a solid-looking weapon and caught a sleeping Braon.

His squawks fell on deaf ears. She hauled him without effort. *Gawen*, if her strength didn't pulse heat through Tieren's body. What manner of creature was she? Regardless of his disbelief, he held Ghilian and Pengfei back when they tried to push past him. They couldn't stop her from taking Braon, not without knowing what those weapons could do.

The box shot up. Tieren curled in his wings, letting Pengfei and Ghilian storm across. He bolted after them, sighing in relief when the box stopped and hovered. She appeared in the square doorway, her heels on the edge. Her voice held a pleading note with a sense of urgency.

Then she was falling, screaming with rage.

He summoned his wings and vaulted to save her, but she flipped mid-fall to land on her feet. Cursing followed before she sprawled on her belly and used her weapon to injure the box. It lurched, weaved, then plummeted, startling a nest of colorful skkeens.

He landed beside her, tucking in his wings as he leaned over her. Pride warred with his need to save Braon. The nervousness at meeting her twitched his fingers.

She rolled over, gripping another weapon—smaller and looking ineffective. Her gasp and his name on her lips shook him, sending fire and ice through him.

She snatched her hand back, a thumb away from touching his jaw. A sense of loss engulfed him like a wet blanket draped across his shoulders. He stepped back to allow her to rise when he wanted to layer his body over hers, feel her skin against his as he'd done in his dreams. She bounded to her feet and drew closer, studying his face with her lips parted. Her top lip curled up on one side as if she smiled through her amazement.

"I can't believe it's you," she said. "I thought I was dreaming, but you're real."

Though he didn't understand a word, he did like her voice; husky, soft, melodic, caressing his skin and sparking shivers to ruffle his plumage.

Everything about her except her garments was like his dreams.

Her brown gaze shifted, and her cheeks pinkened when she scanned his body. Her lips parted again as her breathing roughened. A fluttering in his chest echoed her leaping and dancing heart. Her delicious scent intensified, tickling his nose, and he sucked it in, willing it to remain in his lungs. She extended her hand as if to touch his chest, then took it back with a shake of her head.

Ghilian snapped a shackle over her wrist, the clinking cutting through the sexual tension. Tieren grimaced, not liking the idea of restricting any creature's freedom, let alone his mate's.

"What...?" She studied the one shackle, then laughed, offering her other wrist. "They mean to capture me, NOX."

"Best to play along, Mick. No use revealing your talents just yet." A male voice came out of nowhere.

Tieren spun in a circle but found no male lurking in the trees' shadows.

"Fair enough. I did just steal one of theirs. Kir has the boy, and getting him back is all that matters." She rattled the shackles and smiled at Ghilian. "NOX, scan the planet. Get me their languages."

"She's happy we captured her?" Ghilian gaped, which settled into a scowl. "She doesn't take us seriously."

"You say that like it's easy. Right away, milady. Whatever you need, my goddess. Zip, zap, and bam." The male voice sounded irritated.

She chuckled. "Stop your sass. Just give me something."

"I come in peace, and take me to your leader?" The male chuckled. "Why not strip? Clothing might be offensive to these people."

Tieren cocked his head, listening for the source. She laughed as if the male had said something humorous. Strange how his voice came from her wrist, or perhaps she spoke to a god?

"Help me save the boy. That will do." Her eyes fluttered, and she danced on her heels. "Thank you, NOX. Get me the rest." She faced Tieren and squawked.

With a stunned gaze at Ghilian and Pengfei, Tieren gasped. If she knew their language, why hadn't she spoken to him in his dreams?

"Yes, my brother." At his reply, puzzlement furrowed her brow.

She tapped her foot, then tossed a glance to the sky. "Well, what did he say? And shit, his language grates my throat." She rubbed her neck, jangling the shackles.

"The boy is his brother. How about I insert English into him?" The male's voice tilted upward at the end.

"When we don't know their physiology?" Her tone did the same. How unusual to have a conversation with questions.

"My scans so far show two hearts with the usual organs and four toes and fingers instead of five. He can bear a few words to test."

She frowned. "NOX, no. As much as I need him to understand me, do a full assessment. Make sure it's safe first."

"You're right to be cautious. I'll do—"

"Enough. What is she saying, and who is she speaking to, *atsuna*?" Ghilian handed Tieren a pair of dowo.

He pulled it on under her vigilant gaze, her cheeks pink again. "A god? And no, I can't understand her. She spoke once, telling me of her intentions but has reverted to her own tongue."

"Can you ask her from where she comes?" Pengfei sidled closer, curiosity revealed in his sparkling eyes.

Tieren understood Ghilian and Pengfei's concern, though. They listened to her jabber when Braon's life was in danger. Not that he was allowed to save his brother. "*Kekaseea?*"

While they spoke, she darted glances at the trees, the sky, the waterfall, and the ground. She raised her gaze to his as if she answered to 'mate,' but her eyes had taken on a distant look. Pain slithered across her face, and she winced, spinning on her feet to scan the area. She pressed her palms over her ears, snapping the chain taut.

Tieren frowned. Nothing had harmed her to justify her reactions.

She tried to dig into her pockets with her hands shackled, then with a grunt, snapped them apart, tearing them off her wrists with her fingers.

"*Gawen*, she did not...?" Ghilian gaped at the mangled metal lying on the ground.

Familiar heat coiled in Tieren's loins. Her strength was an enticement on its own.

With each emptying of a pocket, she tossed small cylinders onto the ground beside her weapon, then screamed, stomping her feet as she paced. Clasping her hands to her ears, she whimpered amid curses and pleading.

"NOX, kill me now. This planet's crawling with insects, birds twittering, the waterfall, something burrowing below my feet, and the wind rustling through the friggin trees, as pretty as they are." She paused to listen. "And a bloody ocean." Water leaked from her eyes while she sucked in great gulps of air. "My earbuds are next to my bed, aren't they?"

"Yup, and the cryopens are in the shuttle. Your best bet is to get there fast."

"Frig. I'm going to kill that bastard." She shuddered but kept her hands in place. "Bring the *Jinsei*."

"No can do, oh captain. The Primary, remember."

"Friggin hell. I'm standing here, an alien to these...people. I'm pretty sure I've shot that directive out the window." She shook her head, tossing her braid wide.

"Can you help her, Pengfei?" Tieren motioned for him to come closer when she fell to the ground. She coiled into a ball, sobbing and writhing.

"She has sensitive hearing," the male voice squawked from her wrist. Ghilian leaped a foot off the ground. "I am NOX, and I serve her. We came to steal one of your species."

Tieren clenched his jaw since he already knew this.

"When she realized the chosen sample was a boy, she tried to return him. Taking him violates the Primary Directive. She will get him back for you and will seek revenge on those who took him. I suggest you let her do what she needs to do."

"What's wrong with her?" Pengfei knelt beside her, running a palm an inch over her arm. Blue swirls glowed beneath her skin.

"She is sensitive to sounds, and her...medication is aboard the shuttle."

"Shuttle? Is that the box?" Ghilian pointed to beyond the treeline to where the box had fallen.

As they chatted, Tieren nudged Pengfei aside and gathered Mick into his arms. She cried out but curled into him, sighing when his skin touched hers. He rose and waded into the pond. Her eyes flicked open, and in their brown depths, molten blue spiraled. She jerked, but he met her gaze and held it, silently asking her to trust him.

He shivered when the coldness lapped at his heated body. It was but a small inconvenience, so he ignored it and dragged her into the depths of the pool, grateful she didn't fight him. Underwater, she pushed away from him, her touch sparking memories of other...activities. While she tapped each ear, her eyelids fluttered closed. Peace descended.

He studied her, his hungry gaze taking in her smooth skin and her odd plumage floating around her face in thin strands, the bulk of which was still in a braid. Flicking her eyes open, she surfaced but lay on her back with her ears in the water. He followed but watched her while her five-fingered hands swirled to keep her afloat. Her gaze rested on his face, lingering on his jaw, lips, nose, and stared into his eyes before running over his plumage.

As if he hadn't done this before, he tapped his chest. "Tieren."

"Mick."

And *Gawen*, if his hearts didn't leap at her smile.

Chapter Twenty-Five

Despite the fiery burn of anger coursing along his veins, nausea churned Kiros's gut. He'd never forget Mick's expression when he shoved her out of the shuttle. With his men watching, he could do nothing else. The *Jinsei* was on the agenda from the start. There was no way on Prime Earth that she would have let him take the ship from her, not without a fight.

It had taken all his strength not to check if she survived the fall.

This was for the best, he chanted. At least, she might live. He chuckled when he realized his men's gazes were still on him. "Well, good riddance." The words were like acid on his tongue.

"Pretty thing." Ru smirked, flicking the matchstick from side-to-side with his tongue.

Yes, beautiful, and now S.o.S' enemy. Kiros stared at the white young man, his four-fingered hands clinging to the net. Well, well, not a dragon, but a gigantic eagle or a griffin of ancient folk tales. Surely the Followers would still pay the hefty sum. The kid's shoulders were smooth with no sign of massive wings hidden under the skin. Dare he say it? Magic? He snorted. He was losing his mind if he thought for one moment that magic existed.

But Mick had been right. Stealing this boy was violating the Primary Directive. Breaking rules, laws, friendship, or family ties wasn't unheard of for S.o.S, especially if the credits justified the means.

"Kiros," Wyatt bellowed while gripping the lever with both hands. The shuttle jerked left and right.

"Frig," Kiros muttered and leaped across the compartment to the console.

"NOX's trying to...take control," Wyatt gritted out.

"On it," Seth called and dove into a panel, yanking wires Kiros hoped weren't important.

When the shuttle righted, the tech guru beamed and saluted with two fingers to his temple.

Kiros laughed, but two thunks swallowed his good humor, despite the joy zinging through him. Mick was alive. The shuttle shuddered, then banked sharply, tossing them to the side.

"No," he roared, throwing out his arms to catch onto something. Drys palmed Kiros's forearm, preventing him from hitting the bulkhead.

It took seconds for the shuttle to hit the ground. A horrible grinding and screeching filled his ears. Wyatt screamed. Kiros's men bounced around like coffee beans in a tin. Drys hung from one arm, the other keeping Kiros mid-air. And through it all, their prisoner squawked, despite being safe within the net.

Frig, all this bullshit for an eagle boy?

Kiros dropped to the bulkhead, inches from where Lanek sprawled. His men were banged up with a few cuts and bruises. Nothing too serious.

Aiden leaned over a pale-faced Wyatt. Sweat dewed on his temple.

"And?" While squeezing Wyatt's shoulder, Kiros focused on Aiden. A pulse ticked next to the scar on his brow.

"Busted leg," he said, scanning the shuttle. No doubt looking for something to use as a splint.

Kiros did the same. "Comm Elias. Who knows what NOX will do."

"Right," Drys grunted. "I'd still like to know how the frig he got upgraded."

"Like I explained," Seth huffed, "the buddy I mentioned said Fentus' security is tighter than usual, though there's talk about some fantastic find." He scowled. "He couldn't find out more."

"NOX," Kiros addressed the console. Silence was the worst response. Surely the A.I. would gloat if given a chance. *Friggin hell.* Ice slithered down Kiros's neck. "Tell me we've reached Elias?" He glanced at his men, trying to pry the twisted door open.

"Nothing yet," Seth muttered, stabbing at the wires in the panel. "The connection to the *Jinsei* is active, just getting no reply. The *Sentry's* comms are dead, like the ship had never existed."

Kiros closed his eyes, pinched the bridge of his nose, and almost tossed up a prayer to any gods listening. "Frig, this ain't good."

Not once had he considered they'd be stranded on the planet. Mick's abilities should have raised some concern, but he'd thought they could outsmart her. *Frig. Frig. Frig.* Not taking her rifle was his biggest mistake. But would NOX have allowed them to board the *Jinsei* without her? Maybe he shouldn't have pushed her out of the shuttle. A hostage situation made more sense. Hindsight. He gritted his teeth.

It was what it was, and now, he had to deal with this situation.

The door fell open with a clunk, spilling his men onto the crushed and singed vegetation around the downed shuttle. A boulder showed skid marks, white against the dark gray rock.

Kiros squared his shoulders and released a slow breath. "Status."

Wiping blood off his brow, Lanek gestured to their prisoner. "We need access to the weapon stash. Let's move the boy."

"Do it." Kiros hitched a thumb at Wyatt. "Aiden will see to the injured. There's bound to be a medkit in the shuttle. Drys, find it."

"This was badly planned," Lanek muttered.

"Don't start. How the hell were we to know Mick would be a problem?" Kiros raised his gaze to the sky, praying for a miracle. "If NOX jettisoned the *Sentry*, let's hope Elias was inside the ship." He winced. "If we're stranded here, we have two options."

"Fix the shuttle and get off-world." Lanek scowled. "Its distance fuel-wise is limited. I doubt there are sufficient provisions, and who knows how long life support can sustain us."

"Like you said, we're friggin screwed," Kiros snapped. "Worst case scenario, we're trapped here. We need food. Focus on that, and take Ru with you." He gestured to where the man stood on the edge of the clearing, peering into the surrounding forest.

Wyatt screamed when Aiden set the makeshift splint in place. With Drys's help, they moved the injured pilot to rest against a tree. Both turned to assist Lanek in relocating the boy, net and all. He didn't struggle when they bolted the net in place next to a boulder opposite the shuttle.

The nearby pond meant they wouldn't die from dehydration. But the clearing wasn't defensible. Kiros tried not to calculate the odds of Seth fixing the shuttle. A life planetside had never occurred to him. Nothing in his genetic makeup said he would make an excellent farmer. What the hell would they do? How could they survive? And what other species existed more dangerous than the birdmen? Thankfully, the blasters could be solar-charged. But the shotguns and assault rifles? They *would* run out of ammunition.

And chatting to the locals? Language was an issue. The situation was unimaginable. Like they'd been cast back in time to a medieval era. They'd be lynched, drawn and quartered, dubbed wizards with their magical firepower. Their arrival would trigger the wizard trials of Tau Ceti. He snorted at his thoughts, but the truth rang deep within him.

"Friggin farming," he muttered. Shit, he didn't even know what to plant. Maybe fishing lay in his future, quiet days spent adrift at sea? The image his mind conjured hinted at peaceful times. He had his family with them. That was all that mattered, right?

To find peace, they'd need to conquer almost insurmountable odds. As a young boy, before Solomon had found him, Kiros hadn't dreamt of staying on terra firma. His hopes had been to travel the galaxies. He'd done that. His chest swelled, and he ran a thumb up and down his sternum. Solomon used to say that life took unexpected turns. It was how a man reacted that determined his worth.

Kiros would push for off-world first. If it didn't happen, they would be forced to stay here. At some point, NOX had to bring the *Jinsei* down to pick up Mick. S.o.S. could pounce then.

He grinned then cursed. Sure, sneaking onto a ship was par for the course as a mercenary band. But staying on board with an aggressive A.I.? The chances of NOX killing them in their sleep or sabotaging life support were high. The only person who could guarantee their safety was Mick.

No, he needed another plan. And no matter from which angle he studied this, she was at the center of it. He'd have to do something he hated. He'd have to apologize, perhaps tug on her heartstrings and remind her of their history.

He unclenched his jaw, drew in slow steadying breaths, and tossed aside ideas on what to say. She was his oldest friend. How would her father have reacted to how heartless she was being? Couldn't she see how much this mission mattered to Kir? Could he claim he had some incurable disease? No, she'd expect medical results from her pod.

Summoning the charming rogue he'd once been would be a stretch, but for his men, he would do it.

He gave a decisive jerk of his chin and forced a smile that felt stiff and uncharming. He grimaced, strode to the pond, and winked at his reflection. A few more attempts had the smile of his youth firmly fixed in place.

Time to make Mick fall in love with her old crush.

Chapter Twenty-Six

WHAT THE FRIG?

Year: 2364

Breaking the Primary on Tau Ceti

Cetus Constellation

HOLY FRIG, IF HE wasn't the sexiest man she had ever met. He was unaware of how his nudity bothered her. Not once had he shielded himself from her. He didn't strut or puff out his chest, just stood there as if being gloriously naked didn't matter. In his low-slung harem pants, he was as divine. NOX chirped with Tieren's companions, but she had zoned them out, more than willing to let him hold her, to drown her, if it meant he kept his obsidian gaze on her. As impactful as in her dreams, the way his intensity invoked emotions hadn't diminished. She should be pissed off or sad over Kir's betrayal. But from that to meeting her dream man, her mind reeled. After all, what did she know about Tieren other than he could wield a sword, was an excellent hugger, and was as real as frig was to a curse word. Unable to think, she relied on instinct which had her trusting him, his intentions.

She had thrice been bitten by alien creatures and mutated accordingly, so she wasn't going mad. It was known to happen in the far reaches of space with no one to talk to but the A.I.

With insanity not probable, lovesick fool, that's what she was. And her interest shouldn't be sex-driven after…um, David? Daniel? But that familiar hum in her core *was* sexual, molten hot, and demanding. Not to mention basking in Tieren's volcanic gaze made her feel like she'd come home. Silly, that.

"Better?" His voice rumbled.

She shivered. "Yes, thank you." Gasping, she sat up. "NOX."

"What?" He cackled. "You were busy. I figured a few more words in your repertoire wouldn't go amiss."

"Friggin A.I," she grumbled, rubbing her throat. "I should pull your plug, and I would if I didn't love you, you bucket of bolts."

"Love?" Tieren frowned.

"Shit, did I say that in your language?" She pinched her brow, dreading the impending headache. "Come, the quicker we find your brother, the quicker I can—"

"They have wine," NOX offered like it was consolation for his sneaky behavior.

She cut across the pool's surface and waded onto the bank.

The younger man held out a wineskin. "Sorry about the shackles." He grinned, unrepentant.

"Sorry about breaking them." She gave him a sweet smile to show how unremorseful she was.

He uncorked the wineskin for her.

With a tentative sip, fire burned her throat and exploded in her belly. "Whoa." She savored the tart flavor on her tongue and instant dampening in her ears. "Bottle this." Tipping the wineskin back, she drank deeply while the alcohol rushed to numb her senses.

"You like?" The older male arched his bushy brows. A grin split his cheeks. "I am Pengfei. This is Ghilian. Welcome to Rianus."

"Thank you, Pengfei. I'm Mick. Had I known you were humanoid, I wouldn't have stolen Tieren's brother."

"Tieren?" He smirked. "Yes, well, your NOX says to let you retrieve him. There is a slight problem. Braon is on his Trial of Tolend. We cannot interfere in any of his adventures or else he will not attain manhood and the respect as the future king."

She gaped. "But..." Facing Tieren, she tried not to admire his saturated pants clinging to muscled thighs, nor the way his torso rippled when he moved. "King?"

"*Tsuna* Tieren Fanyell of Rianus, a *pleasure* to finally meet you, Mick." He tapped his chest in a gallant gesture that only spiked the heat churning inside her.

"Mikaela Danvers, hunter of alien creatures." She frowned. "If your brother's to be king but is still young, why aren't you in line for the throne?"

"I have the wrong plumage." He tried to smile, but sadness flitted across his eyes. "I am considered cursed."

"What? You have got to be kidding me." She flicked a gaze at Pengfei with his blinding white skin and hair, so similar to Braon's. Ghilian was dark, but not like Tieren, who gleamed under the two suns like licorice. She drew in his cologne—spicy and addictive. "Who the frig decides this?" She handed the wineskin to Ghilian and paced, slamming a fist into her palm. "Let's kill those bastards, and start a new tradition."

Tieren's laughter slid over her like sunlight on a cool day. *Wow, just...wow.* He was so much better in real life. "I have often thought the same. Regardless, I serve to protect my brother, except during his trial. I cannot interfere."

"But I have, and I will." She gathered the strewn bullets, tranqs, darts, and incendiaries, sliding them into her many pockets. "Come, let us find them. I'll take care of each man from afar." She tapped Flint. "Once Braon is off on his adventure, I'll retrieve what I need from the shuttle."

Darkness crossed Tieren's face and settled into a glower. "If you endanger yourself, female, I will need to—"

"Do what?" She grimaced, massaging her throat. "I can protect myself, Your Majesty."

"To find one's mate is rare. I must follow *and* protect." He folded his arms across his bare chest, and frig, if her gaze didn't snag on those bulging pecs.

"Mate?" She frowned, then shook her head, clearing *memories* of him pinning her on a soft bed. "Let's find my shuttle first." Slipping the rifle over a shoulder, she stomped to the tree line, heading northwest, uncaring that her boots squelched or that her drenched pants rubbed her thighs raw. "Talk some sense into him, NOX."

"What am I supposed to say? Listen here, birdman, thou shalt not lay with mine owner?"

A wave of heat scorched her cheeks. She liked the idea of 'lay' more than she should. Sleeping with alien species with her biological instability wouldn't be wise, no matter how tempted she was. Or how Tieren had managed to bombard her with visions across millions of lightyears. That was some kind of magic mojo, right there.

"Your hearts are in sync, by the way."

She paused, glaring at her arm. "NOX, are you matchmaking?" She gritted her teeth, not needing to have to deal with this *and* Tieren staring at her ass. "Wait until I speak to Dr. Nielson. What the frig did he do to you, my friend?"

"Various upgrades that are noteworthy, along with more detailed maps of the galaxies. The part you find worrisome is the personality modifiers. There's quite a number. I'm dabbling with them to find a mix compatible with an average human."

"Like what?" She resumed her hike, veering around silver-barked trees and bushes in a lovely purple.

"Aggressive. You get your ass to the shuttle and fix this, Mikaela Danvers." Dad's voice tore through her.

She froze. "Dad?" Tears burned her eyes.

"Understanding. This wasn't your fault. Kir betrayed you, us, and killing him will rip a hole in your heart. But, it's gotta get done, sweet pea."

"Enough." She punched her forearm, silencing NOX's impersonation of her father. Explaining why speaking like Dad was cruel would take all her composure, and she didn't have it in her now.

"Who was that male?" Tieren's warmth seeped into her back where he lingered behind her. He had saved her from lust-driven madness by donning a V-collared shirt. Chunky boots hid his four-toed feet, and an honest-to-goodness sword hung from his belt.

"That was NOX impersonating my father." She met his gaze and stared, finding the dark depths hypnotic. "He died a while ago."

"I am sorry, *kekaseea*." He caught her fingers for a gentle squeeze, his touch as hot as volcanic rock.

She whipped her gaze forward and trudged on. He spoke as if there was an unavoidable future for them, as if he would never abandon her, never allow harm to befall her. The little girl in her, who had longed for such a knight, preened under his attention. The mutated woman she was feared the truth in his eyes.

Around midday, they paused at a smaller pond. A sweaty Pengfei hobbled, coughed, and staggered, looking worse for wear. Guilt uncoiled in the pit of her stomach. She had set the pace the poor man had to maintain.

"We could fly there, for *Gawen's* sake." He splashed water on his glowing cheeks, barely regulating his breathing.

"And reveal ourselves and our intentions?" Ghilian shook his head. "Remain here, Pengfei, we will return to you. I would appreciate a hot meal if you have the energy to hunt?"

"Youth," Pengfei spluttered. "I must be present to thwart allegations claiming Tieren interfered." He collapsed onto his ass with his legs akimbo.

"NOX?" She tapped her forearm. "Have Kir and his men abandoned the crash site?"

"What? Now you talk to me?" NOX whined. "Scanning now. Yes, a few hiked southwest to those snowcapped mountains but are now returning."

"The Claren Circle?" Tieren frowned. "That is most unwise. 'Tis bebbayaya territory."

"And what are they?" She arched a brow, doubting that anything could be more fearsome than her last kill.

Tieren cupped her jaw before sliding a stray curl behind her ear. He snagged her gaze and held it. "At the base of the mountains are circular caves holding worm-like creatures with sharp spikes and gaping mouths. They are difficult to kill and silent on their many feet."

"It has six mandibles near its mouth to hold the prey while it bites off chunks." Ghilian raised his face to the mountains, a slight shiver twitching his shoulders. "Its digestion is slow and excruciating, or so I am told."

"Right, so avoid at all costs." She patted her pants, searching for the incendiaries.

"Let us find Braon before a bebbayaya does." Pengfei clambered to his feet and strode past her, renewing the hike when she had yet to quench her thirst.

"Kir has guns." She tapped her rifle.

"Is that what you call your weapons?" Tieren stroked the barrel. "Arrows cannot pierce a bebbayaya's hide, but it has a weak spot beneath its jaw. A warrior must be close enough to reach it."

She frowned. "Let me guess, while avoiding its spikes and mandibles?"

"Yes," Ghilian and Tieren said.

"NOX, track anything slithering, crawling, or burrowing between Kir and the closest mountain." She pushed off the tree and hurried to catch up to Pengfei. "Tell me, when does it hunt?"

"At night." Tieren's warm breath on her neck sent a shiver through her. "The first sun sets in four hours."

"Okay, double time." She bolted, but when she glanced at the men, they were far behind. Shit. She'd forgotten about her preternatural speed. Sighing, she slumped against a tree and waited, doubting a 'whoops, my bad' would be enough of an explanation.

Chapter Twenty-Seven

HELPLESS

Year: 2364

Rianus

Tieren blinked at the spot where Mick stood an instant ago. Panic was swift to strike, squeezing his chest and limiting his ability to breathe. He clenched his muscles, ready to launch himself skyward but took a second to scan the forest around them.

She leaned against a tree hundreds of yards ahead.

His breath escaped in a whoosh, and he stomped toward her, wanting to yell at her, to demand she...what? Gritting his teeth, he halted, fighting for control.

So, she was fast. He sighed, casting a gaze skyward. The *Gawen* had sent him a female he couldn't keep up with and, therefore, couldn't protect. Perhaps, what was needed wasn't the norm. Greeven females submitted to their mates in all things. He couldn't see Mick doing this.

There had to be something he brought to their relationship. Discovering what she needed from him was his first priority.

"Sorry about that. I forget sometimes, and..."

He smiled, capturing her hand to convey he understood. Her breath caught, and color flushed her cheeks. "How are you feeling, *kekaseea?*"

Her heartbeat leaped and danced under his fingertips, tempting him to succumb to the silkiness of her soft skin. He pressed his lips to the inside of her wrist, closing his eyes against the barrage of heat, excitement, and lust charging through him.

"Your...wine is more potent than I'm used to." She gestured to the wineskin hanging from her belt. "Let's hope I don't finish it before we find the shuttle."

"There are ponds along the way." His gaze dipped to her heaving breasts straining the still-damp tunic she wore.

"Why can we not fly there?" Ghilian huffed, bending over to catch his breath. Pengfei straggled, mopping sweat off his brow again. His pale face was a bright red as he climbed boulders toward them.

Tieren frowned. "They will see us coming."

"So, we can fly some of the distance." Ghilian threw out his arm in a wide arc. "It will take longer if we insist on walking."

She grinned, flicking her gaze between them. "I cannot fly."

Ghilian gestured to her legs. "But you are fast on your feet."

"I won't abandon my *kekaseea*..." Tieren settled his gaze on her upturned face.

"We can make it a race?" She bounced on her toes, jiggling her breasts. "Up for the challenge?"

The staccato of his heartbeats vibrated through his chest, and an answering eagerness swept along his skin. "Always."

She blinked, her mouth parted, and for the longest moment, met his gaze with something intense darkening her eyes.

Ghilian whipped off his tunic, bumping Tieren with an elbow. His friend chuckled. Tieren peeled his tunic off too. Not that he broke the connection with her, mesmerized by the play of color across her cheeks as her focus dipped to every inch he bared.

Pengfei stumbled into their midst, gasping for air. "What...? Are we flying?"

She leaned her shoulder against the trunk and watched three Greeven undress. Ghilian stowed his garments in a satchel, then dropped it at his feet. Crunching followed when he changed into his Greeven form. Tieren kept his focus on Mick, needing to know how she felt about such an integral part of him.

Her attention shifted from Ghilian to Pengfei, then settled on Tieren. He summoned his Greeven. She winced when his bones re-formed, but after the transformation, she gasped, holding out a hand as if to touch him. He dipped his head and pressed his temple to her palm.

Her cry of delight soothed his soul, along with her gentle stroking, along his nose, cupping his beak, and down his neck. "You're beauti-ful."

He ruffled his feathers in response.

She laughed. "Ready?"

Ghilian squawked, rushing him, so Tieren smacked him with his wing. Ghilian dodged the strike by picking up his satchel and launch-ing himself skyward. Pengfei did the same, leaving Tieren alone. At last.

She caressed his beak, then held out a satchel for him to grab hold of. When he did, she bolted. If he blinked, he would miss her. Heat engulfed his chest, energy flooded his veins, and he took to the sky.

Her laughter reached his sensitive ears, and instead of flying to the shuttle, he trailed her. Her feet blurred. He caught glimpses of her catapulting over boulders, vaulting from one leg to the other, from one trunk to another. Raising his gaze to the treetops, he judged where best to land, needing to beat her there. With a flap of his wings, he generated momentum, then tucked them into a barrel roll, hoping to gain a little speed.

Ghilian and Pengfei drifted above the trees. Ahead rose Claren Circle's ice-capped mountains wrapped around Leito's Pond, but also the home to bebbayaya. The forest was untouched by Greeven because of their presence. It wouldn't be long before one sensed an intrusion in their territory.

He squawked a command to Pengfei and Ghilian. While they landed, he surged forward, descending on a rock outcropping when Mick broke into a small clearing. She halted, then chuckled despite her slight breathlessness.

"We didn't discuss what the winner gets." She leaned her weapon against a trunk, untied the wineskin, and raised it to her lips, exposing the delicate arch of her throat while she drank.

He dropped the satchel, dismissed his Greeven, and stood before her as she liked him most—naked. "What do you want, Mick?"

"You won." She smiled, darting her gaze everywhere but on him. "You get the prize."

His breath caught. "What is the prize?" He hopped off the boulder and shortened the distance between them.

Her focus shifted to his discarded satchel then she met his gaze. "Like I said, we didn't discuss it."

Another step forward and the salted scent of her skin tickled his nose. "And if you had won?"

"To fly."

He jerked as if she had slapped him. "It's rude to ask a Greeven to carry you."

"Oh?" She dipped her head. "Then I suppose I'd ask for more wine." She offered him the wineskin and shrugged with a small smile.

His fingers brushed hers gripping the wineskin, and heat surged along his skin. She gasped and snatched her hand back. He closed the distance between them until they were less than a wing's length apart.

"But you're the winner, and I'm not a sore loser. Name your prize." She squared her shoulders and waited.

"Anything?" His voice was hoarse, and he blamed her tempting lips pulsing lust through him. When she nodded, he rasped, "I claim a kiss."

Her eyes widened, then flicked to his lips. "A kiss you can have for free." She chuckled, shaking her head, even as she pressed her palm against his chest. Her mouth parted, and her breathing shuddered. She lowered her gaze again but whispered, "Holy frig, he's hot, gorgeous, all kinds of hard and soft licorice."

"Hot?" He chuckled. "Licorice?"

She froze and whipped her head up. Her cheeks paled before flushing a bright red. "NOX!"

"What, oh-divine-seductress?" NOX must have been listening in. Tieren didn't like that he was not alone with her.

She smacked her forearm, then pressed her lips to it to whisper, "He's. *Speaking.* English."

"Well, I did the full assessment as you commanded, found his physiology to be more than capable of handling it, and have been subtly slipping your language into his brain."

She slumped, held a finger up to Tieren as if to ask for a moment, but trembled with barely restrained emotion. "You could have warned me, you bucket-of—"

"Yeah, yeah, bolts and such like. I'm shivering in my circuits." NOX's tone turned bored. "Now, hurry. The ground is trembling with something massive heading for Kir. Save the boy, but let the creature kill the Soldiers of Solomon."

Her focus whipped to the mountains. "There you go being all bloodthirsty again, and don't think this matter is settled."

Her frustration distracted Tieren, but NOX's words resonated with cold sliding down his back. He gripped her forearm and held his lips an inch from her skin. "Bebbayaya, NOX?"

"Yes, my prince."

She glared at her arm. "He gets respect, and I get sass?"

NOX scoffed. "He doesn't know me yet. Give me time."

"How long?" Tieren studied the path ahead, bent to hold his palm to the ground, then searched for Pengfei and Ghilian.

"It's sniffing, pausing, but crawling in the right direction. You have time to reach the shuttle before it does."

"Good." Tieren dropped the wineskin and burst forward, pinning Mick to the trunk, moaning at her softness molding to his edges. The temptation of her parted lips was comparable to her body against him. He cupped her cheeks and buried his fingers in her soft plumage.

"Time for that?" NOX sighed. "No."

Tieren scanned the sky above him, not understanding how NOX knew what he was doing, or worse, planning.

"He's right." Instead of pulling away, Mick slid her palms up his chest and over his shoulders. His eyelids fluttered at her touch. She rose onto her toes for added height and feathered her lips across his. "I've wanted to do that for so long."

His ability to breathe abandoned him, and any thoughts of an impending bebbayaya attack, saving Braon, or killing her people, scattered. He swooped in, capturing her soft mouth, shuddering at the sweet nectar and the strange yet addictive flavor of her. A kiss had never meant more to him.

She moaned, tilted her head, and deepened the kiss. A tidal wave of need crashed over him, and he shoved her against the trunk, spreading her thighs to nestle there. Time slowed, dragging out other pleasures, like the sunlight on his back, the texture of her dowo rubbing his ass, her fingers delving into his plumage. Shivers racked his body, from his scalp, along his back to his arousal.

"This is like those action entertainment thingies when the building's exploding, and the shit's about to hit the fan, then out of nowhere, the man kisses the woman. Like hello, we're about to die here," NOX chatted on. "All you need is to add a musical number to make it a what-the-frig moment."

Mick broke the kiss with a chuckle. "They're called movies, and we're not about to die."

Tieren hadn't understood some of what NOX said, but he didn't care. She was mesmerizing, with the blue swirling in her eyes and her breathlessness rubbing her pebbled breasts against his chest.

"Quit tempting me, and put some pants on." She tightened her voice as if she commanded him to dress but ruined it by trailing her hand from his chest to his belly. He captured her hand to his skin. Her heated softness like warm fur seeped into him.

Grunting, he hid his longing while yanking on his dowo. He pulled his tunic out of the satchel and over his head. Her touch where she tugged on the hem was electrifying. She helped him dress, as if she had the right to.

While running a hand down his chest to linger on his belly, she gazed southwest. "NOX, where's the boy?"

"He's pinned under a net but out in the open. Wyatt's injured and sitting to one side. The others have set up camp with Kir pacing. Seth can't reach the *Sentry* and is panicking."

"Right." She slammed a fist into a palm. "We need to stop the bebbayaya from harming Braon. He's defenseless."

Tieren gritted his teeth. She was correct.

"If you climb onto my back, I'll circle the campsite." She gazed at the mountains again. "Maybe get us between the bebbayaya and your brother."

He jerked as if she slapped him. "No, I will trail you."

She stared at him. "Fine, then grab me by the arms and fly me to a high point. I can snipe from there."

Fiery darkness engulfed him. This was worsening every second. "No."

"Tieren, you—" A blood-curdling screech sliced through the air, coming from the east. "Never mind. Stay here." She bolted.

"*Gawen,*" he squawked. Summoning his Greeven shredded his garments, but he didn't care. He launched himself skyward.

On the horizon, weaving and slithering toward the downed shuttle was a ship-sized bebbayaya, glistening yellow in the fading sunlight. Its mandibles pinched the air as it paused, sniffed, adjusted its direction, and barreled onward, crushing trees in its path.

At the speed the bebbayaya was going, it would reach Braon in minutes. From this vantage point, the campsite splayed out like a map. While Mick's males bellowed orders to each other, one male sat to one side, his leg extended. He had to be this Wyatt NOX mentioned. They had pinned Braon close to a boulder, which wouldn't hide him from the bebbayaya if the creature had good eyesight. It didn't, but it could scent a drop of blood in a hundred-mile radius. When Mick had brought the shuttle down, she had ensured the bebbayaya would hunt this day.

She couldn't have known, and she had done it to save Braon.

Ghilian and Pengfei hovered beside him, assessing the scene as he had done. They waited for instructions.

Tieren swung his gaze, searching for Mick. A soft swish hit the dirt next to Braon. His net loosened. Tieren followed the trajectory and spotted Mick halfway up a tree with her weapon balanced on a thick branch. Another swish gaped the net. Braon shifted closer, tugging the ends down to hide it was loose.

Wyatt hobbled around the edges of the campsite to reach Braon.

Tieren revealed his face enough to speak. "Ghilian, head him off."

"Stop." Pengfei threw his wing across Ghilian. "We must not interfere. Let us see if this male means to harm Braon."

Tieren clenched his jaw. Seconds ticked by while he hovered, waiting.

Chapter Twenty-Eight

"Don't let the men see," Drys said, limping to stand beside Kiros.

"See what?" he asked and gazed away. Drys, the old bastard, knew him too well.

"That you don't have a plan. Perhaps not our best mission," Drys muttered, scrubbing his salt-and-pepper beard.

"Our worst," Kiros admitted. "Our choices are few." He rubbed a hand over his face, wishing he'd chosen a different path. "I need to beg Mick's forgiveness. It's the only way off this planet."

"And pray NOX hasn't harmed Elias or destroyed the *Sentry*." Drys gripped Kiros on the shoulder. "Sorry for steering you wrong, son."

"I should've handled this better. Maybe fueled her silly crush and convinced her to join S.o.S." Kiros pursed his lips. "Instead, I—" He winced, tormented by Mick in that red dress. Wrapping his arm around his torso, he searched for a twinge from his healing ribs. Some pain would be justice for his treatment of her. "I've failed us. Let you down." He swallowed, the guilt eating what remained of his soul. "I can't shake the feeling we're going to die here, Drys." He met the man's gray gaze.

A rueful smile twisted Drys's lips. "Death is inevitable." He gestured to Kiros's wrist. "I suggest you start begging."

If only it was that simple. Regret, despair, and desperation warred within him. He'd frigged this up royally.

Wyatt stumbled around the clearing, no doubt testing the splint. The pale boy watched from beneath the net, not once having tried to escape. Kiros expected an attempt soon. Seth worked under the shuttle while Drys rummaged through the lockers for supplies. Aiden scanned nearby plants, in search of something edible. Lanek and Ru had headed southwest, hoping to find dinner.

Kiros sucked in a deep breath and tapped his wrist. "NOX, patch me through to Mick."

"No, can do, *el traidor.*"

Relief exploded through Kiros, like a burst of bright joy. Speaking to the A.I. flooded him with hope. "Please. I need to...apologize."

"Mick and the prince are having a moment. Interrupting them now would mean my death."

Kiros gritted his teeth and fought for calm. "Tell me, at least, is Elias alive?"

"He and your ship are no more."

Kiros's heart froze. His breathing seized.

"As I see it, Kiros Caldwell, you are stuck on Rianus for the foreseeable future. The chances of you resuming your former life are minuscule."

Kiros raised a fist to the brown sky. "NOX—"

"You frigged with the wrong woman, Kiros."

Mick's voice vibrated from Kiros's wrist. *"...disable any communication between S.o.S and their ship. Empty their berth into the nearest sun. No S.o.S will survive to tell the tale."*

"Frig," he growled. He dropped into a squat, his vision spinning. What the frig had he done? A scan of the campsite had him considering relocating to somewhere safer, but did such a place exist? Mick could still be killed with a bullet to the head. Doing that would sure as hell trap them on this world. No, he had to swallow his pride and beg.

"Release the boy, and perhaps, she will kill you swiftly." NOX's advice had some merit. Sort of.

Kiros glanced at the 'prize' he'd been so determined to steal from her. All the credits in the universe meant nothing if he and his men were dead. "If I do, can you guarantee safe passage off this planet?"

"It's not me you have to ask."

Kiros pinched his brow. Why had he bothered to speak to NOX? The A.I. frustrated the friggin hell out of him. "Patch me through, NOX."

"There's no need. She's minutes away. But it's not her you should worry about."

"It's not?" Kiros frowned, studying the pebbles trembling underfoot.

"Beware...the bebbayaya," NOX sang.

"The what now?" Kiros launched to his full height when Lanek burst through the foliage. Ru was hot on his tail. Their pinched faces and flushed cheeks said it all. Kiros drew his blaster.

"Frig," Lanek rasped as he skidded to a halt beside Kiros. "We were quiet, for frig's sake."

Ru bent over, sucking in great gulps of air. Rumbling pierced the silence. In the distance, trees dipped as if being sucked into a cavern.

"What is it?" Kiros asked, his gaze fixed southwest.

"Like a giant centipede," Ru managed, for once his matchstick missing. He straightened and raised his assault rifle.

"Odds?" Aiden asked, joining them.

"Zero," Lanek spat. "And if by some miracle we kill it," he whispered, "it's not edible. Its spit scorched the vegetation."

"Shit," Kiros breathed out.

"Told you so," NOX sang.

Lanek gaped. "Frig, when did you—"

"Only way off-world." Kiros glanced at the boy, who cowered behind the boulder, curling his wings around him. His blue eyes were wide. He kicked at the net's pegs but to no avail.

Trees creaked and cracked as they tumbled over. Fear coiled in Kiros's gut when a click-click and thundering rumble grew louder. It vibrated the air around him. He trembled but raised his blaster. He refused to blink.

Trees exploded outward as a gigantic yellow centipede emerged, its mandibles twitching and clicking. Too many eyes meant blinding it would take too much effort. Spikes surrounded its body like a cactus. Spit dripped onto the ground as it rose higher, resting on its army of hind legs. It focused on the shuttle. No one moved or...breathed. Aiden loaded his shotgun in slow, deliberate movements, as if doing it at a snail's pace would mute his actions.

The clicking intensified. The creature snapped its head in Kiros's direction, dipped, and brought its great bulk to within a foot of where he stood.

"Looks like we're screwed," Seth called out. "Could someone give me a hand?"

Kiros sliced a glance at the shuttle where Seth's legs stuck out. Ice traveled from Kiros's ears to his toes. He squeezed his eyes shut and prayed.

The creature howled, twisted, and smacked Kiros across the chest. He flew backward, sliding along the dirt. Lanek roared and emptied his blasters while Kiros staggered to his feet. His body pinged complaints, but he squared his shoulders and drew his last blaster. Not that Lanek had penetrated the creature's hide. Bullets littered the ground. Blasterfire painted white spots across its flesh. Nothing hindered it.

A squeal preceded a charge across the clearing. Kiros threw out an arm. Silly that, when the creature barreled over him regardless. Flat on his back, pain cinched his chest, halting his ability to breathe. He blinked at the brown sky, aware of the creature moving from one side to the other. His men's screams filled in the details. Something thunked beside him before half of Aidan disappeared into the creature's mouth.

Kiros cried out, unable to move, to help. He'd done this. With twitching fingers, he tested the thing beside him and met the stickiness of blood.

"Aidan," Ru roared and scooped up the strewn shotgun, getting off a few shots before the creature swallowed him whole.

"Kiros?" Lanek stood above him, his focus on the centipede.

"I'm frigged." Kiros coughed, tasting the salty tang of his blood. "Can't feel my legs, and my chest's on fire."

Lanek glanced at him then. Sadness darkened his eyes. He whipped his hair off his temple and squared his shoulders. "The *Jinsei* has a pod. Let's get you there."

Shrieks preceded metal crumpling as the creature raged against the shuttle.

"Seth's...squashed. Aiden and Ru—" Lanek nudged his head south. "Drys's dead."

Kiros craned his neck and caught Drys's lifeless gaze where he sprawled like a limp doll against the lurching shuttle. Seth's legs still stuck out from under it, blood saturating the soil.

"Wyatt?" Kiros croaked.

"Freed the kid," Lanek spat.

Kiros closed his eyes on a sigh. "I'm sorry."

"Don't go friggin soft—" Lanek screamed. A mandible swept him out of Kiros's line of vision.

"Lanek?" he called. No response came. He was alone.

A shadow swooped across the sky. An ivory bird descended.

Then Mick was there, cradling Kiros's head in her lap. Tears streamed down her cheeks.

He tried to smile, to raise a hand to touch her one last time. Regret crippled him further. Oh, what a fool he'd been. "I'm sorry," he mouthed.

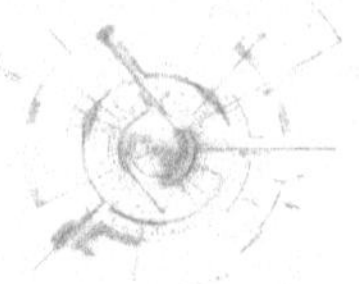

Wyatt had flicked the net back, setting Braon free. But instead of running or taking to the sky, Braon yanked the dagger out of Wyatt's boot. He lunged at the neck of the bebbayaya while it leaned over the bleeding male.

Braon vaulted into the air, using his summoned wings to spin him. He swooped and weaved, dodging the mandibles. One clipped his wing. He tumbled to the ground. Tieren's breath caught. At the last second, Braon regained his balance and exploded upward, plunging the dagger into the bebbayaya's neck.

That wouldn't kill it, but Braon didn't release the dagger's hilt. As the bebbayaya thrashed, it sliced its own throat, spewing yellow blood and acid.

"He is worthy," Pengfei crowed beside Tieren.

While the bebbayaya was in its final death throes, Braon landed on his haunches and hid his Greeven wings. Circling the writhing bebbayaya, he bolted to Wyatt to throw an arm around the male, helping him limp faster and away from the camp.

Mick had leaped from the tree, tossed her weapon aside, and sprawled alongside the bleeding male. Her tears streamed, and her indecision hovered her hands over his chest.

"Kir?" Her voice cracked with emotion.

"Mick," he choked out her name. Red trickled from his mouth.

"Lie still," she crooned.

His gruff chuckle merged into a cough, and blood pooled beneath him. "I'm dead, Mick."

She sobbed, "No, don't say that." Raising her face to the sky, she met Tieren's gaze. "Please."

There was nothing to be done, but he couldn't bear telling her that. His hearts broke into cacophonous beats, and he dove, landing beside her. Cupping her shoulders, he lifted her away, then nodded at Pengfei, who trailed him.

Pengfei shook his head, tossing his braided hair wild. "A beb-bayaya's strike or bite carries much venom, Mick. All you can do is offer a merciful death."

"Um, hate to mention this," Ghilian descended, blasting dust with his wings. "You're too close to the beb—"

Tieren flew out of Mick's arms, almost yanking her with him. She screamed his name. Fire burned across his back. He landed, bounced, and slammed into a tree trunk. Every jarred muscle and bone protested. He sagged, watching with stunned helplessness as Ghilian thrust his sword into the bebbayaya's neck, silencing it, at last.

Mick hesitated halfway between him and Kir.

Something harsh twisted her features, and she gave Tieren her back, choosing Kir over him.

Ice drenched Tieren, spiking fiery shivers through his aching body. In the last moments of his life, she would rather be with Kir than with him. He closed his eyes, drawing in slow breaths as the venom spread, incomparable to the dark forces of despair. He had hoped...longed, and trusted the *Gawen* to choose well, but she couldn't love him. Not when she loved someone else.

Cool hands on his cheeks brought him back to the agony burning him alive from the inside.

"Tieren, hold on." She tapped her wrist. "NOX, bring the *Jinsei*. And please hurry."

"Already on the way, Mick."

She slumped, uncaring that her tears dripped onto Tieren's belly. He had never seen anything more beautiful than her, so close to him, with bright blue in her brown eyes.

A glance to the side showed Kir, unmoving, his neck at an odd angle. Tieren frowned but couldn't speak, with his tongue swollen and his breathing labored.

"Come, Mick." Pengfei tried to pull her away, but she clung to Tieren.

"I'm taking him to my...healer." She glared at Pengfei. "NOX is on his way."

Ghilian crouched beside Tieren, squeezing him on the shoulder. "No one survives a bebbayaya."

"I have to try. I..." She sobbed, pressing her temple to Tieren's chest.

"Clear the campsite." NOX's voice cut through her crying.

All raised their faces to the sky, to the hovering shuttle.

She gaped. "But...how?"

The door opened. Out leaped a male, covered in shining silver and rusty browns from head to toe. "Happy to see me?" He squeaked as he ran toward them, bending to scoop up her weapon.

She slid her arms under Tieren's back, sparking fresh waves of agony. His vision blurred while she carried him into the shuttle as if he weighed nothing more than a squawkling.

Darkness engulfed them when the door closed, and in the flickering lights, he scanned the interior, skipping over Ghilian, who had joined them.

The shuttle vibrated, but when she tightened her embrace, despite the cost of moving, Tieren curled into her.

"NOX, did you fix the old shuttle?" she asked.

"Yup, figured you might need it." Said shuttle jerked and spluttered.

"Thank you." She met Tieren's gaze and brushed his plumage off his temple. Darkness circled his vision, and he struggled to keep them open. She cradled him closer to her, burying his face in her neck. "Stay with me, Tieren."

The salted scent of her engulfed him, and he succumbed to the bliss of oblivion.

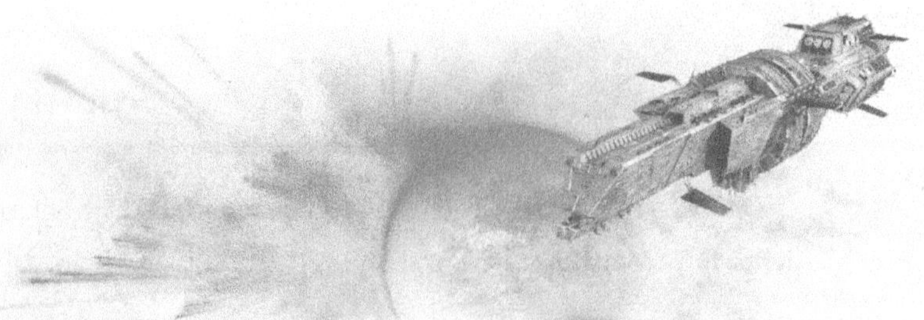

Chapter Twenty-Nine

TO THE RESCUE

Year: 2364

Rianus

THE SHUTTLE TOUCHED DOWN, and Mick bolted, not caring whether Ghilian followed or not. NOX did, tapping on the med console as soon as she slipped Tieren into the pod.

"Do you think it will heal him?" The words squeezed past her constricted throat. Yellow glowed under his skin where the venom traveled.

"I have added his physiology to the database." NOX stood beside her. The soft whir of the pod's scanners filled the medical bay. "It's a good thing Dr. Nielson upgraded everything."

"Except your suit." She tossed him a tight smile. "At the next stop, NOX, I promise you."

"I'll monitor him. You best deal with the other Greeven."

She stilled. "Greeven? Is that what they call themselves?"

"Yup. Oh..." NOX pulled out a syringe gun and pressed it to her neck.

The pinch was short-lived, but the burn of the meds set her neck on fire. "What the frig."

"Dextrorabine. It numbs the senses."

She blinked. "You could have warned me." Gasping, she cupped her mouth. "Why am I speaking with a lisp?"

"It might numb other parts of you." NOX shrugged.

"My tongue?" she garbled. "I could kill you. And here I wanted to thank you for the shuttle and the rescue. But now—" At his stoic expression, she threw her hands in the air. "You don't even know what I am saying." Wiping spittle off her chin, she stomped off.

Sure, the ship's hums and whines were fainter, and her nose didn't sting from the stench of space, but her neck spasmed, and her tongue felt as if it had swelled to ten times its size. Damn A.I.

Ghilian meandered around the docking bay, touching crates and picking up tools. His eyes were wide and his posture stiff. He hurried over as soon as he spotted her. "How is he?"

"I don't know." She closed her eyes at his furrowed brow. "Come." Gesturing to him to follow, she marched to the pod. "NOX can explain how it works. I'm taking a shower."

Worry fired her blood and twitched her limbs. She didn't need to wash, but the water might soothe her. There was nothing she could do but wait, hope, and if God was listening, pray. Nor could she keep herself busy showing Ghilian her ship, not until the drug NOX had given her worked itself out of her system. Dextro-whatever was off the list, not if a numb-tongue was the cost.

After stripping off her clothes, she stepped into the spray. Tears trickled unheeded. Kir was dead, and by her own hands. His blood loss was too much. She couldn't save him. And his betrayal hadn't helped him. Justifications.

Clasping the amulet, she slid down the tiles to her knees and sobbed.

She had gripped his cheeks, slid her fingers into his hair to cup his ears, and pressed a kiss to his nose.

He'd spluttered a smile. "Do it, Mick."

The crunch of bone echoed in her mind, cementing the memory. She would never forget killing him.

He was her friend, family, a tie to her past. Their connection hadn't mattered to him, but it had to her. All those days spent by his side, eager for a smile or a good word. He had tossed their history aside because she hadn't fucked him. Just like that.

Pain squeezed her chest until she sucked in air as if through a straw. The Soldiers of Solomon were no more. Their annihilation was her fault. She'd shot down the shuttle and, in doing so, summoned the bebbayaya.

"Mick, with His Royal Highness out for the count, I suggest we sample the bebbayaya and collect the messed-up shuttle for parts."

She shuddered and wiped her eyes with the heels of her palms. "Good...idea, NOX. Gimme five." With a twist of her wrist, the water stopped.

Still, she hesitated before reaching for a towel. If she kept herself busy, she wouldn't have the time to worry about Tieren or blame herself for killing Kir.

In fresh underwear, jeans, and a tank, she stamped her boots on and braided her wet hair as she hurried to the bay. NOX waited for her inside the shuttle, punching on the console. She paused in front of her small armory to check ammunition. He'd clipped Flint and Locke into their slots. A bottle of grit sat on the console, condensation glistening on the glass. Beside that were her earbuds. She could kiss him.

"Good thinking, NOX. Sample the bebbayaya without having to kill another." She gritted her teeth, hating how uncaring she'd been. "About that, from now we tag and bag, no killing. These creatures don't deserve to be lab rats."

Pouring a dollop into a shot glass, she threw it back. It hit the back of her throat like a sledgehammer. "Argh, after Tieren's wine, this stuff's disgusting." Dropping into the pilot's chair, she threw her heels onto the console's edge and popped the magnetic straps in place. "Ready?"

"Aye, aye, captain." NOX's tight smile was without teeth. Older models didn't have a mouth which served no purpose. All he had were molded lips that could twitch or stretch like pliable rubber. Humming a song from The Pirates of Penzance, he shut the shuttle door and bounced to the console.

She jerked, missing the glass and splashing grit onto her fingers. "Wait, where's Ghilian?"

"He chose to remain with Tieren."

"Friggin' hell, NOX, what if he touches something?" She leaped out of the chair but slammed into NOX's metallic chest. Rubbing her bruised shoulder, she glared at him.

"Deactivated all the panels, buttons, and locked the drawers. He's fine." NOX's lips fell into an Elvis Presley impersonation. "Besides, *I* haven't left the ship, Mick."

Heat burned her cheeks, making her eyes water. "Good point." She slumped into the chair and faced the fore vids. "Might as well tag and bag the other creatures on our radar."

"If there's time. I can't schedule these things when you go off plan with your heroics."

"Heroics?" She huffed. "Name once."

NOX's eyebrow was as pliable as his lips when he arched it, almost touching his grooved hair.

"Fine." She raised her chin in defiance—the act lost on NOX. "I'll behave if the creatures do. Gotta survive, NOX."

He powered up the shuttle, leaving her to twiddle her sticky thumbs. The bottle of grit and messy glass remained untouched, taunting her. Her senses buzzed, the whine and whirl of the engines merged with her deafening heartbeat as a stray blast of air tingled the hairs on her arms. If she was submerged in water, it would be quiet enough to hear her blood gurgling in her veins, her stomach acids digesting, and the tick-tick of her hormonal clock.

She snorted at her silliness. The act of digestion was too quiet. It would be the passage of food through her bowels squelching along. She popped the earbuds in and played the sound file Wyatt had shared, just loud enough to mute some of the noises.

The bay doors opened to NOX's voice warning the nonexistent crew to stand clear. According to space legislature, he was expected to do so. Other than recording it somewhere as a completed task, it made no sense. He piloted the shuttle out of the bay and didn't spin to ensure the bay doors closed.

"Did you lock Ghilian inside the medical bay?"

"Yup. Seemed the wisest course of action. Can't have him accidentally jettisoning himself out of space or worse."

She chuckled. "What's worse?"

"Flying the *Jinsei* into a sun."

"Yeah, that would be bad." She fought an eye-roll, like the man could find the bridge or press the complicated buttons that would auto-destruct or crash the *Jinsei*.

"Probables state you're blaming yourself for S.o.S, so listen to this."

The voice of Kir's old friend Drys filled the tight confines of the shuttle. *"Friends? Kiros, you've never mentioned Mick in all the years I've known you. That ain't a friendship."*

"History, then." Kir's husky voice shot darts of guilt through her. It was too soon.

"Shut it off, NOX." She dug her nails into her thighs, fighting the silent, lethal pain scouring her heart.

He ignored her, holding up a scarred metal hand, instead.

"I doubt you'll see her again, especially after you steal the quarry right from under her." Eagerness drenched Drys's voice.

As NOX had warned, which she had ignored, Kir had deceived her from the start. She caught her breath, waiting for him to reject the truth in his friend's words.

Kiros grumbled, *"Good point."*

A tear escaped, pausing on her lashes before slipping free.

"Having second thoughts?" Drys knew Kir the best. She hoped he was rethinking this plan even though she'd lived through his betrayal.

"Nope. It's a shit ton of credits." A pause followed, and she prayed Kir hesitated because he felt guilty. *"It's a good plan, Drys. Catch a ride, use her resources, and steal the prize."*

Silence fell, well, as silent as her hyper-senses and earbuds would allow. NOX was right to have played her this.

Kir's voice filled the compartment again. *"I say we take the Jinsei and abandon her on whatever habitable planet she lands on."*

"Enough." She slammed the console with the flat of her hand. Dropping her temple on her arm, she willed the crushing vice around her heart to vanish. "Thank you...for revealing this to me."

"You couldn't save him, Mick. His injuries... Well, he could have made it to the pod, and still, it would have been too late."

She raised her gaze to her...friend. An A.I. showed her more loyalty than Kir ever had. "I know." The juddering shuttle whipped her gaze to the console. "Um, random thought. What if this thing crashes? Then we've doomed Tieren and Ghilian to starve to death."

NOX tutted. "It won't crash."

The shuttle jerked as if in defiance. She tightened her grip on the console.

"Why is it so hard for you to remember? I'm still on the ship, Mick."

She chuckled. "Sorry, my friend. You're here with me, pretty much in human form."

He paused and stared at her for four ticks of her heart. "Fair enough."

The shuttle cut through the atmosphere like a rock hitting mud. The jolting rattled her teeth. Instead of strapping herself into the chair, she drank grit straight from the bottle. If she died now, she didn't want to suffer through every crippling sensation.

"Twenty seconds until clear."

She swallowed great gulps of grit. The shuttle wouldn't split apart, but this thing had been inoperable just this morning. "Swoop in with the *Jinsei* and maglift the busted shuttle?"

"That's what I was thinking. I'll tag the shuttle so we can fly in under the cover of darkness. No need to start a panic."

"I wasn't thinking of that when I flew in with Kir." She dipped her chin to her chest. "I'm the worst explorer ever. How many protocols have I broken coming here, NOX?" She threw out a hand to silence him when he hummed as if he gave her question serious thought. "No, I don't want to know. Here's hoping Dr. Nielson doesn't find out."

"Ten seconds." NOX broke into a side-by-side dance step before breaking into song. "Y'know? I was driving Lamborghinis, sipping super-dry martinis..."

She gaped, willing herself not to blink. The shuttle jarring her snapped her out of her daze. Torn between giggling at his impromptu dance act or recording it, she retrieved Flint instead. The bebbayaya was dead, but predators could be feasting on its corpse. Safe rather than sorry made more sense. And besides, the familiar weight on her back swelled her with security.

The fragrance of the planet hit her when the shuttle door opened. Not daring to glance at the bodies littering the site, she hopped out, landing on her feet. A stray urge begged her to bury the last of S.o.S. in a show of respect. Well, Kir at least. Her gaze slipped to the side, and she whipped her head forward, not wanting to catch a glimpse of his body. She hurried over to the bebbayaya lying in a pool of yellow blood. Minutes were all she needed to secure a biosample and vid footage of the creature.

NOX scanned the area. "I'll take care of the bodies, Mick."

Tears pressed behind her eyes. "Where next?" she rasped, then coughed to clear her throat.

NOX closed the door, sealing them inside the shuttle. "Northeast of here are two species, one is waterborne and the other on dry land, and by dry, I mean bone dry. After that, we circle two islands for another two."

"Why so many? Usually, it's one and done." She loaded a few tranq rounds into Flint while NOX shot the shuttle north. They were medium strength, strong enough to slow a hefty animal.

"Fentus upgraded your reconnaissance equipment, which means we might have to hit our pre-visited planets. Just to make sure we have the best they can offer."

"True. I do feel like a long journey, NOX. Just you and me, like old times." Thoughts of Tieren asleep in the pod tormented her. Her heart twinged, and she sighed, wishing she could take him with her. He wasn't a pet but a humanoid species, yet leaving him behind or being apart from him indefinitely, made her shift in her seat. A dull ache had taken up residence in her bones.

"Well, yeah, that's the plan. Tag and bag, babe."

She chuckled at the 'babe.' "So, what did our sparkling new recon equipment reveal? Any details?"

"They look like flying manta rays, and I'm not sure your mutations can handle water retrievals. Maybe you should leave those to me."

"You?" she squeaked. Part of her bubbled with unexpected happiness, as if she wasn't alone in the universe. Another part worried he wouldn't survive.

"I'm waterproof and don't breathe air." He smirked.

She laughed and gestured to all of him. "But you also weigh a shit ton and will sink to the bottom like a lead balloon."

"I can use my thrusters to propel me up."

"Fair enough. We'll let you tag the manta rays. I'll hit the creatures on land. By dry, do you mean desert?" When he nodded, she blasted air out, puffing her cheeks. "Sure, I can handle that."

"I'm monitoring the pod, so the second Tieren starts surfacing from his drugged stupor, we're outta here."

"Thanks. I'd hate for him to wake up, and I'm not there." She sliced a glance at her expressionless friend. "A friendly face, so to speak."

"Waking up to Ghilian's hideous countenance might terrify him." NOX winked which looked like his eyelid hitched half-shut, then fluttered in a spasm. "Whatever you say, boss."

He threw a tracker into the crushed shuttle and hopped into the other shuttle, waiting for her to follow before closing the door. "I suggest you hover over their nesting site while I plunge in."

"I'll attach a grapple in case I need to pull you out. I'll use the winch if need be."

He dropped into the pilot's seat to fly them northeast, away from Claren Circle. As they skimmed the tops of the purple trees, she scanned the ground, searching for Braon and Wyatt. She loved that someone from S.o.S had survived. Ice drenched her, and she froze.

"Wyatt's alive, NOX. Won't he seek revenge?" She shook her head, answering her question. "He's a good guy."

"And if he does turn mean, you'll see him coming, Mick." NOX spared her a glance before speeding across the emerald waves.

The course he had charted zigzagged, dodging flashing blips she assumed were ships. No sailor would spot them and assume the worst.

She groaned at her inability to follow the Primary. Besides, she doubted many explorers managed to obey it all the damn time. Calculating for an individual out on an evening stroll was difficult. The variables were just too many. Still, they should have flown in under cover of darkness.

They were here now. The door slid open, and a gust of salted air whipped her hair back. She breathed it in, wishing she was lounging on a beach, an orange cocktail in hand, and Tieren rubbing suntan lotion on her legs.

The splash as NOX plunged into the waves shook her out of her daydream. With a firm grip on the side of the door, she swung out, catching a glimpse of a shrinking red light the deeper he fell. An iridescent purple creature leaped out of the water, floated a few seconds above it, with the tips of its wings skimming the surface before diving in again. Its beauty was breathtaking. She grabbed a portable camera and attached it to the front of her tank. In time too. Three more manta rays burst out of the water. The setting sunlight brushed across their shimmering scales.

When NOX pierced the surface, attached to his face was a baby ray, fluttering its fins. It slithered around his metallic head before sliding into the sea.

"That was incredible, Mick. I recorded it, but you've got to see it. They have villages, with flat coral homes that shield them." He tossed her the excise dart before swinging into the compartment. Water streamed off him, but he strode with ease to the pilot's seat. The shuttle tilted east, crossing over gray beaches and dunes. She gripped the back of his chair, scanning the horizon through the fore vids.

"I see nothing, NOX."

"Neither do I." He switched the vid to infrared and set the sensitivity. Something shifted, like a glitch or a refresh of the vid. "There." He tapped the glass, rippling the pixels.

Gray rocks with tuffs of tundra rose, shuffled forward, then dropped in a puff of sand.

"Land. I'll tag them. Keep recording, please." She removed the tranqs and loaded excise darts.

After hopping out of the shuttle, she climbed a steep dune and sprawled across the apex, aligning Flint's barrel for a clear shot. The warmth of the sand baked her thighs and belly, as the suns toasted her from above.

The creature wriggled, but as soon as it rose, she released a slow breath and fired. The dart bounced off its rock-like shell.

"Friggin' hell," she grumbled, tugging the dart across the sand to reload.

Sweat beaded around her eye where it rested against the scope. She didn't dare move. The telltale sign of an impending shuffle was a slight tremble in the sand beneath the rock creature. As soon as it happened, she fired. A horrific squeal pierced the air, a mixture of a pinched cat and a bullet ricochet. The ground vibrated while she retracted the dart, drawing the thin cord across the sand. She counted down under her breath; five meters, four.

Splitting her focus between the dart and the creature, she pulled, slow and steady. When two, five, no, seven more creatures burst from beneath the sand, she remained calm, curious as to how they would react. Hovering a few inches above the ground wasn't expected. Yet, despite their outrage at one of theirs being injured, they plopped onto the sand, like pancakes on a skittle.

Her stomach grumbled. Cinnamon buttery goodness. She swallowed a moan. Perhaps when she returned to Rebirth, she could find a restaurant with legit pancakes. Hell, even one of those state-of-the-art replicators that could cook anything other than chicken noodles.

With the dart in hand, she crawled backward, her gaze locked on the creatures in case their attack strategy was a little more destructive than sand plopping. Once inside the shuttle, the door closed, and she leaned against the bulkhead.

"I'm starving."

NOX didn't spare her a glance. "Protein bars are in the locker."

She grimaced at the idea of tasting sawdust where cinnamon should be. "No, thanks. I want something...edible."

"Fentus did restock the mess. You could try there." He shrugged and veered the shuttle southwest.

She snorted. "Right, I have pancakes on the *Jinsei*." But, frig, she sure as hell would check.

Once again, he zigzagged, so that the frigates remained on the horizon. To the west rose a mountain, steepled with massive bird-like shapes circling it. Her first thought was dragons. But this far away, all were in shadow, and since NOX hadn't mentioned heading in that direction, she had to assume there was nothing remarkable about those 'dragons.'

The Renaissance era would be her guess. Soon, the Greeven would reach the industrial era. That's if she could compare their progress to Prime Earth's. They were a long way from breaching their atmosphere and outer space.

"What do you expect with this next creature?" She tore into a protein bar and tried not to focus on its putty flavor or clay consistency.

"I can't explain this one except to say it's a lump?" He tapped the console to display the recon's readings. "Circular, bulbous, with legs?"

She nodded. At least the readings carried more data than head southwest, and X marks the spot. Knowing alien octopus spit acid would have been a tad bit helpful. She stashed the excise darts along with the data crystals into the cryo-tubes, ready for storage or droning. Loading a fresh excise dart into her trusty Flint, she slotted one into a blaster, readying it for NOX.

"Buckle in, Mick. Tieren's surfacing." NOX's warning came too late. The tilt of the shuttle slammed her against the bulkhead, smacking the blaster from her hand. It skidded across the compartment, but she didn't lunge for it. Instead, she yanked the fold-up seat down and strapped herself in.

Tieren. Her heart leaped and danced. Nervousness churned her stomach, and butterflies rose to choke her. "How is he, NOX?" She had to yell above the shuttle's squealing engines.

"Healed. Duh."

She harrumphed. The urge to smack him gripped her. His attitude wasn't appreciated, but her question was a silly one. Tieren wouldn't be surfacing if he wasn't well. What she wanted to know was the state of his heart, and no A.I. could tell her that. NOX could hazard a guess, but then, so could she. Chewing on a thumbnail, she focused on nibbling it to the quick. Anything was better than pestering him with questions. Friggin' A.I.

Chapter Thirty

LIFE/LOVE IS FLEETING

Year: 2364

Orbiting Rianus.

Tieren opened his eyes and blinked at the blurred glass curved around him. A strange world lay beyond it, all white with flickering lights and rhythmic beeps. Ghilian hovered outside, his brow furrowed.

"Where...am I?" Tieren struggled to swallow, his voice jarring his throat.

"On Mick's ship."

"She saved me?" Visions returned of Mick choosing Kir, breaking his neck, then rushing to Tieren's side. She'd carried him onto her shuttle... Heat engulfed his chest and ramped his heartrates. She cared.

"I suggest you relax, my prince. If the pod senses a change in your core temperature, it will sedate you again." NOX's voice filled the white room, but he wasn't present.

"Am I healed?" Tieren tried to sit up within the confines of the pod, and when he did so, it hissed open. Cool air flooded over him, smelling like burned battusks.

"You are well. All signs of the bebbayaya's poison has been eradicated. We are a few minutes out and will be docking soon."

He nodded even though he didn't understand. Sliding off the bed, he rested his weight on his feet but kept a hand on the contraption to steady himself. Ghilian caught Tieren's elbow for added balance. He didn't need it, not when he felt incredible, well-rested. If his dowo and tunic weren't in tatters, he would believe he had dreamed it all.

He settled a dazed gaze on Ghilian. "How is this possible? Did it—?"

"It happened, Tieren. I swear it. I have not left your side." Ghilian hesitated, then squared his shoulders. "Your scars are gone."

"What?" Tieren jerked. He held out his arm to trace the scar running along his inner forearm. One stupid incident with a sword as a squawkling had caused the injury. Smooth skin met the swipe of his thumb. A sense of loss settled in his soul, like a thin coating of darkness enshrouding memories of his childhood.

"My apologies, my prince. With your life at risk, we didn't task the medical pod to ignore your scars."

Tieren raised his face to the square-patterned ceiling, searching for the origin of NOX's voice. He sighed. "It's a small price to live, NOX."

"We are docking now. Mick will head to you as soon as the bay doors seal."

Yet more words he didn't understand, except for Mick coming for him. He shivered, running his palms along his arms. As soon as he could, he needed her to know what she was to him. Since the *Gawen* had revealed her existence, the silent bond between them had grown stronger. The moment she had stepped onto Rianus soil, she had placed herself on this path. Kissing him had decided her fate.

The taste of her lingered on his tongue, saturating every part of him. He would forever taste her kiss, scent her skin, and long for her touch.

An acrid stench burned his nostrils, and he glanced at his ruined garments. He needed to bathe, to change before she arrived. Gritting his teeth, he tore off the remnants of his tunic, letting the strips fall to the glowing floor. A black circle shot out, and he leaped out of its way. It gathered the pieces and vanished into its hole.

Tieren blinked. "What was that?"

"Auto-bots clean." Mick filled the doorway where one hadn't been a second ago.

Tieren's breath seized, and he stared at her in her tight dowo and tunic, her hair in a thick braid draped over a breast. Faced with her exotic beauty, his tongue tied, and he struggled to form words.

"How are you feeling?" She crossed the distance between them, bringing with her the dry aroma of the Coeus Desert.

A fine layer of sand coated her dowo and clung to the thin cloth of her tunic. Her breasts rose and fell with each breath. He dragged his gaze from that mesmerizing action to snag on her eyes.

"Good." Saying anything more would test his mental abilities.

She smiled, caught a thread on his dowo, and tugged on it. "Want to shower?"

"Shower?" He caught her trembling fingers and brought them to his lips. Her warmth seeped into him, and he pulled, easing her closer.

"My version of bathing." She frowned, resting her palm on his chest. "I don't have clothes for you."

"May we return home?" Ghilian hovered behind Tieren.

Mick pursed her lips. "We're waiting for the darkness of night to collect the broken shuttle."

"I'll drop you off and do that, along with the remaining tag and bags." NOX strode into the medical bay, setting shelves and the pod to rights, before nudging his head at Ghilian. "Care for a quick tour?"

Ghilian hesitated, then trailed NOX, leaving Tieren and Mick alone.

Releasing her hands, Tieren wrapped his arms around her, pinning her warm body against his. She gave off heat, as if he basked in sunlight. "We need to talk." With her softness pressing into his body, he couldn't focus past her beautiful brown eyes and the way her breath rasped across his lips.

"Oh?" She glided her hands over his shoulders to tangle in his plumage.

He moaned, arching his back as thrills of iced fire shuddered through him. "*Gawen*, I need you, Mick."

She gasped, "Like in the visions."

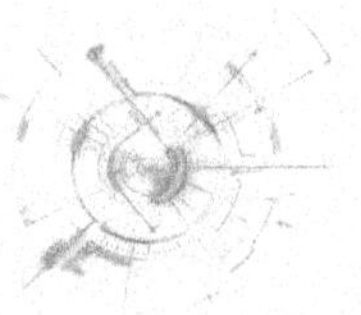

"Yes." A slow, sexy smile spread across his lips and darted fire to her core. "But after a bath."

"My shower—"

"I invite you to enjoy one of my world's pleasures, Mick." He stroked her hair behind her ear. His touch was so slight, yet every one of her nerves focused on it like charged electrons.

She shivered and opened her mouth to accept.

"Descending. Darkness in nine minutes and twenty-three seconds."

She glared at the ceiling, swearing NOX was programmed to cockblock her fun. When she settled her focus on Tieren again, he stared at her, his gaze warmed.

Descending with exquisite slowness, he paused his mouth an inch from hers. Their breaths mingled, and with his heated stare, both pulsed her heartbeat to adrenaline levels. The rush of her blood through her veins deafened her. Thump-thump pierced the din, and she latched onto it, onto Tieren's heartbeats. Hers calmed, matching his, yet that intense fluttering in her chest remained.

When his lips brushed across hers, the warmth, the plump softness of his mouth, and his exotic flavor drove away her thoughts. She succumbed, melting into his embrace. Her breath hitched with a swipe of his tongue. Shivers beset her skin, and she gripped his biceps, trying to be gentle.

A moan tore from him, the sound so primal that it reverberated down her throat. She tilted her head, deepening the kiss. No matter what she did, it wasn't enough. It didn't bring him into her, into every pore.

Running his fingers along her spine exploded bright, white need. She whimpered and wrapped a leg around his thigh. With trembling fingers, she buried them in his hair and held him close. At his guttural growl, heat pooled between her thighs. She flicked her eyelids open to meet his gaze. Hunger and desperation burned.

"Please, Tieren…" She wasn't above begging if it eased the ache thrumming through her.

His breath shuddered, and he pressed his temple to hers. "I want to taste you, Mick, savor every moment. Just a little while longer?" He arched a brow, and she studied his flushed cheeks. His eyes mirrored her desperation.

She uncurled her body from around his and released a sigh when cool air slithered between them. "Do...?" Her voice rasped, and she cleared her throat. "Do you want a tour?"

"From here to the shuttle is tour enough for me." He closed his eyes for a moment, clenching his fists at his side. "I can't focus on your ship, Mick, not when I want you this much."

She cupped his fist, and when he unfurled it, she laced her fingers through his. "Come."

As she led him to the docking bay, she tried not to sneak glances, at his bare chest, at the impressive package tenting his shredded pants. Holy friggin' hell. Focus. Shuttle, land, bath, sex, and in that order. She ushered him inside the shuttle and strapped him into the seat, stroking his chest when she secured the belt. He hissed and gripped her hip, casting a heated look at her. A warning. It spiked her excitement, and she flashed him an unrepentant smile.

Ghilian and NOX stopped her from catching Tieren's lips with hers when they leaped inside.

She huffed. "Ready to depart?"

"Righto, captain." The door slid shut, almost trapping his metallic ass. "I'll drop you off first. Might as well attend to the final creatures while the *Jinsei* collects the old shuttle." He tapped his forearm. "Call when you're ready for pickup."

She didn't want to think about leaving Tieren just yet. Dad's amulet hummed, and she patted it, as if that would calm it. When she was next on Rebirth, she would show it to Nielson. Maybe he could study it and discover its origins and purpose.

NOX answered Ghilian's questions while he strapped him into one of the flip-down seats before assuming the pilot seat. She wasn't going to fight NOX for control when she could snuggle with Tieren along the journey. Besides, when she disembarked, she couldn't be piloting.

Tieren didn't complain when she climbed into his lap. He tucked her head beneath his chin and looped his arms around her, cradling her close to him. With his steady heartbeats thumping in her ear, the whine and groan of the descending shuttle didn't bother her. She couldn't remember when she had last felt...secure, cherished. Perhaps as a young girl, when she'd climbed onto her father's lap and listened to him wax poetic about a new creature in his menagerie.

Tilting her face, she pressed her lips to Tieren's neck, reveling in these emotions he raised within her. If she didn't know better, she would say she was falling— She jerked. *Holy frig. No, it couldn't be.*

His grip tightened, and he twisted to meet her gaze. "What's the matter, Mick?"

She grinned, unable to contain the joy within her. "Nothing."

Doubts pinged across her mind, snatching her happiness. He might not feel the same, and besides, she'd leave him soon. The most she could hope for was a few passionate nights.

Dipping her chin to her chest, she tried to hide her sadness. Tears burned behind her eyes, and her need to cry twitched her nose. She was being silly. Love didn't happen this quickly. Whatever she was feeling was the burn of attraction, nothing more.

She burrowed into his embrace, needing to savor each moment. In love or not, it felt good to be held.

Chapter Thirty-One

SOLIDIFYING THE BOND

Year: 2364

Tau Ceti

The Cetus Constellation

MICK STEPPED ONTO THE platform, gaping at the high peaks in ebony rock, the churning ocean meters below, and the disappearing shuttle as NOX attended to the final tag and bags. Part of her didn't want him to do it alone, worried, but another part of her thrummed with excitement to share this with him. He needed a new suit, and she would damn well get him one. If she could order a humanoid one, even better. On the long, quiet trips between planets, when she missed Tieren, NOX could hug her. She shoved that thought aside, not wanting to trigger unhappiness. She'd yet to ask Tieren to join her.

A stone bridge spanned from the platform to a dark entrance at the base of the mountain. Ghilian crossed it without another word. Tieren snagged her hand and led her in the opposite direction. Beneath the tall spires with massive golden rings was another cave. Warm air fanned her face as a white-robed man hurried toward them.

"Welcome, *tsuna*." He flicked a glance over Mick before bowing. "And guest."

"A private pool." Tieren's imperious tone surprised her.

She dipped her head to hide her awe. Wow, if her body didn't hum, pooling heat in her loins. If he spoke sweet nothings in that tone, she just might see the stars sooner.

He tugged her behind him. They trailed the robed man, who scurried along the rock-carved passage, twisting, and turning until he gestured with a wide sweep to an arched doorway. Without hesitation, Tieren pulled her inside.

The pool was about two meters in diameter, and the darkening green indicated how deep it went. Tendrils of steam rose from the emerald surface. Beside it was a stack of towels, a row of soaps, a jug, and silver goblets. She sniffed, picking up hints of florals and spices, and the sweetness of *jaketta* wine. Glowing stones embedded in the dark rock walls cast off a steady light like entombed candles.

"This is...beautiful." She grimaced at her whisper.

He chuckled and ripped off what remained of his trousers. Heat of another sort flushed her face, and she gasped, unable to drag her gaze from him. She ogled him, as if she hadn't seen him this...exposed. Muscles rippled along his thighs, an impressive, ridged erection bobbed under her perusal, smooth obsidian skin stretched over a taut stomach to his nipple-less chest. She swallowed past the lump in her throat, uncaring that she couldn't breathe. He spun to remove his boots, revealing his carved backside and the hair streaming down his back in wild abandonment.

The water ended mid-calf when he stepped into the pool. He lowered himself with a groan, spread his arms along the edge, then settled his gaze on her.

Right. His turn for a show? She shivered, blaming the moist air for her pebbled nipples. Unstrapping her boots, she tugged those off first. Then peeled off her cargo pants, taking the time to fold and balance them on her boots. Off came her tank top, and she faced him to unclip her bra and slither out of her panties.

"Where are the ledges?" She dipped a toe into the water and hummed at its perfect temperature.

"Around the circumference." His hoarse voice summoned another shiver, and she hurried to slide into the green depths.

Closing her eyes on a soft moan, she let the heat melt through her tension. A quick dunk soaked her hair. She nestled onto the ledge and unraveled her wet braid, tossing the band to the side. His gaze didn't shift from her, prickling her skin under his attention.

"This is better than my shower." She smiled, but it faded under his intense expression.

"Your amulet is familiar to me."

Her interest piqued. "It is? I found it among my father's things. It hums, but I don't know what triggers it."

He closed the distance between them, his proximity suffocating the air out of her lungs. Seated next to her, he swept the amulet into his palm. It hummed, as if on cue. She didn't know what to focus on; Tieren close enough to touch and one hundred percent naked, or that the amulet had reacted to him.

"This is Greeven, Mick." Seriousness cooled the ardor in his eyes.

"Oh?" She took it from him and swiped a thumb over the muscled hawk. It did look like him. "I wish I knew how Dad came by it. He might have journaled it, but I don't have the heart to read through his notes." Her breath shuddered, as the dormant sorrow cinched her chest. She would forever miss him.

Tieren tugged the amulet free from her hand and draped it, letting it fall between her breasts. With a trembling hand, he rubbed his palm over a nipple.

She gasped when a different heat burned outward, curled in her belly, and tingled her nerve endings.

His gaze snagged hers while he tormented her, tweaking, feathering, cupping, until she writhed, unable to ease the throbbing in her core. At her whimper, he pulled away and chose a bar of soap.

"Come, the sooner we bathe, the sooner—" He bit his bottom lip and captured her hand to place the soap on her palm. "My vision of you is in my bed, *kekaseea*. We can return here afterward, to ease the soreness between your thighs." He stilled, squeezing his eyes shut. His nostrils flared, and the grip he had on the pool's edge was white-knuckled.

After caressing the amulet's chain, his touch searing her skin, he pushed away, settling on the opposite side of the pool. He soaped, and with every rinse, rested his gaze on her. She made quick work of the washing part, wanting to sit back, savor the hot water lapping at her, and watch him as he bathed. Stripteases be damned. This 'show' was tantalizing, arcing her desire until her thumping heartbeat drowned out twittering creatures, whispers from others bathing, and the ocean's waves crashing against the rock.

Rising from the pool and climbing out, he unfolded a robe and held it for her. She pulled herself onto the rocky floor, slipped into the robe, and let him wrap and secure it around her. Naked, he padded barefoot along the path.

She pointed behind her. "But...my things..."

"Will be delivered to my chambers." His impatient strides meant she had to hurry to keep up.

"You're naked, Tieren." She hesitated to point that out, lest he hid such beauty from her, but passing Greeven gaped, albeit at her.

Standing on the platform where NOX had delivered them, she peered over the edge at the waves below. Something large slithered around the island. Tiny gray creatures clambered over the rocks.

"Battusks."

At his voice, she settled her gaze on him. A wince preceded the popping and cracking when his wings sprouted from his shoulders. She gaped. Seeing them always sent a rush of excitement through her. When he gripped her hips and launched them skyward, she squealed, throwing her arms around his neck.

She wasn't scared he would drop her, nor did she fear she wouldn't survive a fall. The suddenness of the act, when he had said it was rude to fly her anywhere, was what had her clinging to him. Not that she had the time to admire the disappearing bridge, the glimmer of moonlight off the rings, or the many platforms they flew past. The wind whipped her wet hair, but with her mutations, she didn't feel the chill for long.

"Your speed is incredible." She flicked her hair out of her face when he landed on another platform close to the apex of the mountain.

With another grimace, he vanished his wings and tugged on her robe, unraveling it. It pooled at her feet, leaving her bare for his hungry gaze, she kept her hands at her sides, letting him look his fill.

"I hate to intrude..."

At the feminine voice, Tieren leaped in front of Mick to shield her. "Nona, this is a surprise."

Mick twisted to peer around him. His familiar features on the woman's face announced the connection.

The older woman chuckled. "An unwanted one." In a navy-blue robe embroidered with silver thread, she waddled closer, nudging Tieren aside to rest her pale gaze on Mick.

With a tilt of her chin, Mick didn't bother hiding despite the urge to do so. If there was one thing her dreams had shown her was that Tieren and the Greeven weren't bothered by nudity.

"This is your *kekaseea*?" The older woman circled her. "She is darker than me but lighter than you, a middle ground." She tapped her chin, but her eyes twinkled with mirth. "I can see why the *Gawen* chose you. Call me Nona, and welcome to the family."

A lump in Mick's throat choked her and summoned tears. Tieren had yet to explain this *kekaseea* nonsense. Mate he had called her. She had thought their relationship was fleeting, a few nights and done. Now, having a new family as his 'mate' hadn't occurred to her. She'd been alone for so long. Dipping her chin, she tried to hide her silly tears. They showed up when she least needed them to. Saying goodbye to Tieren meant no more family. Loneliness settled over her like a dark cloud.

Tieren circled his arm around her, snapping her from her somber thoughts. She bowed and lifted her gaze to meet the older woman's. "Thank you, Nona. Please, call me Mick or Mikaela."

The older woman shuffled toward the door. "Come for tea when you're...done." She giggled as the door closed behind her.

"That was unexpected." Tieren chuckled and scooped Mick into his embrace. "Now, where were we?"

Mick splayed her fingers across his chest. He hissed, proving how sensitive he was to her touch despite the lack of nipples. The tremor racing along his skin verified her findings when she ran her thumbs along the peaks where his nipples would have been.

"Something about easing the soreness between my thighs?" She pressed her lips to the dimple in his chin, ran her mouth along his sharp jaw, and sucked on his earlobe.

His breath caught, then he released it on a laugh. "I'm nervous." He ushered her back until her legs hit his bed. "There are differences between our species, and even though the visions revealed how to address those, my hearts want to leap from my chest." He cupped her cheeks, holding her still for a sweet kiss. "I have never wanted a female more."

Sharing how he reacted to her was precious, but as much as she wanted to jump him, she needed to understand. "*Kekaseea, Tieren*. Explain it to me."

He stilled, then brushed the curls off her face, trailing his touch along her jaw. "My mate as revealed by the *Gawen* and our shared visions." He ran his fingers down her throat, across her collarbone to her shoulders, then gathered her close.

"And what does being your mate entail?" She hoped he mentioned hours on her back.

"You're mine, Mick. Mine to cherish—"

"To protect, I remember." She smiled, trying to ease the tension tightening his arms around her. "Give me the limitations, the full impact it will have on my life."

He shifted, spreading his legs wide to nestle her between them. "We cannot be apart."

She gasped and gripped his biceps. "I have to stay on Cetus?" Never see a nebula, a dwarf star, the infinite velvet of space? Instead, endless days doing nothing awaited her.

His muscles rippled under her touch, reminding her that he was naked. That she was naked. Where her breasts squished against his chest, his warmth seeped into her skin.

"No, I stay with you."

She froze. Her eyes widened. Persistent tears clogged her throat. "You would leave your home?"

"Braon doesn't need me anymore, and I want to see what you've seen, Mick." His smile was tremulous but no less beautiful. "If you'll have me?"

Tears slipped free, and she yanked him against her, laughing and crying into the curve of his throat. "Yes, please, yes."

"Good." Crushing his mouth across hers, he squeezed her ass and lifted her to deepen the kiss.

Warmth, joy, and need bombarded her senses, affecting her breathing. She wanted his hands all over her, his lips. He carried her, kneeled, then crawled to sprawl her onto his bed. When he withdrew, he trailed his fingers from her shoulders, along her collarbone, between her cleavage to dip into her belly button.

Fire accompanied his touch, and she shivered, not sure she could bear more of this.

"Let me learn what pleases you, Mick." He stroked a finger along her inner thigh, pausing an inch from the curls hiding her sex.

She drew in a calming breath, closed her eyes, and spread her legs. Her senses burst to the fore, the heat of him near her knees, the spicy fragrance of his skin, her erratic heartbeat matching his, and the slow caress of his fingers across her skin, climbing, nearing the apex of her desire.

When he penetrated her soft folds, stroked across the nub, she moaned, tensing from a wave of exquisite heat. Her limbs trembled, but under his continued onslaught, she dared not move. How she reacted now would determine future intimacy. Restraining her hips, arching, and writhing took all her control. His touch thrummed fire through her core. She needed him to quicken his fingers, to not stop. Whimpering, she gave up control and released her body to the pleasure he summoned from her.

"Tieren, please." She spread her thighs wider and buried her fingers into his bedding.

When he sucked one of her taut nipples into her mouth, shivers rippled outward. She arched off the bed on a strangled cry, riding a wave of sheer bliss, the kind where her brain mimicked stellar explosions.

As she settled, floating down from the best orgasm ever, his adoring kisses across her breasts, on her hips, and fingertips tugged on her heart. His weight nestling between her thighs drew her dazed focus, and she eagerly clung to his shoulders, urging him on.

The pressure at her apex stilled her, then inch-by-inch he slid into her, stretching her. His gaze snagged hers, and he waited after every push, studying her reactions. He trembled as if he struggled to restrain himself.

She kissed him. "Breathe."

He smiled, rested his weight on one arm, and cupped her cheek. "Mick."

The way he said her name like she meant the world to him, fluttered her heart. "I've got you, Tieren." Wrapping her legs around his waist, she thrust her hips up, burying him to the hilt.

He growled, then stilled. "*Gawen*, Mick, you feel...heaven-sent." Shuddering, he withdrew and thrust again, stroking every nerve ending.

Relishing and craving him, she angled her hips, meeting his thrusts. Renewed joy skittered along her skin, her spine, to nestle at her core. "Harder."

He grunted and slammed into her, rocking her back. She offered her body to him, overwhelmed by the rush of fiery need tingling from her neck to her nipples and inflaming her core. *Holy frig.* Stars exploded across her vision and rushed along her senses. She screamed his name.

He roared, pinning his pelvis to the backs of her thighs, digging his fingers into her hips, and stilled. With his arched back, his teeth dimpling his bottom lip, she had never seen anyone sexier. He slumped, crushing her, then rolled her over but cradled her closer while he fought to breathe.

"You're mine to cherish, to protect." She lifted herself to meet his gaze.

He raised a brow and smirked. "Is that so?"

"Want to challenge me?" She swirled a pattern along his collarbone.

"This is forever, Mick." His seriousness startled her.

Instead of panic seizing her chest, an acceptance flooded warmth through her. "I know."

He captured the amulet in his hand, then flipped it open. She gaped, having not known it was a locket. She twisted to peek inside, then frowned. At the center was a spike and nothing else. He pressed his thumb onto it. His white blood stained the metal when he offered her the locket.

"Now you."

She lowered her thumb. A pinch preceded her red blood streaked with blue blending with his. He flipped the locket shut, then crushed her against him for a kiss. Lost in the skilled sweep of his tongue, it took her a moment to notice the strange tugging on her soul.

"Do you feel that?" She paused and flexed her fingers on his shoulder.

He grinned. "Yes." Then rolled her over and kissed her again.

CHAPTER THIRTY-TWO

LET THEM HAVE IT
Year: 2364
Rianus
In the city of Qilaetor
The Royal Chambers

THE CHAMBER DOOR BANGED open, and guards burst in. Their regalia was familiar. Cousin Karlez sauntering in confirmed it. Sighing, Tieren blinked the sleep out of his eyes and threw his legs over the side. With a glance at a curious Mick, he trailed an admiring gaze over her hooded eyes, tousled hair, those lips he had sampled so many times and would do so again, soon.

"What is the meaning of this, cousin?" He shifted, shielding Mick with his chest. Though nudity wasn't an issue to Greevens, he didn't like Karlez gazing at her. "Leave."

Karlez helped himself to wine. He sipped, then smacked his lips. "Consider yourself usurped."

Tieren laughed. "Your timing is perfect." Karlez targeted the wrong royal. He'd always been a fool. "But alas, Braon doesn't need my protection anymore, and..." Tieren tutted, "...your plumage isn't pure enough."

"Braon is a squawkling, and while his Trial of Tolend is unknown..." Karlez shrugged, sucking on his fingers after snacking on a sliver of *ersik* fruit.

It was a day's trip from the mainland. Pengfei would escort Braon and Wyatt to Qilaetor, so poor Karlez hadn't heard the news yet.

"I wouldn't want to be you when Braon arrives." Tieren smirked. Revealing what Braon had killed in his Trial wouldn't be believed, so Tieren held his tongue.

"Bringing in this...female has worsened your situation." Karlez's belittling tone shot fury through Tieren, and he leaped off the bed to march across the room.

"*Tsunari* Mikaela, cousin, so insult her again, and I'll have your wings." He vibrated with restrained fury, praying Karlez challenged him as Assalan had done.

"Tieren, who is this person?" Clutching the sheet to her chest, Mick halted beside him.

"My cousin," he said through gritted teeth.

"What do you mean *tsunari*?" Karlez demanded in Greeven, flicking his gaze between Tieren and Mick, frowning when they conversed in her language.

"Ah, so family?" She sighed. "I can't kill him?"

At her question, the red blurring Tieren's vision eased. He chuckled and folded his arms across his chest. "And how would you end his life?"

"I could snap his neck." She clicked her fingers. "He won't see it coming."

"Yes, I have seen you fight." Tieren slipped his arm around her and pressed a kiss to her temple. "Your skills are breathtaking, Mick."

"So, no to killing him." She snuggled into his embrace, splaying her fingers across his chest. "If they try to hurt you though..."

"Yours to protect." He winked.

"Tieren," Karlez roared, no doubt frustrated at being ignored. His guards shifted, preparing themselves to strike.

Tieren was done with this pointless banter and threats. None of it mattered anymore. He frowned, gazing passed them to the corridor through the gaping doors. Where were his males? If Karlez had them killed, cousin or not, he would die.

Mick straightened her posture, tightened her muscles, then tied a knot in the sheet, keeping it in place. She flexed her fingers into fists, her intent clear.

"Karlez, this is my *kekaseea*." Tieren strode to an alcove, selecting a tunic and a pair of dowo off a carved shelf.

He offered Mick the tunic, then pulled on the dowo. All gazes rested on her when she switched between the sheet and the tunic. Tieren growled a warning, snapping their attention to him.

Karlez gaped. "How?" He flicked a dismissive wrist. "It doesn't matter. I hereby relinquish you of your title."

"With what authority?" Tieren leaned to the side to peer around Karlez. "Where is the Auviphis Order? Nor do I see Ambassador Sugard with you." He chuckled, unable to take Karlez's threats seriously. "And once Nona hears of this, your fate might be like General Assalan's."

Karlez gasped, his pale cheeks darkening. "You would dare—?"

"I dare nothing." Tieren poured a goblet of wine and offered it to Mick. "When will we be leaving Rianus?"

"Whenever you're ready." She sipped the wine and hummed her appreciation, snagging his focus.

His nostrils flared, and he sucked in a sharp breath. "In a few days. I haven't had my fill of you."

Her eyelashes fluttered, casting shadows on her flushed cheeks. He was done entertaining his cousin. Time with Mick was all Tieren wanted.

"Enough," Karlez snapped. "What language are you speaking?"

"English," Mick squawked. She downed the wine, then crushed the goblet with her fingers. "Now, I suggest you leave. My opinion of you is low, and you lack the backbone to be a prince." She dropped the mangled goblet into Karlez's frozen hands.

Tieren grinned at the authority in her voice. She made the perfect *tsunari*.

"Kill her."

At Karlez's order, Tieren roared, bursting forward to grip his cousin by the throat. Mick blurred between the guards until they sprawled on the floor, unmoving.

"I warned you, cousin," Tieren hissed an inch from Karlez's gray-tinged face.

"What...what is she?" Karlez croaked.

Tieren arched a brow. "That's what you ask as your life drains?"

Karlez gurgled.

"Since you're dying, let me share this. Braon killed a bebbayaya without assistance."

Karlez's eyes bulged before he died. Tieren released him, letting his body slump to the floor.

"Wow, what an awesome life you live, Tieren." She danced around the bodies to throw herself into his arms.

"Says the female who hunts creatures?" He spun her and snatched a kiss. Along the bridge to the stairs lay his guards, thankfully unconscious and unharmed, for the most part. With Mick's assistance, he dragged his males into his chambers, all to ensure they didn't roll off the ledge and plummet to their deaths. They would awaken in relative safety.

Lacing his fingers through hers, Tieren tugged her to the door. "Come, let us visit Nona and my surrogate family."

She followed him down the spiral stairs. "Your what?"

"I grew up in the Labyrinth where my plumage matters not."

She scowled. "When the universal genetic database captured the DNA from all newborns, the idea of purists fell to the wayside. The purity of their DNA was called into question. Judging people by their skin color no longer occurs in mainstream galactic living." Her fingers trembled where they touched the wall. "I'm furious it still exists on Rianus, Tieren, but until your technology advances, I can do nothing but fit in."

"I don't know what DNA means, but there is much you will teach me. You are too unique to blend into the crowd, Mick." He brought their clasped hands to his lips for a brief kiss. "I want you to meet Rassin, Meilo, and Zabbica after we visit Nona."

Her breath released on a sigh. "What is Nona to you?"

Tieren paused on a stone step to look at her. "My mother's mother."

Mick grinned. "Your *grand*mother, and now mine to protect."

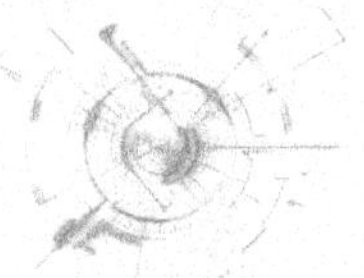

ON THE NEXT LEVEL, Tieren led her along the passage without a railing. Made sense when everyone had wings. A violent sea-scented gust whipped across the slab, whistling in her ears. Distant cries, squawks, and twittering merged with the waves crashing onto the rocks below. Ahead stood two guards with brilliant white hair and skin and resplendent in golden armor.

"Gold?" She stretched out a finger to stroke the breastplate, then snatched it back, lest she offended.

"A rare metal once mined far south of Claren Circle, in the realm of Levion."

"Once mined?" She trailed him, past the vigilant guards.

"The Drueen have become cantankerous, restricting access to the gold resources."

Before she could ask what a droo-een was, he urged her to sit on a stone cube. She hurried to tug the tunic lower and tuck it under her thighs, preserving her modesty. When Nona had seen her naked? She snorted.

"Is it official? I apologize for my poor timing." Nona clicked her fingers, and a servant offered Mick a wine-filled goblet. "I heard you were home, and I needed to know how Braon fairs."

"He is well." Tieren stood behind Mick and rested his hand on her shoulder.

Nona squirmed in her chair, carved with muscular hawks Mick now recognized as Greeven. "Feathers of the *Gawen*, Tieren, just tell me. What did he kill?"

Tieren chuckled. "A bebbayaya."

Nona gaped. Her cheeks turned ashen, then flushed bright white. "Do not tease me so."

"Much has happened, but it is best Braon bears the tale. My knowledge could be misconstrued as involvement."

She harumphed, then settled her blue gaze on Mick. "Tieren says you're a star traveler."

"Yes," Mick squawked, then rubbed her lacerated throat. She offered an apologetic smile before glancing at Tieren. "I wish your grandmother could speak English."

He winked. "Well, ask her if she would like to learn."

Facing the older woman, Mick hesitated. She didn't want to offend, but speaking the guttural Greeven tongue was tiresome. "Nona, would you like to learn my language?"

The woman jerked back, then shook her head. "I am much too old to learn a new language, *abucaah*."

Mick rose and knelt beside her. "Please, trust me."

Tieren chuckled. "I was as skeptical. It will take a few moments, and at worst, you will bear a headache."

Nona gasped. "What sorcery is this?"

Mick shrugged. "Those without fire consider the flames sorcery. My universe has many things I'd believe are miracles. This is possible. It's how I learned to speak…Greeven." She coughed, rubbing her throat again. "I'm not designed to speak your tongue."

Nona rested her hand on Mick's. "I will try."

Tapping her wrist, Mick called to NOX in English. "Please, scan Nona, and make sure she can endure learning English. If so, then leak it. Nothing too sharp, too strong. I want the tiniest headache or none at all."

"On it, boss lady."

Nona squeaked, but instead of sliding away from the disembodied voice of NOX, she grabbed Mick's forearm, giving it a good shake.

Mick layered her hand over Nona's and smiled. "It's my…servant, NOX."

"Scan's complete. Activating language transmittal now." NOX hummed a song, and, by the background tap-tap-tap, he danced to it too. "Regarding the results, it's best if you pod the woman."

"What?" Mick twisted to settle her gaze on Tieren. Ice slithered down her spine to churn nausea in her belly. "Why?"

"She has a lung infection that should be hindering her breathing, but she's hiding this and her pain."

Concern furrowed Tieren's brow. He closed the distance between them and joined Mick in front of Nona to capture her frail hand in his. "Nona, NOX tells me you are not well."

The older woman trembled, then with a pinch of her lips, nodded. "The healers do not bring good news, but how is it you know?"

Tieren growled and lowered his head, as if he fought to control his temper. "Will you suffer through a trip to Mick's ship?"

Nona sighed and offered a twitch of a sad smile. "The journey to the Forest of Iliana was too much for my frail bones, *abucaah*."

Tieren sliced a glance at Mick. She understood what he was asking. A short time in the pod might heal her. They had to try.

She tapped her arm. "NOX, bring a shuttle."

"Already on my way, Mick, and I have prepped the pod."

Tieren smiled and patted Nona's hand. "Soon you will see how Mick saved my life."

"You were in danger?" Nona settled her gaze on Mick, her eyes warming to the blue of a Prime Earth summer sky. "I have not heard you were—"

"The bebbayaya caught me in a full swing of its mandible while we tried to save one of Mick's friends."

"Let me look at you." Nona pushed off the chair onto her wobbling knees.

Rising as well, Tieren spun in a circle with his arms outstretched, then stilled, enduring a thorough examination. Mick smothered a smile at the motherly affection pouring off Nona. She hovered her hands along his back, his shoulders, and twisted his arms to check for hidden wounds.

"There's not a scratch on you." She faced Mick. "I see why he trusts you. At first, I was concerned. You are not of Rianus. But when he carried you like a sack of flour and gifted you with a bonding amulet, then I knew, all was as it should be."

Stroking the chain, Mick arched her brow at 'bonding amulet.'

A knock sounded, and in scurried Ghilian, carrying her boots and folded clothes. She grinned, rose to her feet, and darted to him. "Thank you, Ghilian. I feel a little exposed."

He frowned at her but said nothing, letting her swipe the bundle out of his hands before circling her to reach Tieren.

Mick tugged on panties under her tunic, then her cargo pants. Tall panels provided a secluded area to change, so she slipped behind them and donned the bra and tank top. Oh, to be clothed again. Stamping her boots on, she draped the tunic over her arm and joined Tieren. He pulled on the tunic and captured her for a quick kiss. She lingered on his lips, aching for the feel of their softness across hers.

"*Atsuna*, it is good to see you well. Ghilian spins a most outlandish tale."

"You're not Ghilian?" Mick gaped. "You look just like him."

Tieren laughed. "Mick, Meilo doesn't speak English."

"Oh." Her cheeks warmed.

"I have summoned the Auviphis Order to deal with the bodies in your chambers." Meilo tutted. "First Assalan, then Karlez."

Nona huffed. "I expected as much. He was always an impatient male. No news of Braon's success has reached us. He must have thought now the best time to challenge for the throne."

"It's a good thing you are beloved," Tieren teased. "I cannot fathom why neither of them saw you as a threat."

Nona giggled, and her bright smile removed years off her countenance. "What can little, old me do?"

Tieren scoffed. "You command the Auviphis until Braon is crowned."

"But they do not know this." Nona shrugged. "They assume you do, and I would like to keep it that way."

A humming snapped Mick's focus to the platform. "NOX is here." She needn't have said anything, for in strode NOX in all his metallic glory and with far too much energy.

Nona squeaked with her eyes wide. "NOX?"

"Yes." Tieren captured her hand and slipped it through his bent arm. He steered her toward the platform.

She paused at the sight of the gaping shuttle. It hovered on the edge of the platform with a negligible space between the stone and metal flooring. As she stepped across with ease, Mick slipped past Tieren to buckle her *grandmother* in. This was her family now. She beamed, unable to restrain the wave of joy that fluttered her heartbeat.

"The smoothest ride, NOX." She gripped the bulkhead and snagged Tieren's hand at the same time. Meilo hovered on the platform. NOX held the door open, his stoic face expectant.

Tieren smiled. "We shall return. Let Zabbica know we will visit soonest."

Relief slumped Meilo's shoulders, and he shuffled backward as if the shuttle might bite. His nervousness made sense. She looked like them except for the number of her fingers and toes, but her technology screamed her strangeness.

Tieren whispered to Nona as NOX piloted the shuttle to the *Jinsei*. Mick watched their interaction, able to listen without trying, when he described to Nona how he met Mick, what happened afterward, and the intrusion of the bebbayaya. At his sweet care, warmth barreled up from her core, pooled in her belly, and exploded in her chest. This was *her* man.

"Mick, Dr. Nielson sent a message." NOX's metallic voice sliced through her daze.

"He did? What did he say?"

NOX nudged his head at the empty pilot chair, and she settled into it. Nielson's face appeared on a side mini-vid. She leaned an elbow on the console and listened.

"Ms. Danvers, I need a live replica of the hokou that bit you. It must be as infected. How quickly can you find one?" The screen flickered black.

She frowned. "Friggin hell, NOX, like that's easy."

"It's quite a distance to travel, Mick. We're talking the opposite side of the known universe."

He didn't need to tell her. She spun the chair to settle her gaze on Tieren. He would come with her, he'd said. Taking him to Rebirth would introduce him to space travel. But if he didn't like it, she'd planned to return to Rianus and perhaps call this planet her home.

This hokou mission wasn't a guaranteed success. She tapped the chair's arm, twisting her lips while she considered the options. "NOX, will we be able to scan packs of hokou and pick up a diseased one, or do I need to tag them all?"

"I should be able to modify the reconnaissance scanners to seek out your original mutation. You might have to tag those hokou within range."

She sighed. Okay, so not the entire hokou population, but still, how many could there be in a troop?

The shuttle juddered when it breached the atmosphere. She relinquished the chair to grant Nona an unhindered view of the fore vids.

The older woman gasped, then patted her eyes, catching tears on her fingertips. "That is Rianus and our suns?"

"Breathtaking, isn't it, Nona?" Tieren pressed a kiss to her temple.

She laughed and swatted him away, then squeezed his forearm. "Thank you, Tieren and Mick for insisting I come. I can die a happy female."

Minutes later, when the pod's dome enclosed Nona, Tieren looped his arms around Mick from behind, folding them under her breasts. "Thank you, Mick, for doing this."

She swept his gratitude aside with a wobbly smile. "I'm doing this for my family." And she meant it.

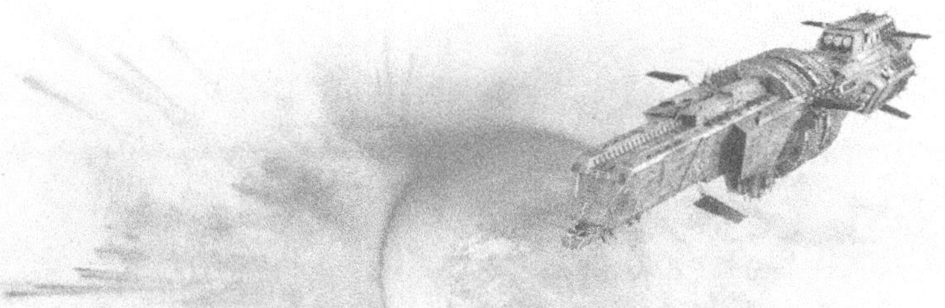

Chapter Thirty-Three

HEARTS CONTENT
Year: 2364
Rianus
In the city of Qilaetor
The Labyrinth

Tieren couldn't smother his smile. Fully healed by Mick's magical pod, Nona danced with Meilo as if she was a squawkling. Her eyes twinkled as bright as her glowing cheeks. Mick taught Ghilian how to arm wrestle. Even though he and Ghilian knew of her phenomenal strength, they had been at it for a while. Zabbica served platters of fruit, weaving between the Labyrinth inhabitants. A giggling Hali clung to a dancing Rassin, her face flushed. Imsal smoked a pipe, waving an arm in animated gestures as he retold the times of war. A small band of males played their instruments, merging from one song to another. Tieren tapped his foot along with the beat and raised a goblet to his lips.

Meilo relinquished an inexhaustible Nona to another dance partner and strode toward him. He fell in beside Tieren, his chest rising and falling as he struggled to regain his breath.

"We will miss you, *atsuna*." He accepted the goblet Tieren offered him. Pausing before he took a sip, Meilo sliced a glance at him. "All is readied, and your chest and weapons loaded on the..." he frowned, "...shuzzle?"

It took all Tieren's control not to chuckle. Instead, he left Meilo uncorrected. "Thank you, my friend." He faced the crowds with his focus remaining on Meilo. "Promise me you will protect Braon and Nona."

Meilo nodded. "Ghilian and I will not fail you, *atsuna*."

Tieren slapped him on the shoulder. "You have never failed me. I am the blessed male to have such loyal friends."

Meilo's eyes glazed, and he lowered his chin to his chest. "This isn't forever, is it, *atsuna*?"

"No." Tieren grinned, rocking on his heels. "I look forward to no obligations, Meilo. To learn new things and to spend time with my *kekaseea*." On cue, he searched for Mick, but when he found her not with Ghilian, he scanned the crowd. The cold fear crushing his chest eased when she danced past with Hali on her hip. Other squawklings trailed her, skipping and singing. Every few steps, she swapped squawklings, swinging them until they squealed with delight.

"If she was not yours...," Ghilian said by way of greeting. He grinned, showing he was teasing. "The evening is drawing to a close." He gestured to the dwindling bonfire at the center of the market square. "Meilo has packed Imsal's armor as well, Tieren. We're not sure what you might encounter...up there." He pointed with a finger to the rock ceiling.

"I'll be fine, mother."

Ghilian's cheeks flushed, but he pushed past his embarrassment with a fake-aged voice. "Do take care, *abucaah*. You are not redundant, yet."

Tieren threw an arm across his and Meilo's shoulders, yanking them into a hug. "Any news on Braon?"

"He and Wyatt are crossing to Qilaetor as we speak."

Meilo grinned. "We await Pengfei's announcement."

Pengfei. Tieren would miss him, but the male wouldn't be free for a while. Once he announced what Braon had killed, he and the Auviphis Order would return to the scene to verify the claim. Only when they docked at Qilaetor with confirmation would Braon be crowned.

Tieren didn't want to wait for the inevitable. As Mick danced past, he released Meilo and Ghilian and lunged across to capture her arm. She settled a bright smile on him, fluttering his heartbeat.

Lowering the squawkling, she fluffed their plumages, then slid into his arms. "Is it time?"

His chest swelled when she snuggled against him. "Yes." Excitement pulsed through him, and he tightened his hold.

"I could sleep." She smothered a yawn.

He tucked a curl behind her plugged ear, captured her chin, then raised it for his descending lips. After a sweet kiss, he tucked her into his embrace. "Is NOX close?"

"On my way, my prince."

At NOX's confirmation, Tieren swept through the crowd, bidding his family and an energetic Nona farewell. It had been years since he'd traveled away from his home and for an extended period that he dreaded the tears. This was an exciting time, but he'd miss those dear to him.

"If I had not seen Mick's ship and our beautiful planet on the return trip, I would feel anxious for you." Nona squeezed Mick's arm. "But you are in safe hands, *abucaah*." She kissed Mick's brow and Tieren's cheek. "Bring back wonderful tales and mayhaps a squawkling?"

Tieren snorted. "I will try, especially on the latter."

As he stepped onto the platform, he raised his gaze to the dark sky, seeing the stars as something more than twinkling lanterns. He drew in a deep breath to savor the tang of the ocean below and the heated rock around him.

"We can stay longer."

It was sweet of Mick to offer, but he wanted to clear a path for Braon. Yanking off his tunic, he offered it to her before summoning only his wings. Launching them skyward, he swooped, swirled, dived, and climbed until they touched down onto his platform outside his chambers. A massive chest waited there. He shuddered to think what Meilo had packed for him.

With his wings hidden, he donned the tunic and wrapped his arms around Mick, admiring the view, his chin rested on her shoulder. A blast of warm air blew back his plumage as the shuttle lowered in front of them. The door slid open, and NOX leaped out, lifting the chest as if it weighed nothing. Mick nudged Tieren into the chair, buckled him in, then climbed onto his lap.

NOX closed the door and slid into the other seat, singing a jaunty song about the wind sweeping the plains. Tieren cuddled Mick closer and refused to blink when the shuttle shuddered, then broke free, smoothing as it flew toward the silver-black ship, *Jinsei*. This was his new life, and without watching the image of Rianus disappearing behind them, he smiled.

He was free.

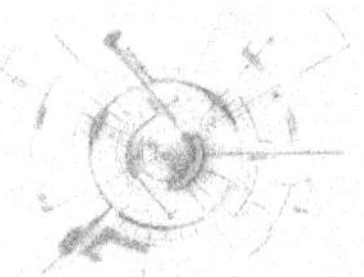

SNUGGLING AGAINST TIEREN'S BODY while Mick surfaced from sleep was the moment she cherished the most. Knowing he was with her, that she was no longer alone, filled her with waves of warmth, of love. She had yet to tell him though, unsure whether his species could love.

It was a silly fear when loving his friends and family was demonstrated at the bonfire. Still, she hesitated. After rubbing his arm wrapped around her, she twisted to kiss his shoulder and along his jaw. He mumbled something but tightened his embrace until every hard dip and rise of his body pressed against hers.

"Morning, *ateeko*." His sweet 'my hearts' squeezed her breath from her lungs. It was just an endearment.

"Morning." She dipped, nuzzling his neck rather than reveal her tears.

"I am almost done with one journal. Your father led a fascinating life." Tieren rubbed his chin across her temple. "It's been four days since we left Rianus, and judging by the number of journals he has, I will be at this for a while."

Tieren had taken to trudging through Dad's journals in the hopes of discovering where and when the amulet had come into play. Between his quiet reading sessions, ravishing her, and NOX teaching him how to pilot, Tieren had fallen into a routine he enjoyed.

Occasionally, he would sing along with NOX, or hum a show tune he couldn't remember the words to.

Mick had never thought she would know contentment. "Wanna shower?"

He flicked an eye open and smiled. "Just shower?" His voice hoarsened when he rubbed a certain hardness across her hip.

"Before you waste another hour, we have an incoming message from Rebirth, marked red alert."

Mick stilled at NOX's intrusion. She flipped out of bed and stumbled, snagging her feet on the sheets. Tapping the vid mounted to one wall, she waited for NOX to put it through.

"Ms. Danvers, Rebirth needs you." Nielson's face dominated the screen. His disheveled hair alarmed her. "An alien creature hitched a ride on one of the mining siphs. We have managed to trap it on a lower level but at a considerable loss of life. Security staff are dying too fast to retrain, and frankly, no one is signing up. I don't blame them. I need *you*, the famous Shikari."

"I'm days away, Dr. Nielson. At full power, I might be able to shave some time off, but not much. How long has it been trapped? What am I dealing with?" She didn't bother responding to the shikari bit, whatever that meant.

"We'll try and keep it trapped. I'll send through what footage we have. Just get here, as fast as you can. Fentus will pay for everything."

The screen flickered from his face to still images of a gray lizard-like creature with four legs and two arms. Webbed fingers merged into razored claws. Armor plated its underbelly, and sharklike teeth ran the edge of its spine to the tip of a thick tail. It had no eyes she could identify, which meant its sense of smell was well-defined. Flesh and tendons matted the saber teeth filling its gaping mouth.

The video footage showed its quick movements, blurring as it leaped and lunged from one security officer to another. Corpses lined the corridors and causeways, and in the background, the pseudo-joyful lighting of the bars flickered. A body slid across the vid, smearing blood on the metallic flooring as it did so. The sharp jerks implied the creature feasted.

The whine of the *Jinsei* shook her free from the shock. NOX had increased the speed, and without her earbuds in, the grind of metal when the ship adjusted to the thrust reverberated in her ears.

"Whoa, what is that?" Tieren circled her waist from behind. The warmth of his chest against her back eased the tension twisting a knot in her belly.

"Something I need to take care of. NOX, find out what the friggin hell Nielson meant by Shikari."

"On it."

Tieren pressed a kiss to her neck. "It looks like a Drueen without their wings."

"You've mentioned them before." She waited for Tieren to continue.

"They live far south of Qilaetor."

She gaped as realization dawned. "Do they change too?"

He nodded. "With larger wingspans than Greeven. They are voracious warriors. We used to be at peace, but maintaining it became too exhausting. They're volatile by nature. For the most part, we avoid each other."

So, NOX steered her and the S.o.S. to the wrong side of the planet, away from finding the dragon-like shifters. She couldn't shield their discovery from the Followers for long, but at least, their exploitation wasn't at her hands.

Spinning within Tieren's embrace, she claimed a short kiss.

He pinched her chin, forcing her to meet his dark gaze. "You are concerned."

"I'm but one mutated woman, Tieren."

"You are not alone." His tone was gentle." Train me to aid you, Mick."

"No, I need you safe." She bit the inside of her cheek, willing her tears to vanish.

"As I need you safe." A slow smile crawled across his lips. "I have just found you, Mick, I cannot lose you."

"You can be my eyes, tell me where it is, where it's heading." She wanted him somewhere inside a security console, far from the action.

He shook his head. "NOX can do that."

"NOX will be with me, herding the creature." Right into her sniper range but her instincts screamed that this would be close combat.

"I can do that."

At Tieren's determination, anger burned a fiery path through her, and she would swear her blood sizzled. "NOX has a metallic body, replaceable. You're not."

"I am a warrior, *ateeko*, with fast reflexes. Do not fear that I cannot aid you."

She pushed away, needing to break the temptation of his body and that bewitching smile. "I...I don't want to worry about you. If it's just me, then I can react instinctively."

He has my heart, can't he tell? Losing him will kill me. She...she couldn't grieve again.

Closing the distance between them, he spun her to face him. "I love you too, but understand this from my perspective. I must be beside you, Mick. You're mine to protect."

She froze. Had she said that aloud? Heat flooded her cheeks. She cupped her face, wishing the floor would swallow her. Her heart thumped in her ears, and her stomach swooped and dived as if it was joyful. "What did you say?"

"Silly female, I love you. I wanted to tell you after your pod healed me but didn't want you to think my love wasn't pure, that I confessed out of gratitude."

She gasped, ignored the tear slipping past her defenses, and launched herself into his arms. "I love you too."

"I know." He grinned, enduring her feathered kisses. "You killed Kir to save me, Mick."

She stilled. Yes, she had.

"To end this argument, I can be beside you and assess the vid footage at the same time." NOX sighed. "You keep forgetting this, Mick."

"I do." She grinned. "Now, be a dear and browse through the A.I. suit catalog. Mommy and Daddy need alone time."

NOX groaned when Tieren swooped in for a kiss.

EPILOGUE

THE SHIKARI

Year: 2364

The way station, Rebirth.

MICK STEPPED OFF THE ramp onto the Rebirth's docking bay. Everything was the same as a week ago: the desanitizer, the crowds, and joyful announcements. With the bustle, the mining siphs traveling between the station and Grus in the distance, she would never have suspected something dangerous lurked in the lower levels.

Tieren spun in circles as he strolled, gaping and gasping like a tourist. She laughed, laced her fingers through his, and tugged.

With security trailing him, Nielson barreled toward her, his cloak flapping. He parted the crowds like Moses had divided the Red Sea.

"Ms. Danvers." He pumped her hand, his smile splitting his cheeks wide. "I'm so relieved you've arrived." Gesturing to Flint on her back, the daggers, and blaster strapped to her person, he spoke to the security behind him. "Give her full clearance, and...her gentleman friend." He blinked at the sword sheathed to Tieren's belt.

Mick hesitated, unsure how to introduce Tieren. NOX came to the rescue, thumping his metallic feet when he jogged to them, splitting the crowds. Folks squealed and dived to the side.

"My prince, your dagger?" NOX flicked the scythe-shaped blade and offered it to Tieren.

"Prince?" Nielson's cheeks flushed, and he twitched between a bow and a curtsey.

She smothered a chuckle. "Of Tau Ceti, or as he calls it, Rianus. I've studied the footage, Dr. Nielson. Where is the creature now?"

Squaring his shoulders, he stepped aside, granting a security officer the opportunity to address her.

"Mikaela, it's good to see you." Daniel grinned, running his gaze over her. "I never thought our rescue would be at your hands. Dr. Nielson assures me you are more than capable."

Tieren growled and shifted between them, his hair ruffling in agitation. "*My* princess."

"Oh." Daniel blushed but threw out a hand. "*Princess* Mikaela, welcome. We have the creature trapped eight levels below. The public pods have been disabled." He tilted to the side, peering around Tieren to make eye contact with her. "The people think it's a gas leak."

She cupped Tieren's elbow, and he jerked, sliced a glance at her, then slid to the side.

"So, a cargo pod?" Gesturing to Daniel to lead the way, she waited until he did, along with his officers. She paused, placed a palm on Tieren's chest, and halted him. "Remember, *ateek*, I love you."

A slow smile curled Tieren's lips. "Noted."

She held his gaze, then nudged her head. "Let's kill this thing. NOX?"

"Patched into the feeds, Mick. It's banging on the pod doors." The thump-thump of NOX's feet granted a small measure of comfort.

"It's intelligent." Visions of a blue-white, ten-tentacled octopus came to mind. Its tilting head had denoted a thought process behind its many eyes.

Daniel picked up the pace, so Mick caught up to Dr. Nielson. "It's best you watch from Security Control."

He hesitated, and when his gaze lowered to the dagger on her belt, he grimaced.

"I'll save the corpse for you, Dr. Nielson."

"Clive." He smiled. "And thanks, Ms. Danvers, for doing this."

"Mick." She hitched her thumb at the exit. "Now get to safety."

Daniel and his secs held the cargo pod open. Dented metallic sides, no windows, and flickering lighting cast an ominous tone to what awaited them. She brushed aside that sharp tug in her stomach.

After the doors shut, the pod chugged downward, with everyone watching the numbers tick. Except for Tieren, who fixed his gaze upon her face.

She laced her fingers through his. "I'll go in first."

Various men voiced their opinion on this, so she released Tieren, formed a fist, and punched the metal side of the pod, molding it into a perfect replica of her hand.

"I said, I'll go in first."

A strained silence thickened the air.

NOX broke it a few minutes later. "It's on the far side of the corridor. Slip in, Mick, and find a high point. I'll stride down the center as a decoy."

It was a good plan, and damaging NOX's A.I. suit was the preferred option.

"We'll hold back and cover you when needed." Daniel tapped the multi-phaser he held to his chest.

"No heroics." She rested her gaze on each man, then for longer on Tieren. "I mean it." Unable to control him and not wanting to, she still needed him safe. The doors opening saved her from saying more.

Shredded bodies litter the floor. The sharp, metallic tang of blood burned her nose. The humid air assaulting her was stale with an acrid stench hinting at urine. No sound other than gaming jingles, sales pitches, faint music from the bars, and electric shorts spluttered and sparked.

She stepped out of the pod.

A high-pitched screech tore through her, the scratching and thudding following it.

"Stay back," she whispered while nudging bodies aside to clear a strip of floor. Unlooping Flint, she dug into her pockets and removed armor-piercing bullets. After sliding one into the barrel, she sprawled on the blood-smeared floor, then lined up the other bullets for easy loading.

"Ready?" NOX hovered to the side.

At her nod, he thump-thumped along the corridor, stomping the bodies in his path. Bones crunched. She winced, silently apologizing to the dead's loved ones.

Another squeal sent shivers along her spine, but she steadied her breathing. The spicy scent of Tieren's skin tickled her nose, and she sighed, accepting that he guarded her while she lay there.

When the creature made its appearance, she gaped for a second, before peering down the scope. The crown of its head brushed the ceiling panels. Red glowed on the edges of its underbelly and at the base of the serrated teeth along its spine. It didn't charge NOX like she'd hoped. It waited, assessing, sniffing her, Tieren, and the sec officers shielding the pod doors.

A deep rumble fluttered the armored plates at its throat. It shuffled its feet, like an enraged bull about to charge a matador.

"What are you waiting for?" she roared.

It tilted its head, assessing her as she scanned its body, searching for weaknesses. But nothing revealed itself. She could only hope the bullets pierced its armor.

When it moved, it took her and NOX by surprise. He flew to the side from a wide swipe of the creature's arm. She didn't take the time to look at him, focusing instead on the creature charging and blurring. Drawing in a deep breath, she held it and fired. It struck, then fell off its body, leaving a red circle. Good, it bled. She fired again, aiming for the same spot, but it twisted at the last moment.

The distance between them was shrinking. One more shot, then she would draw her dagger. But as she fired, so did the sec officers behind her.

Fools. It would only enrage the creature, and now, under a barrage of fire, she was pinned to the ground until they'd exhausted their phasers' power banks.

Time was of the essence. "Halt," she bellowed.

They did.

She leaped, left Flint on the floor, and drew her dagger and blaster. Bolting forward, she zigzagged, leaping over bodies, kicking off the sidewalls, anything to confuse the creature's senses. NOX scrambled up and banged on the wall, spiking sharp reverberations through the corridor. Daniel and his men did the same, moving around to disorientate it.

This bought her the opportunity to close the gap, but she still had to kill it. Vaulting on top of a credits automated teller, she caught a dislodged pipe and swung herself, landing on the creature's back. It squealed, then thrashed, trying to dislodge her. She clung to its ridged spikes, wincing when it sliced into her palm.

Ideas zipped across her mind. She tossed each aside. It reared onto its hind legs, sliding her down. She cried out as the spikes tore at her clothes and skin beneath. Her dagger snagged. She tightened her hold on its hilt. Her legs flailed, but she tucked them in just as the creature landed on its front feet, crunching more bones beneath them. The action plunged her dagger into its flesh.

Another squeal proceeded a violent spin that slipped her farther toward its tail. With one flick, it could dislodge her, despite the wound along its spine. Plunging the dagger under the plates layering its head seemed the best option. Gritting her teeth, she withdrew the dagger and thrust it in higher while gripping the spike for leverage. Withdraw, stab, grip, and repeat with its howling piercing her sensitive hearing. Fleeting movement showed NOX and Tieren ready to strike, taunting the creature with bellows and banging on the bulkheads.

She was close to its head, but its blood and hers made things slippery. With one more push, she buried the blade under the plate at the base of its skull. She threw herself off, rolling when she landed before bolting toward Tieren. He tossed her his dagger and gripped his sword with both hands. The weapon slipped through her fingers. She hurried to wipe her palms on her thighs before scooping up the blade.

Tieren roared a warning, but it was too late. The creature pinned her to the floor face down. Tieren leaped onto its back, burying his sword into its flesh, with his summoned wings keeping him aloft. Daniel and his officers opened fire. The creature's armored plates absorbed the pulses in riotous color.

She struggled to roll over. It thumped her down. Pushing back, she shoved her backside in the air, using the power of her thighs. The resistance was incredible, her throbbing back bore the brunt of it. As soon as she was high enough off the ground, she flipped in mid-air and swung her arms wide, searching for holds. She latched onto its arms and pulled herself from under its front feet. With a final grunt, she yanked herself at its throat, releasing one arm to angle the dagger.

With one stab up and under its jaw, the blade met the point of Tieren's sword—a dual strike. Blood burst outward, drenching her. She dipped her face to lessen the amount she swallowed. Then she floated backward. Tieren had flown her away from the squealing creature in its final death throes.

She stumbled over a body when her feet touched the floor. He tucked her into his embrace, shielding her within the drape of his wings as he ushered her toward the cargo pod. Lessons learned from the bebbayaya, but having him there drowned the last ounces of loneliness layering her soul.

She grinned at him. "Easy."

He chuckled. "Not my idea of easy. Look at you."

"I'm not shirtless." She trailed a bloodied finger down his chest. At his shiver, she laughed. "NOX, let Clive know the creature's his."

"Mick, that was…" Daniel gaped. "I didn't know you could…" He squared his shoulders. "That explains why you took on Ramirez and his partner alone. Well done." He flicked his fingers at his officers. They scampered along the corridor, searching for survivors.

At the ding of the cargo pod, Tieren ushered her aside and let NOX choose their destination. He dipped his head as if to kiss her, but she stank of blood. She pressed a bloodied hand to his chest, stopping him.

"Later, after a shower. Then I'll thank you properly for that rescue." Facing NOX, she assessed the scratch marks across his metallic body. "Order a suit."

"It's waiting for me." His lips twitched. "Oh, and all the footage I sent through to Dr. Nielson regarding your hunts is why he calls you Shikari. It means huntress in some ancient dialect."

"Makes sense." Her arm vibrated with a series of messages. Scanning a few, she grunted at the jobs offered to her. A colony had a bug infestation. A mine had a snake-lizard problem. Another had ginormous bats burning their crops. And one from Dr. Nielson confirmed she had access to the accommodation again. He promised to visit later.

Slipping away from Tieren, she selected the upper floor, then cuddled into his arms. "NOX, have clothes delivered to the room."

The door slid open, and NOX nudged her and Tieren out. Then with a stiff finger wave, the doors closed on another full-bodied, tinny version of the Pirates of Penzance.

"Ms. Danvers." A familiar bald man glared at her. His midnight black tunic fell to his knees, over gray leggings, and white slippers donned his feet.

Ah, she remembered him. Cason something or other. "You."

"Yes, I am sad to say." He glanced at Tieren. "It seems you did not contact my employer as expected."

She shrugged. "I lost the crystal."

"As I thought." He held out his unblemished palm, this time with two crystals balanced on it. "Please do not lose these. Rebirth is not my favorite destination." He ran a disparaging gaze along her bloodied and shredded clothing, then took a wide birth before sashaying down the passage. His two men followed, stoic as before. Their whirring hearts announced them as A.I.

"Care to explain?"

She smiled at Tieren and laced her fingers through his. "Come, let's bathe."

After a thorough wipe on her ruined pants, revealing her healed lacerated fingers and palm, the door opened for her. Into a data slot, she slid a crystal. Tieren strolled around the suite, admiring the view, touching objects with puzzlement while she ran the bath.

But when her mother's voice filled the suite, Mick hurried to the sitting area. The face in the vid froze her steps. "Mom?"

The woman looked like Mick, same brown hair and eyes, same nose and lips, just older, tired, despite the perm-cosmetics enhancing her features. Her surroundings were nondescript, with no passing planets, siphs, cruisers, or iconic structures. She could have been anywhere in the known universe.

"I can't go into detail on these things. I have much to explain. If Cason Themis is as good as they say, he has found my daughter. You're not safe, Micky. I'm in the Libra constellation. Come find me." She stroked the vid like when she used to brush a curl behind Mick's ear. "And be careful."

"Your mother?" Tieren wrapped his arms around Mick from behind, resting his chin on her shoulder.

"Yes. I thought her dead. Looks like we'll be making many stops on the way to Leo." She unstrapped his weapons, tossing them with every nudge of her hips. "A shower then a bath."

He did the same, leaving a trail of boots, ammunition, and weapons before her trousers pooled at her feet. Off came her shirt with one firm yank, then he pinned her to the wall. She activated the spray and tilted her head for his descending kiss.

ABOUT THE AUTHOR

Sevannah's a romantic at heart. Across science fiction, fantasy, paranormal, and contemporary genres, you will discover new worlds and lovable characters she's created. Her books are action-packed love stories of alpha men meeting stubborn women and finding happily ever after.

MARRIED TO A HIPPO-WHISPERER and the force-is-with-him, she, a live-long-and-prosper, manages to navigate her world with humor and passion. With two full-grown children, a Labrador, a pug, and a kitten named Peanut, her life is filled with chaos and merriment in the center of South Africa. And yes, the weather is sunny and hot.

Words she lives by: "Know your pothole and dodge it. Don't work in a pencil factory if you're a vampire."

Sevannah loves to hear from her readers. You can find and connect with her at the link below:

https://linktr.ee/Sevannah.Storm

Thank you for taking the time to read *The Shikari*. If you enjoyed the story, please tell your friends and leave a review. Reviews support authors and ensure they continue to bring readers books to love and enjoy.

https://sevannahstorm.com

SOUL FORGED

Know-it-all Oriana agreed to travel with aliens who need women. But she didn't agree to abduction, life/death battles, and escaping with a bossy, arrogant man. She was sabotaged, attacked, and kidnapped, but she is far from beaten. Forced to participate in an alien battle arena with no promise of freedom, she has to forget the loss of her family and focus on surviving.

Enyl has given up hope. His people are dying due to a genetic modification gone awry. Darkness is consuming his warriors, and his world, as he knows it, will end. His father, the king, has rolled out a plan to save them all. But Enyl doubts a solution will be found in time.

And when a compatible female is found...and lost, he must rescue her, a human female capable of surviving despite all odds. However, freeing Oriana serves to anger the aliens holding her captive. Ensuring she is cared for—as per Etterian protocol—he is stunned by the strong connection between the two of them. Such a bond was only experienced between Etterian mates.

Is she his salvation or is that wishful thinking on his part?

Read it here:

https://books2read.com/u/mlAWr9

FATE FORGED

SUN FORGED

The Gifting Series #3

Meeting a drop-dead gorgeous man, who falls onto a knee the first time they meet, sounded too good to be true for Ava. Of course, with her luck, he had to be an alien. Thrust into an unknown alien world, meeting weird and scary creatures, and fearing for her life, Ava tries to survive as best as a hairstylist can.

Kanzo never expected to find a life mate, a Dar Eth. Since he was young, he was taught that pairings were rare with fewer females born. The statistics on finding his Dar Eth would be slim to none. Instead of dreaming and longing for companionship, he focused on being the best male possible, to end his life on a battlefield with honor. But when he experiences the Ethera—the life mate force, and is blessed with his female, he isn't prepared for the level of pain, pleasure, and need she invokes within him.

Unable to save her as she's teleported from him, the dark consuming pain in his chest drives him into a blinding rage. With no idea who stole her or where to begin the search, he will scour the known universe to find her, to hold the female he never wanted.

Read it here:

SEVANNAH STORM

https://books2read.com/u/3n5vaB

WAR FORGED

The Gifting Series #4

Being kidnapped by aliens does not sit well with Quinlan. Not only would her seven guardians give her hell if she doesn't attempt some sort of escape, but she refuses to be at anybody's mercy. With her practiced military skills, the help of an underground lounge singer and a personal assistant, she takes over the alien slave ship. Not knowing how to fly the damn thing, she sends a distress signal. ...The rescue comes swiftly in the form of a bronzed man with exquisite ice-blue eyes. Leaving her to ask the true question: has she just given up her newfound freedom for a gorgeous man who seems determined to have her for eternity?

As Elite Supreme Commander of the Etterian Forces, Xan answers a distress call in Earth English. That is all he did. The female who captured the slave ship shows remarkable skill, making her a warrior in her own right. Said skills should be respected and honored. Except she is his Dar Eth, calling forth the Ethera—the soulmate bond. How can he protect his female when she can do so herself? What can she possibly need from him? What can he offer a female, not Etterian but human? Not that he can think clearly in her presence when she scents so good and makes him want to kiss all of her.

Maker help him.

Read it here:

https://books2read.com/u/bz1QGD

STAR FORGED

The Gifting Series #5

Macy is feeling a little left out, as usual. Who would have thought moving from one planet to another wouldn't change that loneliness? She is never alone these days since Etterians guard human women with an urgency she understands. But the lack of companionship is like a dark aching abyss inside her chest. On some days, it threatens to implode, and Macy Mitchell would cease to exist. Looming is her impending meeting with King Xeus of Etteria. How is she supposed to keep her shit together when presented to royalty? Not after she ran from the last king she met.

For Xeus, the void expands daily. Duty, honor, concern for his dying people, and endless loneliness fill his life. Having decided to search for pairings among other worlds, he is pleased his son found his soulmate among human women. It doesn't mean that Xeus's loneliness and longing haven't ended until he stumbles upon a crying female. Meaning only to soothe, he is spellbound when her presence brings him peace. Unable to resist, he forms an attachment to a female he can never have

Read it here:

https://books2read.com/u/3nXgp5

SHADOW FORGED

Forty-year-old Caroline is too old to start dating and too bored with her vibrator, but what other choices does she have. On the day she burns her shirt and breaks a fingernail, she meets Etterian warriors. As part of her job at E.S.A. (Earth Space Association,) she must 'entertain' the hot-as-apple-pie Chief Engineer she suspects isn't who he claims to be.

Operations Commander Malo, Head of Espionage, must act as an engineer and ambassador, hoping to invite human females to visit Etteria and save his dying race. From Princess Oriana, he has strict instructions to distrust humans. What he finds he cannot trust are his emotions and his body whenever in the presence of the human ambassador, Caroline. She does not believe in soulmates or in a forever with him. Convincing her to choose him is the greatest task ever set before him, one he cannot afford to fail.

Until she is stolen from him. He calls in favors, utilizes all his resources to find her. And *when* he does, he is never letting her off his battleship...or his bed.

Read it here:

SEVANNAH STORM

https://books2read.com/u/bPNd8j

EARTH FORGED

The Gifting Series #7

Guilt hounds Izzy, who caused her sister's injury and subsequent blindness. But no matter how she cares for Simone or what she sacrifices, it doesn't ease the ache in her chest. With Simone and naive Caro, her best friend, Izzy's role as protector is fully realized. The cost? Hiding behind quirkiness, pseudo-joy, and giving up her hopes and dreams. What she needs is a knight in any armor. After all, beggars can't be fussy. She has no idea that armor, in her case, means black military and that a knight could come in any color, specifically bronze.

Oyaz wants to find his life force, his soulmate, and he'd like her to be human. Earth's females are soft, amusing, passionate, and their scents rival a garden of hahyt blossoms. His task is to guard their planet that promises so many salvations for his males. It's a duty he's pleased to perform, one he would die for. When Operations Commander Malo orders Oyaz to retrieve a human female, he's eager to oblige. That it would lead to his salvation is something he couldn't anticipate. What he hadn't planned for is an ambush that costs him more than his memory, the loss of his soulmate.

Now what? Nothing in their training prepared him for this.

And yet, despite not remembering kneeling for Izzy, he longs to claim her with every inch of his soul.

Read it here:

https://books2read.com/u/31V82D

LUST FORGED

Ex-socialite Leona wants nothing more than to enhance the mechanics within sex-cybs, not to mention improve their performances with their 'lovers.' It's a job where she's safe in an all-woman factory on Callisto, and far from her matchmaking mama. When the chief engineer is incapacitated, Leona's required to gift—her term would be pimp—sex-cyborgs to prospective clients. On an Etterian battleship, surrounded by gorgeous males, she tries not to think of sex when it's her work, especially with the Sub-Commander Aaro whose neon-blue eyes are the stuff of her erotic dreams.

As a diplomatic favor, Aaro must abandon his task to guard Earth, and perhaps find his Dar Eth or soulmate, all to protect cargo en route to many worlds, including the dangerous and unpredictable Yithia. Princess Oriana is most concerned for the two human female engineers determined to ensure the deliveries are successful. A simple enough mission until one human enters Aaro's cargo bay, dropping him to his knees.

But revealing to independent Leona that she's now trapped in a marriage isn't something Aaro can bring himself to do. He violates all he stands for, every ounce of honor by not telling her the truth. All in the hopes that she will choose to love him.

Read it here:

https://books2read.com/u/3LdA1w

SOL SURVIVOR

Vic's dream was to expand the solar farm her mother left her. Instead, she must survive as an arena gladiator for Carne Corp. to pay off her father's gambling debts. Now her dream is ultimate freedom which is granted to the arena champion. At last, the future she planned for is within her grasp, but when Carne conspires against her and augments her against her will, she flees into outer space, hoping to disappear. A chance encounter with an unknown alien species awakens her sexuality. Plans go awry, and there is much she must defeat before she can truly be free.

Meorri aac Drafe is on a mission to find who assassinated the Ivoyan Ot he was tasked to protect. As a Qaldreth warrior, his tribe's honor rests on finding the killer. Forming an unheard-of union with a servant Ivoy, the other witness to the crime, they locate the killer's homeworld. There, Drafe encounters a female like no other.

To regain his honor, he will need to ask for her aid, go against his protective instincts, and endanger her.

Hunted by Carne, Vic must trust her heart, life, and newfound freedom to a Qaldreth warrior she cannot resist.

Read it here:

https://books2read.com/u/bajAZa